Why?

The question had plagued Star ever since Austin picked her up at 4:30 a.m. After sixteen hours on the road, she still didn't have a clue about why he really wanted to help her.

She could take at face value his comment about being bored and needing a challenge. She understood restlessness better than most, but that was far too simple. If she knew anything at all about Austin Tack, it was that he was a complex individual.

Why in Sam Hill would he drop everything to go gallivanting through the Rocky Mountains? He knew this trip was so much flailing around in the dark. A waste of time. A fool's errand. But Austin was no fool....

Which meant he knew something he wasn't telling.

Dear Reader,

What if someone out there looked exactly
like you...and that someone had committed a
murder?

When author Sheryl Lynn asked us this question,
we were intrigued—and we hope you will be,
too! Harlequin Intrigue is proud to present
our latest subseries, MIRROR IMAGES by
Sheryl Lynn.

Last month, we were pleased to bring you
Dark Knight, the first book in the MIRROR IMAGES
subseries. Now, be prepared to turn the page and
enter a world of danger and desire in the sequel to
Dark Knight. We hope you enjoy *Dark Star!*

Regards,

Debra Matteucci
Senior Editor and Editorial Coodinator
American Romance and Intrigue

Dark Star
Sheryl Lynn

Harlequin Books

TORONTO • NEW YORK • LONDON
AMSTERDAM • PARIS • SYDNEY • HAMBURG
STOCKHOLM • ATHENS • TOKYO • MILAN
MADRID • WARSAW • BUDAPEST • AUCKLAND

To Pamela Wood-Young, for support,
inspiration and wide-eyed enthusiasm.

ISBN 0-373-22336-6

DARK STAR

Copyright © 1995 by Jaye W. Manus

Colorado

• Denver

• Colorado Springs

• Pueblo

• Gold Coin

CAST OF CHARACTERS

Star Jones—Her twenty-six-year quest to find her parents will end only when she can bear to remember.

Austin Tack—An impossible search is nothing compared to the challenge of this private eye winning Star's love.

Jerry and Karen Jones—The young couple vanished twenty-six years ago—because of a murdered woman?

Rowena Waxman—Few mourn this murdered woman.

Betty Brownley—The newspaper owner always thought there was something fishy about the Jones family disappearing.

Doyle Sloane—He admits he had an affair with a murder victim, but so what, he's the mayor and the brother-in-law of the richest man in the county.

Stuart Hagan—He's rich, mean and powerful enough to get away with murder.

Queenie Hagan—She's been on her deathbed for over forty years, rising only when her family is in peril.

Michelle Hagan Sloane—Humiliation and estrangement are her crosses to bear.

Isadora Hagan—She's the orneriest, loudest, pushiest woman in the state, and she likes it that way.

Mark Waxman—He knows who murdered his daughter, and one of these days he'll figure out what to do about it.

Dave Crocker—This one-horse-town cop is about to get a hands-on lesson in how to solve a murder.

Chapter One

"A woman who can't smile at her own sister's wedding," Austin Tack said, "must be remembering a lost love. What's wrong, Jones?"

It figured *he* would notice, Star Jones thought. She dragged her gaze away from the sea of revelers filling the Crystal Hotel's grand ballroom. Forcing her mouth into a smile, she looked up at the private eye.

He cupped flutes of champagne between his fingers. He offered her one.

Mmm-mmm, who would have thought he could clean up so nice? Wearing his usual biker bum clothes, the man was so handsome he could stop traffic. In the charcoal gray tuxedo he wore for his role as best man, he looked spiffy enough to cause a cat fight. Which, considering the admiring looks he'd been getting from every female, young and old, all during the wedding and reception, just might happen before the night was over.

She plucked a flute from his hand, then wondered what to do with it. She never drank. "Nothing's wrong, Tack. I'm having a grand time." She saluted him with the wine.

He caressed a faux-marble column with his big, sun-browned hand. "That's right. You like hiding in corners." His velvet dark eyes captured hers.

Stop staring at him like he's something tasty on the menu, she ordered herself, and arose from the dainty chair. Rustling taffeta made her grimace. She swatted at her bulky skirt. Her maid-of-honor gown was ridiculously heavy and stiff, and her dyed-to-match slippers made her feet feel like hot lumps.

Austin took the dainty champagne flute from her and set it on a small table. "Forgot you don't drink. Sorry. How about cake, instead?"

Forgot she didn't drink? Not likely. As a private investigator, his powers of observation were honed to almost supernatural sharpness. He was always catching her off guard with how much he noticed about her. He was like a cat, always watching, always aware.

He saw too much.

"Either Dana or Kurt put you up to baby-sitting me. I don't need it, thank you. I'm fine."

"You seem uncomfortable. You haven't touched the buffet."

Stroking a finger under his silky lapel, she said, "There's a passel of women here who don't know your usual duds are antique jeans. Take advantage of it. You might get lucky."

"I'm doing my best," he replied with a smile. A killer smile, sweetly serene.

Her heart lurched. She lowered her eyelids.

"So what's bothering you, Jones?"

Since Austin was her new brother-in-law's best friend, she'd gotten to know him fairly well in the past few months. He was a charmer with a soft, husky voice and a soothing demeanor. He was eccentric, what with his mumbo-jumbo mysticism, but he was surefooted, too. She didn't think she'd ever met anyone with so much self-confidence. Or anyone as smart as him, for that matter.

One of these days she might respond to his flirting and find out if he was serious. But not today. She felt too lousy.

"Don't you approve of Dana and Kurt getting married?"

"Sure I do!" She hugged her elbows. "They're perfect for each other. Can't think of a better match." She liked Austin, but her problems were none of his business. They were nobody's business but her own.

A flash of white caught her attention. Her twin sister was leaving the ballroom. "Pardon me." She gathered her skirts and followed Dana.

Star left the ballroom and found the giddy bride in the ladies' room. Dana had removed her veil and headpiece, but still wore her bridal gown, a confection of lace and seed pearls that shimmered with every movement.

Everyone claimed Dana and Star were identical. Aside from both of them being blond, blue eyed, tall and thin, Star didn't think they looked alike at all. Dana was beautiful.

So why did they do it? Star wondered. How could they? Dana was perfect, an ethereal fairy creature. Matthew and Greta Benson, the couple who had adopted Dana, thought the sun rose and set on their only child. So how could their biological parents dump Dana like a stray?

Dana caught sight of Star in the mirror.

"There you are!" Dana exclaimed. "I was looking for you."

"Not more pictures, I hope."

"The photographer is finished. I just wanted to see how you are doing." She gave her flaxen hair a final pat and turned away from the mirror. "Are you having a good time?"

"Sure." Star glanced at her image and barely recognized the rose-swathed creature looking back. Borrowed pearls encircled her throat and dangled from her ears. More makeup coated her face than she normally wore in a year. Her short hair was stiff and shiny with mousse. "You'd best feel honored. You're the only person I'd wear a bow on my butt for."

"You look so pretty. About fifty men have asked me to introduce you." Dana laughed and caught Star's hands in both of hers. "How was the ceremony? I swear, I was shaking so much I barely remember any of it."

"Perfect. Everything's right as rain. I don't know how your mother pulled it together. There must be five hundred people out there and every one of them is happy as a pig in mud."

"Mom lives for a good party." Carefully arranging her voluminous skirt, she sank onto a brocaded settee and fanned her flushed face. "I still can't believe I'm Mrs. Kurt Saxon." She extended her left hand and admired her carved gold wedding band. "Ms. Dana Benson Saxon. *Mrs.* Saxon."

No! Star protested silently. You're Mary Jones. Don't you remember? Star and Mary, born on Christmas Day. Inseparable twins, a team . . .

"Ms. Dana B. Saxon. That'll be it." She kissed her ring. "I am so happy, Star. I keep pinching myself to make sure I'm not dreaming."

Star sat beside her sister. Mild panic squeezed her ribs. This was Dana's big day. Star had no right to feel so miserable, so lost and disconnected. "Has Kurt told you where you're going on your honeymoon yet?" She made herself look interested.

Dana huffed an exasperated sigh. "No. I can't weasel it out of him, either. You know him and surprises."

Kurt Saxon was as charming as a politician, sincere as a priest and fun-loving as a kid—an irresistible combination. "For such a big jerk," Star said, "he sure does have a romantic streak."

Dana waggled an admonishing finger. "Ah-ah, now that we're married, I'm the only one who can call my husband a jerk." Her smile faded and she cocked her head. Her big blue eyes softened with concern. "Is something the matter?"

"No." Yes. Shut up, don't spoil her mood, her day—Dana deserved better. Star stared at the toes of her rosecolored pumps as the emotions of loss and loneliness welled until she could barely breathe. "I was kind of hoping to talk to you before you left. Now that the wedding is over and all. But I reckon—"

"About our parents?" Dana asked. "Oh, Star, not today, *please*."

Star jumped to her feet. "I'm sorry. It's just that—they should have been here today! They should have seen how wonderful you are and what a good man you found."

"I know how much you want to find our parents. I'd help you if I could."

"Why can't you help? I never forgot you. For years and years, I looked for you. I didn't forget. Don't you remember anything? Just a tad?"

"Nothing. Please believe me, Star."

She fingered the flocked wallpaper. Self-loathing churned in her belly. This wasn't Dana's fault. According to the Bensons, Dana hadn't spoken a single word for months after they'd adopted her. Her silence had been so profound, some folks had thought her retarded or brain damaged. Whatever had driven her into silence had also wiped out her past. Yet Star hated accepting the truth. It hurt.

"Maybe it's for the best that you can't find them. They could have been alcoholics or drug dealers or child abusers. Maybe our parents weren't married. Our mother might have been forced to give us up for financial reasons. If they were concerned at all, they'd find us."

Star's memories were from the sketchy perspective of a four-year-old, but she remembered enough to know that, once upon a time, their parents had loved them.

"You're obsessed with this, Star. I don't think it's healthy."

That stung. She'd spent her entire life looking for her family and now her twin implied she was nutty for doing so. "Aren't you even curious, Dana?"

Her sister fiddled with seed pearls sewn on her wedding dress. "I'm not unsympathetic, but I get the impression you think I'm not trying hard enough. Please look at me."

Star made herself meet the blue eyes that matched her own.

"I love you, Star. You can't know how happy I am we found each other. If I knew any way to help you find our parents, I'd do it. You know that, don't you?"

"I reckon," she mumbled.

"It's the truth, honey. I'd like nothing more than to see you as happy as I am."

"Forget it. I won't bring it up again." She stroked a finger across her breast. "Cross my heart." She meant it this time, and that hurt most of all.

Dana took Star's hand and entwined their fingers. "When Kurt and I return from our honeymoon, we'll see what we can do. Okay? Kurt knows zillions of people all over the country. And Austin will help. Finding missing people is his specialty. You'll—"

"Dana!" Kurt Saxon's call echoed inside the lounge.

Star and Dana leaned together to look around the wall separating the ladies' lounge from the arched entryway. Resplendent in his tux and tails, his gray eyes sparkling with besotted adoration, Kurt tapped an impatient finger against his wristwatch.

"The music is starting, babe. Everyone is waiting for us to lead the dancing."

Dana shot Star a grin. If Dana didn't hurry out of the ladies' room, Kurt would come barging in. She gathered her skirt in both hands and hurried to her groom. Kurt swept her into a lusty embrace, kissing her soundly.

"Save it for the honeymoon, Saxon," Star called.

Kurt gave her a wink. He caught Dana under her shoulders and knees. Over her laughing protests, he carried her back to the grand ballroom and the cheering guests.

Ashamed of herself, Star went in the opposite direction. As she walked down the staircase in the Crystal Hotel, it struck her how perfect this glittering, palacelike setting was for Dana. They might be identical twins, but they lived in different worlds.

Dana had been an honor student, was educated in the arts, music and dance, dressed in the nicest clothing, and never lacked in material comfort. She and her father were partners in a lucrative real-estate sales and management company. She owned a showcase home and was now married to a man who worshiped the ground she walked upon. Why should Dana care about finding the people who had discarded her so long ago?

Star stepped outside into the muggy September night.

The sky was clear without a trace of wind to disturb the lake behind the hotel. The Dallas skyline formed a neon picture show on the inky water.

Star took a moment to catch her breath. The air was thick with moisture and the weedy smell of the lake. Sweat trickled between her breasts, but the thought of returning to the reception pained her. She didn't belong.

The time for hopefulness was over. Dana wasn't Mary Jones anymore. She wouldn't, couldn't, help find their parents. That was that.

Acceptance walked hand in hand with terrible loneliness.

At the edge of the lake, she sat on a bench and listened to the soft chuckles of ducks and geese settling in for the night. She slipped off her shoes and smiled in sheer, tingling pleasure. She looked right and left. Seeing no one, she stood and hiked up her skirt and petticoats. Her panty hose clung stickily to her skin, but with a few wriggles and tugs, she peeled them off her legs.

Heaven. She worked her bare toes against the cool grass.

A soft wolf whistle startled her.

Austin Tack stepped into the glow offered by tier lights along the path and Chinese lanterns strung in the trees.

"There's something unnatural about a man so quiet. Quit sneaking up on me." She rolled the panty hose into a tight ball and slipped them inside a shoe.

"And miss the view?" He sat beside her on the bench.

She tucked her bare feet under her skirt. "Why are you following me?"

"I needed some air." He lifted his chin and worked loose his bow tie. He removed the top two studs of his pleated shirt.

Star watched him from the corner of her eye. His tuxedo jacket fitted perfectly to his broad shoulders and tapered waist. His snowy shirt emphasized the dark burnished gold in his skin. The only thing she didn't like was the way he'd pulled his hair into an unobtrusive ponytail. She preferred his wolf-tawny hair hanging free past his shoulders.

"Have I told you how nice you look today?" he asked.

"Look, Tack, let's make a deal. No cracks about this ice-cream sundae I'm wearing, and I won't say a word about the headwaiter's gig Dana strapped on you."

He chuckled softly. Leaning forward, he rested his elbows on his knees. He stared at the lake. "What's up, Jones? You look like you lost your best friend."

"Get off my back."

"Is it your parents?"

She snapped her head around. Irritation faded as quickly as it had arisen, leaving her empty and lonely and sad. She needed to talk to someone.

"They should have been here today." She plucked a blade of grass and pulled it between her fingers. "They should have seen Dana. She'd make any father bust with pride. Did you see Matthew? He's about floating. Our real daddy should be looking like that, too."

Austin stared at the water.

"When I was searching for Dana, I worried about contacting her after I'd found her. I mean, what would she want with someone like me? But I kept thinking, she's got to know something. She can help me fill in the blanks."

"She can't."

His flat statement said it all. She picked up her shoes. "Why am I telling you this? You probably think I'm nuts, too."

"Not me."

Uneasiness gripped her, and she forced a soft laugh. Austin Tack was the kind of man who encouraged trust. She didn't want to trust him, or anybody. Trusting herself, only, suited her. Life was safest that way. "What do you care?"

He turned his head enough for her to see the light reflecting in his dark, wise eyes. "We're friends. I like you." He leaned a little closer and waggled his eyebrows. "You've got great legs."

This time her laugh was genuine. Standing, she stretched, and worked a finger under the scratchy taffeta neckline.

"You'd do anything to find your parents."

The profoundly simple truth shook her. "You mean, like spend every penny I have? Lie, cheat or steal? Sleep with some guy for information? That kind of anything?"

"If you say so."

She didn't need to say so. Her life was a testament. Every job she'd ever had, every place she'd lived, every person she'd gotten to know, all were connected somehow to her search. Maybe she was obsessed—or nuts. "Nothing I've done has come to any good. I'm missing my parents' names and birth dates. You're the pro, you know what I mean."

"So who told you finding them is impossible?"

"Figured it out myself." She walked along the concrete path edging the lake.

Austin appeared at her side like a shadow, matching her stride. God only knew what thoughts lurked behind his hypnotically calm expression.

Don't like him, she warned herself. She had no time for a man. Especially a man with a talent for getting under her skin. "If you're fishing for a job, forget it. I've hired private eyes before. It was a waste of money."

"What do you know about your parents?"

"Give it up, Tack."

"Giving up implies hopelessness. What do you know?"

She wished it were Dana asking these questions. "I have a photograph of my daddy taken in 1968. His name is Jerry."

"Short for Gerald or Jerome," Austin offered.

"Jeremy? Jeremiah? Who knows? I have a letter, too. A love letter, I reckon, all full of mush and stuff. Dear Snuggle Bear, with love from Pookie. Some clue."

"Let me look at what you have."

She stopped next to a cypress tree. The muggy air surrounded her like a drift of diaphanous cloth.

"Thanks for the offer, but it's useless." Useless said it all. She looked back toward the brightly lit hotel. For the first time in her life, she felt utterly without hope. The pain rose again, tightening her throat. "Do you have any idea how many people named Jones live in the United States?" She shifted the shoes to her other hand, knowing if she'd been smart she'd have brought along a pair of sneakers. "You can't find them. Nobody can."

"I found you."

That brought her up short. The biggest surprise of her life had been the day Austin Tack had shown up on her doorstep. On Dana's behalf, he'd tracked her from Dallas to Wichita Falls.

"That was different. I hadn't been missing for twenty-five years." She managed a wan smile. "You knew what I looked like."

"Scared I'll find something and prove you wrong?"

She stiffened her spine. "Even if you did, I'm strapped. That is, if I was stupid enough to waste my money on another private eye."

He reached overhead. Leaves rustled. A twig snapped. "I thought you'd do anything."

Annoyed by his silky suggestiveness, she started walking again. Again, he fell into step beside her.

"You're one cool cowpoke, Tack, but deep down inside, you're just like all the rest."

"How's that?"

"Food and sex. That's all men care about."

"I see."

"No denials?"

"I'm considering if you're wrong or right."

He had the most screwball method of arguing she'd ever run across. She wondered if anything ever got his goat. "Men do math with their brain. All other thinking is handled by auxiliary organs."

He laughed unaffectedly. "Desiring food and sex are perfectly natural. Only sick people don't want food and sex."

"That's not what I'm talking about."

"Isn't it? I'm trying to understand why you think food and sex are evil."

She punched his shoulder. "There you go again, trying to muddle me up. What I'm saying is, the only reason a man does anything for a woman is because she either feeds him or beds him."

"Food and sex are basic to life. As far as good reasons go, you can't get much better than that."

"Yeah, well, what if I don't want to cook or sleep with you?" She stopped again and faced the lake. She was tempted to throw the shoes and hated panty hose into the water. A gesture to express her frustration at having to finally accept Dana's disinterest.

"That's your prerogative. In which case, tell me, what difference does it make *why* I arrive at an answer as long as I find one? Let me help you."

Tempting, very tempting. "I can't pay you."

"A favor."

"I don't accept favors."

He made a soft, amused noise. "I'm a vegetarian."

His comment threw her. "So?"

"You'd probably toss me in the lake if I asked you to sleep with me, so cook, instead. Food instead of sex."

She moved along the path. "Nice offer," she said, knowing he was following. "I'll think about it."

"In the meantime, let's go back to the party. You owe me a dance."

"I owe you nothing."

"Social requirement. Best man and maid of honor have to dance."

In spite of her desire to brood in her own well of misery, her shoulders straightened and her clothing didn't feel so restrictive. "You have a rule book?"

"I left it at home."

Dancing with Austin Tack had to be better than feeling sorry for herself. Except, if she returned to the ballroom she'd find herself watching Dana. She'd wonder again how their parents could have discarded her like some unwanted trinket.

Austin took her shoes and set them on the path out of the way. Drawing her into his arms, he said, "The night makes its own music. Hear it?"

She listened to the faraway hum of hotel activity and the even fainter sound of highway traffic. Crickets and other insects chirped and buzzed. Water burbled gently against the shoreline.

They danced on the warm pathway, turning under the stars. He moved slowly, gently, seemingly content to hold her. Lulled by his gracefulness, she half closed her eyes and allowed herself to feel the pleasure of the night.

When he stopped, he continued to hold her. She breathed through her mouth to cool the air. Her gown was wilted like a sunburned flower, and her face and throat were damp and hot. The heat of his hand seared her waist. His healthy, masculine scent had a honeylike undertone. She leaned closer, savoring the unusual smell of him.

He kissed her. His lips were moist, carrying a sweetish taste that reminded her of fields of wildflowers. A light kiss, friendly and without demands, yet she greedily absorbed the smooth texture of his lips and the cool, questioning dart of his tongue.

Her sudden desire to kiss him more fully and explore the heady sensations he roused disturbed her, scared her. His hand tightened on her waist and trembled. His sudden tension crackled, exciting her. One more second, and he'd enfold her in his arms—

She whirled out of his grasp. Her lips tingled, and the heat weakening her knees had nothing to do with the muggy air. Panting, fighting the urge to rush back into his arms, she tried to convince herself he was just like any other man who saw her only as a body.

Except...wanting him felt as natural as being hungry. Wanting him threatened to drive every other thought out of her head.

"If your rule book calls for more, you're out of luck." She grabbed up her shoes and hurried away.

STAR LIGHT, STAR BRIGHT, first star I see tonight...

Austin shook his head and hair whipped his cheeks. The ridiculous ditty refused to leave his brain.

Try again.

He drew a deep breath, shifted his knees slightly, and closed his eyes. One deep breath, two, draw air deep down toward the diaphragm, relax, exhale— No good. He could feel the hardwood floor under his buttocks. Traffic sounds outside his apartment distracted him. He heard a fly buzzing against a window.

Star Jones weighed heavily on his thoughts.

He knew what part of the problem was: boredom, ennui, a lack of challenges and mental workouts. The center he sought was heavy with rust.

Life was too short for routines, and he'd fallen into the rut of one routine after another. He glumly studied the bank of computers, fax machine and recording equipment which were the major tools of his trade. From this small apartment he could touch the world. Such ease of communication left him intellectually flabby.

Star's search for her parents was exactly what he needed. Lacking her parents' full names and birth dates did make the search impossible—for most. The majority of private investigators he knew wouldn't touch a missing-persons case without them. As Goethe stated, however, the intelligent man finds almost everything ridiculous, the sensible man hardly anything.

Austin Tack was forever a sensible man.

Except, he thought with wry honesty, where Star was concerned. Around her, his brain turned to pudding.

The doorbell rang. He unfolded his legs and rose, taking a moment to stretch his arms and arch his back. The Bogart clock on the wall read three minutes until 6:00 a.m.

He answered the door. As if wishfulness had conjured her up, Star Jones stood on the concrete stoop.

At the wedding, she'd been lovely, but her discomfort had made her seem like a doll dressed for a window display. Now, in her tight jeans and a black T-shirt—its Harley-Davidson logo molded over her small bosom—and with the rising sun forming a halo around her silky cap of pale hair, she was stunning. His heart did a little hop, skip and jump. His blood warmed in remembrance of their kissing. "Good morning."

She stared for a moment at his naked chest before lowering her gaze to his bare feet. He wore only gray sweatpants for his morning meditation.

"Did I wake you?" she asked.

He caught the challenge in her voice. Which meant she probably wanted something, but feared rejection, so she came at a ridiculous hour, expecting him to be irritable or unfriendly. It was the classically paradoxical behavior of a wounded soul. He said, "No."

She handed him a foil-covered pan. "Red beans and rice, Cajun-style."

He smelled onions and tangy hot peppers. His stomach growled. "Thanks."

She reached inside her T-shirt and pulled out the beaded medicine bag she wore on a rawhide lace around her neck. The only time he'd ever seen her without it had been at her sister's wedding. Tattered and missing beads, the leather was dark with age. For a long moment she peered inside the bag before finally handing him a photograph and a letter.

Her throat worked with a convulsive swallow. She appeared braced for him to say, yes, definitely, her search was impossible.

The letter was written on pale blue paper, yellowed on the edges and brittle on the folds. The photograph showed a young man in Western clothing smiling shyly at the camera. On the back, in faded ink, was written, "Jerry, 1968."

Were she anyone else, he'd invite her inside for a cup of tea or coffee and they'd discuss her problem. Instinct held him in place, blocking the doorway.

She didn't trust him. The jut of her chin and the tension in her shoulders said she expected him to try for a bit of sex to go with the food. She'd interpret any action on his part as a threat. Winning her trust—more than finding her parents—was exactly the kind of challenge he craved.

"'He's mad that trusts in the tameness of the wolf, a horse's health, a boy's love or a whore's oath,'" he quoted.

She cocked her head, and her eyes narrowed. "How's that?"

"Shakespeare, *King Lear*. To which I add, or a private eye's optimism. I'll be in touch."

She nodded uncertainly. "I'm still staying at Dana's."

"Cool. See you later." He closed the door. Through the peephole, he saw her surprise. He grinned and silently told her, Not everyone is out to hurt you, punkin. I can prove it.

Excitement he hadn't felt in ages filled him as he settled down to work.

The letter lacked so much as a date. Addressed to Snuggle Bear from Pookie, it was short, plaintive and lacking details. The handwriting was crabbed and childish and the spelling was so bad as to be funny.

Interesting, but until he learned more, he reserved judgment.

The photograph, on the other hand, offered up some interesting information.

Exactly forty-eight hours to the minute after Star had handed him her precious mementos, he stood on Dana's doorstep. Star answered the doorbell quickly enough for him to know he hadn't gotten her out of bed.

She grinned and nodded. "So that's how it works with you. Don't get mad, get even."

"And I thought my motives were pure." He offered her a large manila envelope. "I'm taking a little vacation to Colorado. Want to come?"

Chapter Two

Pure excitement shook Star to her toes. Austin Tack knew something—he'd found something. Her fingers tightened on the edge of the door. She stared hopefully and with vague fear at the envelope. This could be a joke. He could be teasing. She looked at Austin again. His mild, steady gaze said he was dead-on serious.

Shrugging, she said, "Reckon you might as well come on in. No sense giving the neighbors cause for chatter." She took the envelope and stepped aside, inviting Austin into the house.

As he entered, she covertly studied the snug fit of his blue jeans. His gray T-shirt hinted at the compactly sculpted muscles underneath. Catching him bare-chested the other morning had been pure candy for the eyes. If the private detective had flaws, they sure weren't in the physical development area.

He cocked his head slightly, as well as his eyebrows. His twitch of a grin said, "Caught ya looking."

She lifted her chin and hugged the manila envelope to her breast. "Are you for real about Colorado?"

"I aim to please."

She bet he did. He followed her to the kitchen. Once there, he looked around at the stacks of boxes and the counters piled high with pots, pans and miscellany. Kurt had moved into his new wife's home with enough cookware and gadgets to stock three kitchens. Star cleared off the breakfast counter.

Kurt's big black-and-silver tomcat claimed the space. He squeaked a pleased greeting at Austin. "Hey, Snooky, how's it hanging?" Austin ruffled the cat's ears. "Settling in okay?"

"That cat's a regular lord of the manor," Star said. "You'd think he was paying the mortgage." Watching the private eye love up the cat gave her heart a pang. She adored animals, but had never lived anywhere long enough to feel right about owning one. She filled two mugs with freshly brewed coffee.

Austin put Snooky on the floor. The cat began rubbing his head against Austin's boots. "So how goes your job hunting?"

Ever since the wedding, when Dana had finally and forever crushed Star's hope that the two of them could pool their memories, Star had been in a slump, unable to motivate herself into doing anything useful. "I haven't decided if I want to hang around Dallas."

"I thought you had your future all mapped out."

"Dana has my future set in stone," she corrected him, and grinned fondly. "According to her, I'll get my real estate license and work in her office and make tons of money. When one of the houses on this cul-de-sac comes up for sale, I'll buy it and we'll be neighbors."

"And that's that," Austin said.

She held up a finger like a preacher emphasizing a point. "Don't forget the part where I marry one of the fellas she sets me up with. We'll have a passel of kids and trade off baby-sitting."

"Good plan," he said agreeably.

"Dumb plan." She shook her head in wonder at her twin's rosy vision of the future. "Dana's got a nice life and all, but..."

"Domestication isn't your thing."

As she turned, she glimpsed her reflection in the shiny surfaces of the double-oven doors. She winced at the sight of herself wearing no makeup, baggy old shorts and a sweatshirt with ripped-off sleeves. Worst of all, a tuft of hair rose from her forehead like a little flag. Austin had arrived just before her morning run. She hadn't even showered.

He'd notice if she ran upstairs so she could smooth her hair and put a coat of mascara on her eyelashes. Wanting to do it, anyway, irritated her. It didn't matter a lick what he thought of her looks.

When Austin bent over to pet the cat, she finger-combed her hair. For herself, she told herself, not for him. "So why are you going to Colorado?"

"Educated guess," he told her.

Unable to wait for him to start explaining, she opened the envelope. Her photograph and letter were enclosed in glassine protectors. She pulled her medicine bag from inside her shirt and placed her mementos inside. Relief washed through her to have them back where they belonged.

Included in the envelope were a stack of eight-by-ten photographs. She leafed through them. After a few seconds she realized they were blown-up details from her father's photograph. "What educated you? I've been to Colorado lots of times."

The photos had an almost cartoonish sharpness, the outlines crisp. An enlargement of Jerry's belt buckle caught her eye. It wasn't completely crisp. One side of the rounded buckle was plain as day, but most of it faded into gray.

"Your father was a cowboy," Austin said. "Not of the drugstore variety, either."

Unable to decide if he was stringing her along in an attempt to impress, or if he spoke a simple truth, she watched his eyes.

"I analyzed the photograph. What you see is computer-enhanced imagery."

What Star knew about computers could fill a postage stamp. "It's not real?"

"Think of it as a Chinese painting where one or two brush strokes suggest a flock of birds. The mind's eye fills in the details. I give the computer an image, and it acts as the eye."

He arranged the photographs into a mosaic representing an almost life-size image of Jerry Jones.

She was impressed. "How do you know he's a real cowboy?"

"Elementary, my dear Jones." He framed a glossy print with his long, supple fingers. "This belt buckle is a rodeo prize. He won an event somewhere." He pointed out where the letters *FIRS* were visible. "First prize."

"Phony cowboys can buy those things anywhere."

"True. One circumstance does not a conclusion make. Look at this image. This is the inside seam of his jeans. Notice how it's worn almost white. That's caused by friction." He turned on the stool and hooked a foot over his knee. He pointed out the wear pattern on his own jeans. The inside seam along his thigh was frayed, the stitching worn through in spots, but the color matched the rest of the fabric.

"Like friction from a saddle." She gave up trying to hide how impressed she was. She pulled her gaze away from his leg. No sense complicating matters by letting him see her untoward, and completely beside the point, interest concerning how nicely the blue denim encased his long, strong thigh.

"Now look at his boots." He moved her attention to another photograph. "Check out the scars on the toes and uppers. That kind of wear comes from rubbing against a stirrup. Plus, he's got brand-new heels. Real cowboys tend to keep their boots."

She'd studied the photograph for hours on end and never noticed any of this. She rested her elbow on the countertop and her chin on her fist. Her father being a cowboy made sense. The smell of horses, and more so, the heavy, earthy stink of stockyards, sometimes triggered memories, bringing them so close to the surface she could almost, though never quite, grasp them.

"The year was 1968," he continued. "The peace movement, hippies, long hair. Only Wall Street types, jocks and cowboys were this clean-cut."

"What about the military?"

"Indulging in a bit of wild guessing, I'd say he's too fresh-faced. No edge to him. I imagine he was waiting for his draft number to come up."

"Think he was drafted and skipped to Canada?" Or killed in Vietnam, she almost added, but couldn't bear to put the thought into words.

"I tried running a computer search of service records. Without his social security number, it's an exercise in futility."

She tried to imagine her father as a draft dodger, or worse, killed in a steaming jungle— She shoved the thoughts away. "You still haven't said, why Colorado?"

"We know for a fact this photograph was taken prior to your abandonment at the orphanage. What do you remember about being abandoned?"

Irked by his use of the word *abandonment,* she mulled over how doggone little she did know. "There was a woman. I know she wasn't my mother, but other than that, not much. We were in a car. A big car. I remember being on the floor behind the seat. She kept telling us to be quiet, not to say anything. It was night, mostly." She could almost smell dirty carpet warmed by a car heater, and hear soft, baby-animal-like cries, and see pinpoint stars through a curved back window....

"Jones?" He sounded worried.

She blinked rapidly and shook herself. It was embarrassing when people caught her zoning out like that.

"What were you thinking?" he asked.

"I don't know, Tack." That was the blessed truth. What she felt in her heart was as real as the fingers on her hand. But what she actually *knew?* In some ways, remembering a little was worse than remembering nothing at all. She lowered her gaze to the mosaic of computer enhancements. "I remember being angry and scared and missing my parents. That much I know for certain." A psychic shiver made her scalp crawl. "Something terrible happened. I can almost see it sometimes. It's like a word right on the tip of my tongue, but I can't get it."

"An accident?" he mused. "A car wreck? Plane crash?"

She shrugged helplessly.

He tapped his fingers against the stoneware counter tiles. She focused on his hand. He wasn't overly large, not quite six feet tall and lean, but he had big hands with long, muscular fingers. Black hair grew thickly on his arms, emphasizing the taut cording of his forearms and heavy-boned wrists. Nice hands that looked capable of doing anything he set his mind to.

"All I know for sure is, a woman drove me and Dana to the orphanage. I don't know who the woman was or why she dumped us. Nobody connected with the orphanage knows anything about her." She cradled her coffee cup and inhaled the aroma. "So tell me about Colorado. And don't be playing Fred Astaire, dancing around the answer."

"I like to cover the angles."

"You like to drive me nuts. Why Colorado?"

"It's a place to start." He picked up an enhancement that contained only the background scenery. "I showed this to a botanist. He says the combination of aspen trees, scrub oaks, pines and grasses are indigenous to the Rocky Mountains."

She envisioned a map of North America. The Rockies covered territory from New Mexico practically to Alaska. She bit her lip to keep from demanding "Why Colorado?" again.

"Now look at this." He picked up another photograph.

Puzzled, she peered closely at it. It showed part of a white expanse marked with letters.

"It's a road sign. Jerry is standing in front of it in the original. It's probably fifteen or twenty feet behind him."

He pointed out details. "Part of the word *welcome* is visible. This is an Elks emblem, which makes me think it's a town marker. Here on the bottom line the letters *C-O-L-O*. My money says it spells out Colorado."

She could have kissed him. She almost kissed him. The look in his velvety eyes said he wouldn't mind a bit. "Maybe my folks were vacationing. Passing through."

"Possible. Or he might have been riding the rodeo circuit. But, notice." He tapped a glossy. "The aspens have lost most of their leaves. Tourist season is over. Rodeo hadn't yet moved into indoor arenas, so they wouldn't be holding any events in the Rockies at that time of year. Also, he isn't wearing a coat and his sleeves are rolled. It could have been an exceptionally warm day, but chances are better he's acclimatized. I think we're seeing where he lived. So what do you think?"

Fingering the edge of a photograph, she blew a long breath. Now that he'd pointed all this out to her, she couldn't believe she hadn't noticed it before.

Still, even eliminating the eastern plains, Colorado was a big state. In the past few years she'd taken jobs that allowed her to travel, everything from being a courier to driving a truck. In all the miles she'd logged in Colorado, she'd never once felt a twinge of recognition or met anyone who recognized Jerry from the photograph.

Austin knew where to start looking. That was certain as sunset.

"I think I owe you dinner, Tack. And tomorrow I'm heading for Colorado."

"So am I."

Star waggled a finger at him. "Thanks for the sentiment, but I travel alone."

"You need me."

"I don't need anyone. Never have, never will." She couldn't force much conviction into her voice. In two days, Austin had learned more about Jerry Jones than she had learned in the past twenty-five years. She gathered the photographs into a neat pile. "But, just out of curiosity, where in Colorado should I start?"

The corners of his mouth curved. "*I'd* start wherever it feels right."

"That's no answer," she muttered.

"It's the best you're getting, Jones. Take it or leave it."

She tried her frostiest glare. He smiled. She grumbled and huffed. He kept smiling.

"Stop being so pigheaded and tell me."

"Information is a valuable commodity." He chucked her chin tenderly with a knuckle. "He who knows, goes."

She slapped his hand away from her face. "Why are you doing this? What do you want from me?"

"I'm bored."

Nonplussed, she blinked rapidly.

"A metaphorical piece of cake has the same effect on the brain as actual cake does on the gut. Life's too easy. I'm getting flabby in the brain." He placed a hand flat atop the stack of photographs. "This will be hard work, a challenge. I want to do it."

His speech was too matter-of-fact to be anything other than honest. Even so, there had to be a catch. There always was. "Okay, I can understand wanting a challenge and all, but you're a pro. Pros cost money."

"I'm not worried about money."

That made him a minority of one. "I won't be beholden to anyone."

"I'm going to Colorado regardless. I need a vacation."

An answer for everything. She refilled their coffee cups. He knew something—he had an idea about where to start looking. A yearning to know what he knew gnawed at her insides. "You're one stubborn fella."

"I prefer persistent, but that has nothing to do with it. You need me, Jones, whether you like it or not. Ideas are floaters. They drift, waiting for someone to find them. I no longer ask where my hunches come from. I follow them whenever they occur. I'm following this one to Colorado."

Hardheaded so-and-so, she thought sourly. She didn't need the distraction. She sure didn't want to be in his debt.

"You're looking at me as if I'm withholding information." He gestured at her with his coffee cup. "I told you all I know. Jerry was a cowboy who either ranched his own spread or worked for someone else. And that photograph was taken in the Colorado Rockies in the autumn before you were abandoned. It'll take a lot of digging before I feel certain about anything else." He paused, his intense gaze boring into hers. "Digging I intend to do in Colorado."

She turned her attention on the cat. In his insistence on being fed, *now,* he wound in and out of her legs. She pulled a box of kitty kibble from a cabinet. "Just out of curiosity," she said, trying not to sound too interested, "what do you charge?"

"My standard rate is three hundred a day plus expenses. But it's flexible. Depends on the job."

That fixed it. Three hundred dollars a day could go through her savings like a goat through an ivy patch. He might as well have stated a fee of a million bucks and put an end to the discussion forever.

"I can't guarantee anything, Jones, except to tell you that I always do my best."

The computer enhancements kept drawing her attention. She'd spoken to countless private investigators. Most had said her search was impossible. One had spent six months on her behalf wading through adoption bureaucracies in an attempt to find Dana—in the end, Star had found her sister by spotting her photograph in the newspaper. Another P.I. had been an out-and-out crook, taking her money and feeding her phony reports until she finally wised up.

Yet here, for the payment of rice and beans, Austin Tack laid hope on her table.

She owed him.

"I need to think on all this, Tack."

He nodded agreeably. "You can tell me what you think at dinner tonight. Eight o'clock. My treat." He rose lithely from the stool. "My pleasure."

A warm shiver trickled through her belly. Arguing with him would be a whole lot easier if, one, he'd argue properly, and two, if his face and voice weren't sexy enough to melt stone. She tossed her head. "Have it your way. Eight o'clock."

He gave her a slow, sensual smile that made her suspect he didn't believe her tough-girl, hard-as-nails act any more than she did, and then he was gone.

"IS IT TOO EARLY TO CALL?" Star asked her brother-in-law. Her hand sweated on the telephone and she shifted her grip. She wiped her palm on her shirt, but after a four-mile jog in eighty-degree-plus heat, it didn't do much good. She took a quick sip of water.

On the other end, sounding slightly tinny through the telephone connection between Dallas and Cancun, Mexico, Kurt assured her, "Not for me, honey. 'Course, Dana is still snoozing. She's a real slugabed."

Jealousy arced through her midsection. Dana was probably drunk with love. Everything she looked at, every sound she heard, every object she touched, would be so beautiful she'd be aching with joy. She was most likely dreaming about filling this pretty house with pretty babies.

Dana would never be lonely.

She forced a cheerful tone. "You wore her out, huh?"

"I'm working on it." Kurt chuckled wickedly. "What's up? Do you have a problem? Want to talk to Dana?"

"Don't wake her." What was up? She wanted to ask Kurt if Austin was trustworthy, but dollars to doughnuts, he'd say yes. Same thing for asking if he was successful at finding missing persons. Kurt's loyalty to Austin ran deep. "Just pass on a message. I'm taking off for Colorado. I'll talk to Dana's mom. She can use her key to get in to water the plants, and I reckon she'll keep your cat. Don't know—"

"Colorado?" he interrupted. "Why?"

"Personal business."

"Don't play mystery lady with me. What's up?"

His big-brother tone touched her. "Just pass the message on. Tell her I'll call—"

"Not good enough, honey. Did you get a job? How long are you going to be gone?"

Star scowled at the telephone. As an attorney, Kurt often sounded as if he were giving her the third degree, even when he didn't mean to sound intrusive. It was his way of showing he cared. But she owed him nothing by way of explanation.

"Are you still there?" His voice was getting louder.

He'd awaken Dana and she'd want to speak on the phone. Star would end up telling her about Austin's lead. Dana's worry, concern and preference that Star seek counseling rather than their parents would come shining through. "Keep it down," she said. "Don't wake up Dana. Hush."

"Ah-ha!" he exclaimed triumphantly. "You don't want Dana to know where you're going. I get it. A little advice—"

"I don't need advice, Saxon," she growled through her teeth. "Just pass the message on."

"I know what you're up to. You're off looking for your parents. Go for it, but call Austin."

Her breath caught in her throat. Had Austin contacted Kurt? No, that wasn't the way either man operated. "Why should I? That is, *if* I were looking for my parents."

"He's good." He paused before lowering his voice. "And he likes you. So no sense beating your head against a wall. Austin knows what he's doing. He can help."

"I'll think about it. Pass the message on."

After she hung up, she chewed on a thumbnail. In a way, Kurt had given her an answer to the question she'd wanted to ask. She glanced at the stack of computer-enhanced photographs. She didn't need Kurt to tell her Austin was good at what he did.

And he likes you....

That was the tick in the dog's ear. He liked her; she liked him. No use denying it, she liked him a lot. If he were merely physically attractive, she could handle it. There was a lot more to Austin Tack than what met the eyes. He was easy to talk to—too easy. His ability to see straight to the heart of a matter was downright spooky at times.

If he got too close, if she allowed his dark eyes to see into her soul, he'd discover the true reason she had to find her parents. Even thinking about it hurt so much, she'd never told anyone. She suspected she wouldn't have to tell Austin Tack. He'd figure it out all by himself. Once he found out, he'd despise her.

Whatever had happened to her parents was somehow her fault.

She was the bad seed.

AUSTIN HELD THE DOOR to Rick's Place open for Star.

Rick's was a hole-in-the-wall restaurant run by an aging hippie who happened to make the meanest green chili stew north of the Rio Grande. The interior, all dark brick and dirty yellow lighting, had the look of a 1960s beat dive—as if at any moment a cadaverous young woman garbed in black would step to the center of the floor and begin spouting an ode to oxygen.

Head high and shoulders back, Star glided inside. She glanced at a couple seated at a table.

A woman behind the cash register waved, telling them to sit anywhere. Austin led Star to his usual booth. She moved immediately for the seat facing the front door. He guided her toward the opposite side. She resisted.

"I always watch the door," she said.

"So do I."

She pulled her elbow from his grasp and slid onto the bench—facing the door. She grinned tautly at him, until he sat beside her. He plucked a menu from the wire holder on the table and gave it to her.

He ignored her glower and admired her appearance. She wore a forest green silk blouse. The color heightened the rich blue of her eyes and the creaminess of her skin. She smelled fantastic, too. A hint of . . . *Chanel?* he guessed.

"You look great, by the way," he said. "Nice blouse."

"I borrowed it from Dana's closet." She fingered the low neckline. "I don't have any fancy stuff. And—well, I didn't know how nice the restaurant..." She actually blushed. "It's just a shirt."

She'd shoot herself in the foot before admitting she wanted to look nice for him. Entranced, he repressed a sigh.

Rick appeared, wiping his hands on a stained apron. A blue bandanna kept his straggly gray hair off his sweat-shiny face. As he smiled at Star, his eyes gleamed with interest. She met him with a cold expression.

"So, Austin, my man," Rick said. "Lemme guess, gorgeous blonde, a smoky dive. You must be after a ring of international jewel thieves." He laughed as if he'd told the world's funniest joke. "Any friend of the Tack-man's is a friend of mine, lovely lady. I'm Rick."

"Star," she responded, unsmiling.

Rick lingered a few minutes, telling Austin about losing a waitress and hiring another. He'd followed Austin's advice to the letter about checking the young woman's background and references before hiring her.

Listening patiently, Austin nodded. He sensed Star relaxing beside him. She must be figuring out that Rick was essentially harmless. The old hippie wandered back to the kitchen.

"So your friends do their own P.I. work."

"A few phone calls and the right questions can tell him what he needs to know."

"Not a wise business move for you."

"I prefer friendships over business." He put down his menu. "Especially when they cook like Rick. I recommend the green-chili enchiladas. And a pitcher of iced tea to wash them down."

She replaced her menu in its holder and folded her hands atop the table. For a long time she stared into space. "I'm done thinking." Her low, throaty voice held a raw honesty that barely concealed the tender vulnerability so close to the surface. Life had hurt her, but it had made her strong, too.

"You're hired. For three hundred bucks a day."

He'd broken his own rule and made an assumption: he'd assumed they were friends and she understood his motives transcended a mere business deal. He'd work for expenses alone. "My fee is negotiable."

"I'm not good at negotiating." She fiddled with a paper napkin, curling the corners. "Three hundred seems fair. *But,* we stick together. No offense, but I trusted that last yahoo to do right by me and he strung me along like a prize-winning bass."

Being put into the same category as a yahoo pricked his feelings.

"I'll handle expenses. Gas, hotel, food, whatever. I can't afford surprises."

It took a few seconds to recognize he'd been insulted. Considering her background, her distrust wasn't surprising. What did shock him was feeling hurt. He'd thought he'd matured enough to resist taking hard knocks to his male ego. It was disconcerting to learn he wasn't immune.

A waitress arrived with a bowl of chips, salsa and a pitcher of iced tea. Austin filled their glasses before setting to work on Rick's special-recipe salsa. It was hot enough to make his eyes water.

Star lifted her tea and examined the moisture beading on the textured plastic glass. Suddenly she looked at him, her eyes glittering like jewels. "And no funny business, Tack. None at all. This is business, so keep your hands to yourself."

Nice. Not only did she put him in the same class as the crooked P.I., she also lumped him with every other man who'd ever given her cause for dislike or disgust.

He dipped a tortilla chip in the salsa and ate it. The peppers worked their seething magic. He washed it down with a healthy swig of tea.

"It's my terms, or no terms, Tack. That's the way it is."

To which he replied, in his head, *We'll see about that, punkin.*

He offered his hand. "You've got yourself a deal, Jones."

She sealed the bargain with a firm, cool-skinned shake. Relief flickered in her eyes and relaxed her mouth. His wounded feelings stopped stinging as his heart went out to her. She'd taken a big step in accepting his help.

Living up to her expectations could prove to be the biggest challenge of his life.

Chapter Three

Why?

That question had plagued Star ever since Austin had picked her up from Dana's house at 4:30 a.m. She'd wondered all across Texas, the northeast corner of New Mexico and up Interstate 25 through Colorado. After sixteen hours on the road, she still didn't have a clue about why he really wanted to help her.

She could take at face value his comment about being bored and needing a challenge. She understood restlessness better than most, but that was far too simple. If she knew anything at all about Austin Tack, it was that he was a complex individual.

Why in Sam Hill would he drop everything to go gallivanting through the Rocky Mountains? If all he had to go by was that her father had been a cowboy and had once lived in Colorado, then he knew this trip was so much flailing around in the dark. A waste of time. A fool's errand.

Austin was no fool.

Which meant he knew something he wasn't telling. He intended to dazzle her with a stroke of brilliance. A comforting thing to anticipate, and for which she would be properly dazzled.

Working her shoulders, she shifted on the seat, watching the dark plains roll by. At least he was a pleasant travel companion. No chatter, no dillydallying or obnoxious habits.

"Tired?" he asked. He fiddled with the radio and found a rock-and-roll station out of Colorado Springs. He kept the volume low.

"Not really." He'd refused her offers to drive part of the way. Doing nothing mile after mile made her antsy. It gave her too much time to think. "So this three-hundred-bucks-a-day rate of yours. That's based on eight hours?"

"More or less."

"Snooping pays pretty good, then. Thirty-seven fifty an hour."

"Forty bucks an hour." In the glow of the dashboard lights, his smile looked lopsided and sad. "I mean it, the fee is negotiable. I'm not doing this for the money, Jones."

"Yeah, yeah, it's 'cause I'm a great cook." She gave the dashboard an affectionate pat. "Have to pay for these hot wheels somehow."

He laughed with her.

His beige Ford was as pure vanilla as anything that had ever rolled out of Detroit. In Dallas, Austin tooled around on a monster Harley-Davidson motorcycle. She'd expected his car to be just as macho. A Porsche maybe, or a low-slung Corvette.

"Laugh if you want," he said. "But I've never been burned by a subject in this baby."

"Too nondescript to notice, huh?"

"Blends right into the scenery." A John Cougar Mellencamp song came on, and he bobbed his head in time with the hard-driving rhythm. "So, tell me about yourself."

"There's nothing to tell." She pulled down the sun visor and flicked on the vanity mirror light. She fluffed her short hair with her fingers. She dug a tube of lip balm from her pocket and smoothed it over her dry lips.

"The more I know, the easier it is to pluck those floating hunches."

She flipped the visor back into place. "Is that so?"

"Straight-on truth."

"I bet your life is ten times more exciting than mine. How'd you get to be a private eye?"

Traffic was picking up. The northern horizon glowed from the lights of Colorado Springs. Star figured they had about twenty miles to go and then they'd stop for the night. As to where they went after that, she hadn't a clue.

"I was a cop in the marines. Special investigations. I liked it. I have a talent for digging."

She fingered a strand of his shoulder-length hair. "It's hard to picture you as a jarhead." She gave his hair a friendly tug.

"I fell into the corps by accident. When I was seventeen, I boosted a car and got caught. The judge gave me a choice. Jail or military service."

Her mouth dropped open. "*You* stole a car?"

His smile turned mischievous. "I'm flattered you're surprised. Don't be. My youth was, as they say, misspent. I was king of the joyriders."

"Unreal."

"It's the same old story. Broken home, alcoholic parents, bad neighborhood, poor schooling. Half the kids I grew up with are either dead, addicted to something or in prison. Getting caught was the best thing that ever happened to me. The corps taught me discipline and self-respect."

This wasn't what she expected. For all his rebellious appearance, he came off as a straight arrow through and through. He was smart and spoke like an educated man. "I never figured you for a bad boy, Tack."

"Not bad," he said. "Angry. What about you? Were you an angel or a bad girl?"

She gave a start. Did he know? An urge to tell him about herself filled her chest and throat. I was worse than bad, she wanted to say. I did something unforgivable, and that's why my parents are missing and my sister can't remember. If I can't find them, I'll never be able to say I'm sorry.

Instead, she asked, "What made you angry?"

"Life in general. My mother drifted in and out. We'd go months, sometimes years, without seeing her. My father worked at a meat-processing plant. When he wasn't working, he was drinking. He hated everything and everybody. Communists, politicians, rich folks, women, blacks, Indians, Mexicans, anyone who wasn't a Texan, most Texans."

Sympathy and horror mingled. How could he be so nonchalant? "Did he...beat you?" Her voice dropped to a whisper.

"Once a day and twice on Sunday," he said airily.

"None of my business," she muttered, looking away. "I'm sorry." She was sorry she'd asked. The world was full of cruel monsters who shouldn't be allowed anywhere near children. She hated them all.

"Growing up tough isn't all bad. I learned more before I was eighteen than most people learn in a lifetime. Adversity tempers the steel in the soul."

No, this was wrong. He was feeding her a line, telling a tall tale. She had yet to find a trace of bitterness in his face or see it in his actions. No one could emerge from that kind of experience unscathed. "You must hate his guts." If he said no, she'd know he was lying.

"Hate consumes energy rather than creating it. The best thing my old man taught me was how not to hate."

Right. "You're a better person than I am, Tack."

"Not necessarily."

"So I reckon you're all lovey-dovey now. Pals."

He took a while to answer. The air inside the car changed, grew colder. Star rubbed her upper arms. Uncertainty shook her as his change in mood was telegraphed. Maybe this wasn't a tall tale, after all.

"He died almost fifteen years ago. Liver cancer. I got a discharge from the service in order to care for him."

"After what he did to you?" she asked suspiciously. He was telling the truth. She felt it. The knowledge shook her to her toes.

"When I was a kid, I thought he was seven feet tall and breathed fire. Cancer reduced him to a frail, bedridden, frightened old man. Seeing him like that, having our roles reversed, gave me the chance to understand him. He wasn't smart or compassionate or well educated or kind." He glanced at her; she hung on his every word. "I finally understood that in his own way, he'd done his best for me."

Her lips tightened stubbornly. Where was his anger? His bitterness? Where were his scars? "There's nothing to understand. He abused you!"

"Just like his father beat him and his father was beaten before that. It's a pattern I chose to break."

Her forehead tightened. Her joints ached with tension. She clamped her arms over her chest and slumped back on the seat. "I think you're fooling yourself. Pretending like everything's hunky-dory."

"Do you think forgiveness is impossible?" he asked.

His gentle question arrowed straight to the center of her darkest fears. If forgiveness was possible, then finding her parents offered her hope of redemption and peace. If it wasn't, then her entire life had been wasted in perverse self-punishment.

"Forgiveness is like anything else, Jones. You choose to do it. Or not."

It couldn't be that simple. Nothing ever was.

"I'M READY TO CALL IT a day," Austin said.

Traffic moved fast along I-25 as it snaked through the center of Colorado Springs. The road was rough and poorly marked. Orange traffic-construction signs promised repairs soon.

Star pointed out a motel sign and he left the highway. The motel was a block away from the exit. A few cars were parked before units, but there appeared to be plenty of rooms left vacant.

"We may be here a few days."

Star paused with her hand on the car door. "Is this where you mean to start looking?"

"Uh-huh."

She glared askance. "I've been though here lots of times. I've called all the Joneses in the phone book, I reckon. What are you thinking you'll find?"

"This is as good a place as any to start. If we bomb here, we'll try Denver."

"That's it?" She grabbed her backpack off the floor-board. "Brilliant, detective, just danged brilliant."

Her sudden anger bemused him. He watched her stomp into the motel office.

Star returned shortly with a key and directed him to the unit at the end of the row. She met him inside the small, plain room. Ghost scents of thousands of previous occupants mingled with the smells of industrial-strength cleanser and a faint mildewy undertone from the air conditioner. The furnishings consisted of two double beds, a dresser and a plastic table with plastic chairs.

"One room?" he questioned as he tossed his suitcase on a bed.

She fussed with her duffel bag. Her actions were stiff with irritation. "If you've got a problem, I'll get another. But since we'll be here *a while,* it saves me a couple bucks."

He got it now. She thought he was withholding information. He shook his head. "This isn't a snipe hunt, Jones."

"I'll believe it when I see it." She tossed her duffel on the floor, and it hit with a solid thud. She spun around to face him. Her voice quavered with accusation. "Shoot, I can snoop around like a pig in a nut pile just as good as the next guy. What do I need you for?"

He held up his hands, palms toward her. "I told you what I felt certain about."

She glowered at him.

The major advantage in working alone was that he didn't have to explain his thoughts before they were clear in his head. He had, however, all but blackmailed her into hiring him. He supposed he owed her an explanation. He spread open a map of Colorado.

"The disappearance of twin four-year-olds should have made the news in one form or another."

"You think I haven't thought of that?" She edged closer to him in order to see the map.

"Then you know as well as I do that you could spend the next twenty years running data searches." He placed a finger on the map. "Even narrowing our search to one state makes it a big job. Fortunately for us, Colorado has a relatively small population. As far as major news stories go, Colorado Springs or Denver will be the place to find something."

"If anything is here." The fire left her eyes.

"We could have stayed in Texas and conducted searches by telephone and computer. Except, I've learned that fitting bits and pieces together is a lot easier when you can see the puzzle."

She fingered her lower lip as she studied the map. Austin studied her, drawn by the angle of her cheek and the way light played in her pale silver-gold hair. Staying in the same room with her might prove a problem, after all. Or at least highly uncomfortable.

She traced a line from Colorado Springs to Denver and then west to Grand Junction and south to Pueblo.

"I see," she murmured. "When you don't know what you're looking for, it's best to be there when you find it."

Her insight delighted him. "Exactly."

"You're not holding anything back?" she asked hopefully.

"I'm playing straight with you. You know what I know."

She crammed her hands in her back pockets and rocked on her heels. Emotion flickered across her face as she stared at her shoes. "I don't know why I'm being so impatient with you. I'm not usually such a . . . you know. . . ." She looked at him. "I'm sorry."

She was starving for information, he'd given her a taste, and now she wanted the complete menu. He understood. "No problem." He took his shaving kit from his suitcase. "I'm going to hit the shower."

He'd reached the bathroom door when she said, "Don't you ever get mad? Blow up? Shout?"

"Sure I get angry. But no, I don't blow up."

"Never?"

"Not anymore." He entered the bathroom and closed the door.

A quick shower and scrubbing his teeth refreshed him. Toweling his hair, he left the bathroom. The room was empty.

Star's small backpack and the green-tagged room key were missing. She'd left a note propped against the pillows on a bed. She'd gone in search of drinks.

He flopped onto a bed and stretched out full length, flexing his arms, legs and back until travel-stiff joints popped luxuriously. He held Star's note to the light. He was no graphologist, but he knew a little about handwriting analysis. He'd seen it work often enough to know it was a useful science.

Star's handwriting was small and precise, the letters well-formed. Her signature intrigued him. The *S* looked almost lowercase. The cross stroke on the *T* was barely visible. It seemed as if she didn't wish to draw any attention to herself. Or possibly, she had something to hide.

Star returned, carrying a plastic bag from a convenience store. She locked and chained the door behind her.

"Soda pop and springwater. Take your pick." She lined up cans and bottles on the table.

While she showered, he went over his mental list of things to do. He'd wanted a challenge and this certainly qualified. He'd never taken a case where the information was so scanty or so old as to qualify as ancient history.

Nor had he ever taken a case with such high personal stakes. Blow this case, blow his chances with Star forever. It was as simple as that. Failure wasn't an option. He scowled at the ceiling.

Star came out of the bathroom. Her hair glistened wetly and her skin shone with heat. An oversize T-shirt reached midthigh, but it clung in places to her damp body. Her slender legs were well muscled and shapely, her ankles delicately sculpted.

Desire jolted him, weighing his chest and tightening his jaw. Breathing turned into a chore. He had to concentrate to keep from sounding like a raging bull.

He examined closely the physical effect she had on him. At thirty-seven years old, he was no slave to his hormones, and long hours of training had taught him rigid control.

It's emotional, he thought with a measure of amazement. He'd gone his entire adult life managing to rule with his head instead of his heart, and look what happened. He'd fallen for a woman who saw dark motives in his every action, who didn't trust him and who probably didn't even like him.

Nope, failure was definitely not an option.

STAR AWAKENED AND PEERED groggily at the small radio-clock anchored to the nightstand. Six-thirty, mountain standard time. Shivering gripped her, and she pulled her knees higher. The room was freezing.

Austin's bed was empty. Heart in her throat, she sat up and listened. Silence. He'd dumped her, sneaked away, leaving her and her bad temper stuck in Colorado.... She grew aware of a man-shape in a corner.

Austin sat in lotus position—legs folded, back erect, and his hands resting, palms up, on his knees. A thin shaft of gray sunlight touched his face. With his face relaxed, he was so beautiful it took her breath away. Not even the dark stubble on his lower face detracted from his serene beauty.

She watched his chest rise and fall in steady breaths. His hands were perfectly still, the fingers curled as if waiting for something to alight on them.

His eyes opened.

In the half-light, his eyes were black and luminous, emanating peacefulness. Fine eyes, quick with intelligence, truly a window to his soul. Her body warmed. She wanted to touch him, fingertip to fingertip, palm to palm, to absorb his quiet energy flow.

As light increased, turning from gray to silver, his face emerged from the shadows. The strong, solid line of his cheek. The sharp delineation of his chiseled jaw and chin above the corded column of his neck. Glints of gold in hair turned tawny from the sun.

"Good morning," he said.

His voice startled her. Heat flushed her face.

"Are you meditating?" she asked.

"Yes."

"Does that mumbo-jumbo stuff work?"

"At times. It never hurts." In a single graceful motion he rose. He raised his arms toward the ceiling and arched his back, stretching so every muscle rose in relief.

And what muscles they were.

He wore only a pair of gray sweatpants. The way he stretched pulled them tantalizingly low on his hips. She stared at his wolfishly lean belly, bisected by a thick black line of hair. A shiver racked her thighs. Her mouth went desert dry.

It had to be her age. She'd crossed that line the magazines wrote about; she'd reached her sexual peak. How else to explain why merely looking at him aroused her and made her skin itch with longing.

"I didn't mean to disturb you." She eased off the bed. Her bare legs tingled where his gaze touched. "Uh, reckon I'll leave you be while I go..." *Kick myself for getting into this mess.* "Run a few miles."

She fled into the bathroom. Once garbed in her ragged running clothes, she felt more in control. Without so much as a glance his way, she left the room.

Running proved almost as big a mistake as staying in the same room with Austin. By the time she returned, her chest burned and her head was so light she felt a little sick. She flopped onto the bed and gasped. The textured ceiling shimmered and swirled before her eyes.

"Are you all right?" Austin asked.

"No...air...can't...breathe." No wonder Olympic athletes came to Colorado Springs to train. If the altitude didn't kill them, they'd develop the lung capacity of racehorses.

"Ah." He nodded in sympathy. "High altitude, over six thousand feet. It takes a while to get acclimatized. You shouldn't push it."

She'd figured that part out herself. She gave him a baleful look.

"Drink extra water, too. The humidity is practically zero."

"Thank you, doctor."

He'd dressed in jeans and a flannel shirt. A black leather jacket lay on his bed. He was ready to go.

After she dressed in jeans and a sweater, Austin drove them to a pancake house. He ate yogurt, cereal and wholewheat toast. Oxygen deprivation aside, she was starving. She devoured a plateful of pancakes, sausage, eggs and hash browns. Austin studied a city map and a copy of the local newspaper, the *Gazette Telegraph*.

Sated finally, she pushed her plate away. He made another notation on the map. She couldn't imagine what he found that could have anything to do with her parents.

"What are you doing?"

"Looking up the obvious." His enigmatic smile teased as much as it frustrated her. "Do you like surprises?"

"Not particularly."

"Too bad." He folded the newspaper and set it aside. "Then pay the bill, Jones. We have work to do."

Austin drove north. Except for the towering mountains to the west, Colorado Springs from the highway was uninteresting looking. Brown and dusty, its trees having mostly shed their leaves, the town sported the usual fast-food restaurants and motels, interspersed by businesses and factories.

Austin left the highway.

"Tell me where we're going," Star pleaded.

"The Pro Rodeo Hall of Fame."

She laughed. "Are you kidding?"

"Like I said, we start with the obvious."

"Oh, come on. My folks dumped us so they could run away and join the rodeo? That's not obvious, it's dumb."

"The majority of missing people are missing because they want to be. Often they change their names. Sometimes they change their appearances. Some assume completely new identities."

"What's that got to do with a tourist trap?"

"Once a hobbyist, always a hobbyist. Some of my best leads have come from clubs, hobby groups and professional organizations. They tend to be as compulsive and intrusive as government bureaucracies in keeping records, but they're usually a lot more cooperative about sharing information."

Expecting a shabby roadside tourist trap, Star wasn't quite prepared for the modern building with a bronze statue of a broncobuster towering over the parking lot.

Star stepped out of the car. Despite her sweater and jacket, goose bumps rose on her arms. Her breath was visible in wispy puffs. There was snow on the mountain peaks. She shivered, wondering if they would end up in the mountains. If they did, she'd resign herself to freezing.

Inside the museum, they stopped at the admissions desk. Star's first impression was how empty the place seemed. The entryway was spacious and the walls were practically bare. Star and Austin were the only visitors.

A young woman behind the counter asked if they were PRCA members. Star shook her head and paid the five-dollar admission fees.

Austin leaned an arm on the counter. The young woman responded with a flutter of mascara-fat eyelashes. He asked, "Do you have a research library in here?"

She frowned. "Uh, we have books for sale in the gift shop."

Austin pushed away from the counter.

The woman began a spiel about a movie and tour. Star cut her off with a wave of her hand. "Can we look around on our own?"

"Help yourself." She turned a radiant smile on Austin. "Look all you want. If you have any questions, just ask. That's what I'm here for."

I bet it is, Star thought.

The young woman leaned over the counter to watch Austin walk away. She was all but drooling over the way he filled his jeans.

Star narrowed her eyes. Was it just Austin, or hadn't she ever noticed before that women were as bad as men when it came to ogling a good-looking passerby? "On TV, private eyes use fast guns and faster fists. Looks like you've got different weapons." She slanted an impertinent look at his backside.

"As a proponent of nonviolence, I'm a strong believer in the value of honey over vinegar."

"Uh-huh. Especially with ditsy girls. I bet that honey just oozes."

His smile did funny things to her knees. "Do I detect a note of jealousy, Jones?" he asked in a silky purr.

He'd pull teeth easier than gaining an admission like that. "In your dreams." She stopped in the middle of the small room they'd entered and looked around at the boots, saddles and photographs on display. "What are we looking for?"

He produced the enhanced image of her father's belt buckle. "We'll start with this."

There were a few belt buckles displayed in the cases, but none resembled the buckle in their photograph. They walked down a hallway. On both walls were boards listing Pro Rodeo Cowboy Association awards. The dates only went back as far as 1982. Star read every name. None was a variation on Jerry Jones. She followed Austin into the main museum.

"This is more like it," Austin said.

Dominating the museum was a life-size bronze statue of a boy and a dog playing with a lariat. Glass cases lining the walls were filled with saddles, trophies, spurs, belt buckles, photographs and other memorabilia. Scattered throughout the museum were displays containing circular stands. Each was topped by a small bronze statue of a rodeo event. The statue bases were engraved with the names of championship cowboys.

Star started with the first plate listing saddle bronc champions: 1956, Deb Copenhaver, '57, Alvin Neison, '58, Marty Wood, all the way through 1964 when Marty Wood won again. The plates encircled the statue base. She read each name. None of them was Jerry Jones.

Meanwhile, Austin drifted along the display cases, studying the belt buckles inside.

There were more events in a rodeo than Star had ever considered: saddle bronc riding, bareback riding, bull riding, calf roping, steer roping and team roping. Which one had drawn her father into the arena?

On the steer-wrestling display she found the name of John W. Jones. A surge of excitement made her muscles jump. He'd won a championship in 1970.

"Hey, Tack, I found a Jones." She pointed at the engraved name.

Austin looked behind her at the big display case highlighting the careers of champion steer wrestlers. She followed his gaze and saw photographs of John W. Jones. She grasped her medicine bag through her shirt. She didn't need to bring out her photograph to know John W. Jones's face wasn't the one she sought.

Elation left her as quickly as it had arisen.

They spent hours in the museum. Star read every name and studied every photograph. Finally, she said glumly, "He's not here."

"Interesting place, anyway," Austin replied, and gave her shoulder a friendly pat. He headed into the gift shop. There he thumbed through books and magazines, finally selecting a copy of *PSN, Prorodeo Sports News*. Star paid for it.

"This is the Hall of Fame. Champions only. Let's go on over to headquarters."

"What headquarters?"

"The rodeo association. It's right across the street."

The man they spoke to at the PRCA headquarters studied the photos of Jerry and the enhancement of the belt buckle for a long time before conceding he couldn't identify the man or his buckle. Austin left his card with their hotel number written on it. The man promised to call if he dug anything out of the archives.

"Well, gee, Tack, that was fun," Star said as they walked to the car. "What next? Go to the zoo? Ride up to Pikes Peak? Hit a few gift shops?"

"Patience, Prudence," he said with a smile. "I'm a long way from licked."

Shiloh Dawn

Chapter Four

After leaving the rodeo association headquarters, Austin drove them to the Penrose Public Library in downtown Colorado Springs. The library was a rambling building, modern and businesslike, yet pleasant. An odd-looking statue welded together out of bronze leaves into a man's shape graced the entrance. Folks around here sure liked their statues, Star mused as she followed Austin into the building.

"Obvious choice number one didn't pan," he explained. "Now we'll examine obvious choice number two."

Obvious to him, maybe.

For years, she'd been exploring the obvious. Her method had been to go through every telephone directory she found, seeking Jerry—or Jerome, Gerald, Jeremy, Jeremiah—Joneses. She'd also checked courthouses in every city and town for birth records. She couldn't even remember how many record files she'd searched. The trouble was, she'd done most of her looking in Texas. "What's obvious?"

"If your memory is true and it wasn't your mother who took you to Dallas, then we're probably looking for something illegal or disastrous."

"Like a kidnapping?" Being kidnapped had always been her most comforting fantasy. She and Dana had been spirited away by evil crooks. One of them, the woman who'd taken them to Dallas, turned out to have a heart of gold, unable to bear what the bad guys had in mind for the little girls. All these years, her parents had been searching as frantically for her as she had been for them.

A kidnapping couldn't possibly be Star's fault.

Austin laid a hand on her shoulder and looked her straight in the eye. "A possibility exists that your parents were killed in an accident. Are you prepared for that?"

She drew in a deep, steadying breath. "Just as long as I know. That's all that matters." *You're fooling yourself,* a voice nagged in the back of her brain. *It mattered very much. They had to give her the chance to make amends.* "You don't need to be protecting me from anything, Tack. I'm not exactly a stranger to bad news."

"We could also be looking at a custody dispute. If your parents had been in the middle of a nasty divorce, one or the other might have abandoned you rather than allow the other to have custody."

She flinched. Out of the thousands of scenarios she'd envisioned over the years, that was one she hadn't considered.

He showed his palms. "I've seen stranger things."

They set to work. The library had a complete record of newspaper files on microfiche. The *Gazette Telegraph,* the local newspaper, had been reporting the news in the area since 1878. Since the photograph of Jerry had been taken in the fall of 1968 and Star and Dana had been abandoned in April 1969, the two of them read every word of every article printed during that time frame.

Nothing.

Star leaned back on her chair and rubbed her sore eyes. Her rear end ached from sitting on the wooden chair. "This is a bust, Tack. Any more bright ideas?"

He poked her shoulder with a stiff finger. "We still have an hour before they close. We've barely scratched the surface."

"What else can we look for?"

He ticked off on his fingers. "Birth announcements, wedding announcements, divorce decrees, obituaries, police blotter reports, real-estate sales." He patted a viewer. "All of it listed right here."

His matter-of-fact optimism fascinated her. If he felt any frustration, he sure didn't show it. "What if we don't find anything like that?"

"We look someplace else. *After* we've exhausted all possibilities here." He gave her a lopsided smile. "I told you this isn't impossible, and I believe it. But I never promised it would be easy." He indicated the viewers with a sweeping gesture. "Your parents existed. We know that's a fact. We know they had twin girls. That's another fact. From those facts, we can make a few guesses. They were probably married, owned property, held jobs, attended school. Any or all of those things means they left a paper trail. We're handicapped because we lack vital statistics, but we can collect anything that looks promising and go from there. If we can get a full name, then we can gain access to all kinds of records."

"Is this lesson number one, Mr. Detective?"

"Austin Tack's hands-on course," he said with a wink. "You, too, can be a private eye. The real number one lesson to learn is—" he held up a finger "—when skill and experience fail, there's always persistence."

Her admiration for him went up another notch. He didn't merely preach patience, he lived it. Calm, surefooted, undaunted by blind alleys or setbacks. She had much to learn from this man. She vowed to pay attention.

She resumed searching through the stacks of microfiche. She felt positive her birthday was December 25—memories of birthday parties mingled with Christmas trees were too vivid to forget. Of the year, she wasn't sure. She had to have been at least four when she and Dana were abandoned, but they may have been five and small for their age. She started her search in 1964. Every time she found the name Jones, she wrote down the information in her notebook.

Austin grunted. Alerted by the *ah-ha* sound of it, she looked at him. He was slouching, glowering at the viewer screen. The short hairs lifted on the nape of her neck.

"You found something," she whispered.

"I don't know." He pointed to a story headlined Body of Missing Woman Found.

Dated August 4, 1969, the story told how a woman, Rowena Waxman, had been reported missing earlier that spring. Two teenagers on a fossil hunt had found her badly decomposed body.

She read the story twice. "Charming," she said dryly. "What's it got to do with me?" A bad feeling tried to stretch its way over her head like a rubber cap.

He exchanged the microfiche sheet in the viewer for another. He pointed out another story dated a few weeks after the first. Authorities had declared Rowena Waxman's death a homicide. They were seeking information about a man named Jerrod S. Jones. Jones was described as a white male, six feet three inches tall, with blond hair and blue eyes. He'd been employed as a ranch hand near Gold Coin, Colorado. It was believed he was traveling with his wife and two daughters.

Star's heart thudded against her rib cage. Jerrod Jones... Jerry Jones. Not Gerald or Jerome or Jeremy or Jeremiah. Jerrod. She rubbed her medicine bag with nervous fingers. Her vision grayed.

"Homicide? That means murder," she said in a voice gone rough. She cleared her throat. "That can't be right. Can't be."

But it is....

He jerked a thumb over his shoulder. "Find a state map and look up Gold Coin."

As if from far, far away she heard a woman. "Jerrod Scott Jones! I'm gonna feed your supper to the dog if you don't get in here right now!'' The voice was high and clear, full of laughing exasperation. Accompanying the voice was the ghostly scent of frying bacon and yeasty hot bread.

''Jones? Star.'' Austin caught her upper arms in a tight grip.

Startled, her entire body jerked. Her knees buckled. If he hadn't been holding her, she might have fallen. Overhead lights glared into her eyes, and they blurred with pained tears.

''What's the matter?'' Austin eased her onto a chair. ''You look ready to pass out on me. Want some water?''

His anxiety was so far removed from his usual calm, she wanted to laugh. She feared if she opened her mouth, she'd cry. Breathing hurt. A mass invaded her chest. Unnamed fear squeezed her from every side.

Crouched at her knees, Austin rubbed one of her icy hands. ''Talk to me.''

''It's him. We found him.''

''We don't know Jerrod Jones is your father. The bit about the daughters makes it seem possible, but we need more proof. The library is about to close, but we can do more research tomorrow. Relax.''

She felt it in the core of her heart, right where it counted. The shock of recognition was so strong, it was akin to being slapped awake or doused with icy water. Her knowledge was as real as knowing the sky is blue and mountains are high.

Jerrod Jones was her father, and the awful thing that happened so long ago concerned the death of Rowena Waxman.

''NO, I DON'T WANT anything to eat,'' Star snapped as she stalked into the motel room. ''Stop treating me like I'm made out of glass!''

She flung her jacket on the bed. She wanted to kick the furniture and punch the walls. If the lamps weren't bolted into place, she might have thrown one. At some point during the short ride from the library to the motel, the fear had become too overwhelming. She mustered anger to keep the terror at bay.

What was the old saying? Careful what you wish for, you might get it. . . .

Jerrod Scott Jones. Rowena Waxman. Homicide. The tangled past lay at her feet, daring her to pick it up and unravel it.

Austin paused in the open doorway. "I know you're upset. But you're reacting too soon on too little information. We don't know enough to draw conclusions."

"We ought to find out he's been convicted and executed before I get excited, right?" Her skin felt too tight; her temples throbbed. Fear swallowed her, consumed her, stripped her sensibilities down to raw emotions.

"Even if Jerrod Jones is your father, we don't know if he was a suspect. The article merely said the police were seeking information about him. So calm—"

"Look, Tack!" She whirled on him and planted her fists on her hips. "If I want the voice of reason, I'll say, please say something reasonable. Otherwise, just butt out!"

"If you say so." He nodded graciously, backed up a step and closed the door.

His silent departure stunned her. Echoes of her harsh words and hateful tone made her wince. Austin was doing exactly what he'd promised her he'd do. Here she was, acting like a waspish bitch, wanting to kill the messenger. Anger drained from her body like syrup from a jar, leaving her empty and sticky with shame.

She hurried to the door and tore it open. There was nothing in the parking place in front of the room except an empty paper cup and a few cigarette butts. Austin was gone.

"Doggon it," she muttered through her teeth. He wasn't getting paid enough to put up with her crap. By all rights,

the private eye ought to just hightail it back to Dallas—
without her.

HOLDING THE KEY poised to enter the lock, Austin hesitated. Star should be over her upset. Or then again, maybe
not. Her passions ran deep; no halfway measures with her.
His instincts had said to leave her alone, let her work out the
shock in her own way. He hoped he'd been right.

He steeled himself and entered the room.

The television was on, the volume turned down low. Star
lay under the covers, propped against pillows on the bed.
She appeared calm.

He glanced at the television. It was a nature show about
a coral reef. Divers followed an octopus into its lair. "Good
reception."

"Cable."

"Still mad?" He offered her a small white paper bag.

She stared at it a long moment before she struggled upright and took it. She peeked inside the bag and a smile
trembled on her lips. She pulled out a dangling pink worm.
It wriggled, shiny in the lamplight. "Bait?" she asked.

"Gummy worms." He held out another bag. "I brought
you a sandwich, too."

"You're a weird guy." Her smile faded and she lowered
her head. "I'm sorry as can be for yelling at you. When I get
scared, I get mad. I don't mean what I say. It just pops out.
It would be a whole lot easier if you'd yell back."

"Apology accepted."

Her smile reappeared by tremulous fractions. She held out
a hand. "Did you eat? Give me your receipts."

"Not necessary."

Her hand remained steady. "We have a deal. Cough it up,
Tack."

He handed over receipts from a sandwich shop and from
a gas station where he'd fueled the car. "I'm weird, you're

hardheaded." He winked. "We're quite a pair." He headed into the bathroom.

As he brushed his teeth, he noticed the small waste can next to the sink was filled with soggy-looking tissues streaked with mascara. She'd had herself a good cry, then.

He changed into his sweatpants.

When he joined Star, she had taken a few bites out of the sandwich. Smacking her lips, she peered suspiciously at the filling. "This has to be something healthy and good for me. What is it?"

"Eggplant sauteed in olive oil, with mozzarella on honey whole wheat. Like it?"

She pulled a face. "One of those big purple things?" She tried another bite. "Never ate an eggplant burger before."

He stretched out on the bed and hooked his hands behind his neck. From the corner of his eye, he caught the surreptitious glances she darted his way. She ate hungrily, finishing the sandwich. She licked her fingers, her tongue pink and kittenish, and his heart skipped a beat.

It's a test, he told himself. Think of her not as a beautiful, desirable woman, but as a friend. A companion and partner. Don't dwell on her corn-silk hair or the sinuous curve of her ear. Forget her eyes have the blazing depths of perfect sapphires.

And don't even think about her long legs and pretty knees.

She tossed the wrapper in the waste can, and sighed, heavily.

Sorrow whispered in the sound and pierced him. "What's the matter, Jones?"

She shook her head as if to say "Nothing," but her expression spoke volumes of something.

"That article knocked you for a loop, but it isn't time for worrying yet. We don't know Jerrod Jones from Gold Coin is your Jerry."

"It is," she said softly. "Don't ask me how I know, but I do."

"Did you remember something?"

Her eyebrows scrunched over a distant gaze. "Kind of. A woman." She cupped a hand around the side of her mouth and called softly, "Jerrod Scott Jones, time for supper."

He sat up and looked hard at her. "Scott?"

She nodded. "Don't ask me where that comes from, but I'm sure as sitting here his full name is Jerrod Scott Jones. Only one person ever called him Jerrod Scott. Only one…"

Goose bumps rose on his back and arms. Her face looked as if she were a million miles and a lifetime away. He'd held private doubts about her ability to remember anything concrete that had occurred when she was four years old. The sureness of her statement erased those doubts.

"Even if he is," Austin said, "we don't know he was involved in the murder. Being wanted for questioning means nothing by itself."

"Quit trying to sugarcoat it, Tack. I know what I know. Something bad happened." She bolted upright and hugged her knees, curling within herself. "Real bad."

He wanted to go to her, hold her, let her know feeling the fear was all right and she was strong enough to withstand it. Intuition cautioned him to respect her space.

"Right about now," she said wearily, "I'm thinking Dana is right. Let sleeping dogs lie, don't examine gift horses— you know what I mean. Maybe I don't really want to know what happened."

"Your choice."

She slanted an annoyed glance at him. He could feel her desire for him to make a decision for her. If he told her to quit now, she might very well do so—and be relieved.

But all decisions must come from her heart. "Looking for truth is like looking for a specific pebble on a beach. It's a tough job. The beach is covered with muck and sharp shells and broken glass. Most people give up before they start."

She burrowed back down inside the covers and watched television. Finally she said, "It's a doggone big beach." Her smile warmed him. "You've got quite a gift for words. It's like you open my head, take what I'm feeling and say it out loud."

A tenuous connection at best, but he was reaching her. Nearly absurd pleasure filled him. "How long have you been looking for your parents?"

"Forever." Her medicine bag lay on the bedside table. She rubbed it, her expression pensive. The old leather was worn shiny in spots. "I used to run away from the foster homes, looking for my family. I got tagged as a delinquent, but I didn't care. Social workers tried to tell me my folks were dead. Some said Dana didn't exist, that I made her up. Like I was crazy. A split personality or something." She closed her eyes. "Nobody believed me. Nobody helped."

"You never stopped believing."

"I get to thinking they threw me away, discarded me like so much trash. That's when it's really hard. That's when I think maybe Dana is right. I should go into therapy or get married and just get on with my life."

"Which would be a mistake."

"So how come you don't think I'm crazy?" She snuggled beneath the covers. Her large blue eyes locked on his face.

"I understand quests."

She chewed over that one. "What do you mean?"

He rolled onto his side to face her and propped his cheek on his hand. There was only two feet of space between the beds; he could touch her with little effort. But the gap between their souls was wide and treacherous, filled with traps. One misstep and he could lose her forever. He kept his hands to himself.

"Of all the animals, only man questions his own awareness." He extended a hand, palm up and open. "We're all looking for answers."

Her upper lip lifted. "You're talking mystical."

He denied it with a shake of his head. "It's as basic as breathing. Quests give meaning to our lives."

She hitched the blankets higher on her shoulder.

"A grave injustice was committed when you and Dana were torn from your family. Your quest is to right the wrong. The answers belong to you, and only you can find them. Those who expect you to stop are the crazy ones, not you."

"I should just keep looking until I die?" she asked.

"Or until you find what you're looking for."

"And then what?"

"And then you find another quest." He shrugged. "It's the nature of the beast."

She fell silent. She watched the undersea scenes on the television. The drone of the show's narrator was background noise. Wind rippled against the window. Traffic rumbled and rushed on the nearby highway.

Talk of quests made him think of his own life. His was a quest for inner peace. It surprised him to realize he'd found it. He felt good about himself. The demons of the past no longer had the power to control him. It was time for bigger and better things.

"So where did you go tonight?" she asked. She kept her gaze on the television.

Her too-careful, I-don't-give-a-hoot tone made him smile. "Around."

"Meet anybody?"

"No one in particular." He turned his head. Her eyes were lost in the shadows.

"That's all? You didn't go for a . . . drink or anything?"

She wanted something, but he was unsure what it might be. Her vibes were full of conflict. "A sandwich shop. Gas station. Nothing exciting."

"You didn't go to the police?"

Uh-oh. Big shift here. "Why would I go to the police?"

"My father is wanted in connection—"

"Stop." He sat up on the bed and draped his arms over his knees. "Lesson number two, Jones. Never create facts out of speculation."

"But the newspaper said . . ." Her voice trailed away. She sat up, too. "That woman was murdered."

"And the authorities wanted to find your father. If the reporters got their facts right, then we know that in 1969 your family was in Gold Coin, Colorado. We know a woman was reported missing around the same time you were abandoned in Dallas. We know her body was found several months later."

"And the police want my father."

"They *did* want him. He could have been a witness. Or a friend of hers. Or a relative. They could have found him, questioned him and let him go. I refuse to speculate until I know more. You're shaking your head. What's the matter?"

"Nothing." She rested her chin on her knees.

She clammed up. Emotions tangled around her, blocking him out. She wanted to speculate, but speculation was a bad habit and potentially dangerous, leading to conclusions based on emotion rather than fact. After a few minutes, she left her bed and entered the bathroom.

He lay back down and watched the watery wonders flickering across the TV screen.

He must have dozed. Her appearance at his side startled him. Head high, arms rigid at her sides, she stared down at him. The blue-silver light from the television bathed her in shifting shadows.

He wondered if he was dreaming.

"I'm freezing."

Definitely dreaming. He wanted her so much he'd created this fantasy. He scooted over and raised the covers.

Always watching his eyes, she eased onto the bed. The mattress sagged as her long legs smoothed against his. His skin crackled and every nerve ending sprang to life. She touched his chest. Her fingertips parted the thick curls, tickling him. Everything inside him dropped, then rebounded, centering in his loins. Desire flared, shaking him.

This was no dream.

He caressed the back of her head. Her hair was as soft as rabbit's fur. "What's this?" he asked.

"Don't talk." It sounded like an order, but he sensed it was a plea.

He grasped her neck and drew her down for a kiss.

Ah, but she was sweet. Her cool lips tasted of peppermint. Under his hands, her neck and back were tender, yet firm, all delicate lines and fascinating angles. Her skin was silk and smelled of heady woman-musk.

He teased her with his tongue and her lips parted. A tentative flick answered him and hot emotion tightened his chest. She curled her fingers in his hair, tugging his scalp. She kissed him hard, her mouth hot and hungry, meeting the thrust of his tongue with an eager clumsiness that made his blood roar.

He'd wanted her for so long, he scarcely dared believe she was actually in his arms.

He stroked her back. Her T-shirt rode up on her hips and he eased both hands underneath and spread his fingers wide to gather as much sensation as possible of silky-soft skin, firm muscle, and the delicate arches of her rib cage.

She broke the kiss and gasped.

He nuzzled her neck, tasting sweet saltiness. "Star..." he whispered. "You're so beautiful."

Soul mate, the other half of his whole. She moved her leg, stroking him, and a groan was wrenched from his throat. Heat melted him.

She abruptly twisted and half raised herself. The arm she rested on quivered, her biceps taut. Her eyes were black; she panted through her mouth. The dark intoxicating scent of desire rolled off her skin, arousing him to greater heat. Her T-shirt had caught under her hip and it stretched tightly, molding over her small, perfect breasts. Her nipples thrust against the fabric, beckoning his touch.

Something wasn't right. He loosened his hold on her. He forced his thoughts into focus. She'd gone rigid.

This was more than not right, more than new-lover jitters or second thoughts. She was afraid. Possible reasons raced through his mind. She'd been raped or abused—but no, she'd come to him, willing and aroused. She wasn't physically afraid of him. Perhaps he'd inadvertently angered her. Except if he had, she'd let him know.

Experimentally, he rubbed her upper arm. She flinched and quivered. He withdrew his hand. "What's wrong, punkin?"

"We have to get one thing straight." Her chin trembled. She stared above and beyond him, her expression pained and on the verge of tears. "You're a real nice fella and all—sexy, too. Only don't be getting any big ideas. After sex, I always sleep alone. That's the way it is."

Snooping around in people's lives had greatly diminished his ability to be surprised or shocked. That, however, was one of the oddest things he'd ever heard a woman say. Her little speech had the effect of a gallon of ice water dumped on his lap.

She didn't want him.

At least, she didn't want the intimacy he had to offer. That, he suspected, was at the heart of this: intimacy scared the hell out of her. She was prepared to give, but not accept; willing to bare her body, but not her soul. She'd lie flesh to flesh with him, but only after erecting a solid wall of rules and terms to make sure their lovemaking never transcended her barriers.

Desire ebbed, replaced by weary sadness.

He might be able to kiss away the wariness in her eyes. He might be able to win her trust with gentle hands and tenderness. He might even be able to earn enough of her confidence so she'd tell him what it was she really needed.

Might wasn't good enough. Not for her; not for him. He still wasn't exactly certain what he wanted from her, but he knew without doubt it wasn't impersonal sex.

He placed a hand gently against her cheek. "Then it's only fair to tell you, punkin, after *love*making, I never sleep alone." He patted her cheek, then grasped her upper arms and firmly urged her off the bed.

The thwarted ache in his groin was nothing compared to the astonished hurt on her face. Running on instinct, he could only pray he'd done the right thing.

He rolled to his side, his back to her. "Good night, Jones. See you in the morning."

Chapter Five

Star had never been so embarrassed in her life. A restless night spent tossing and turning hadn't helped. A killer run on the steep hills of Colorado Springs, which left her legs wobbly as cooked spaghetti and her lungs on fire, hadn't helped. Sitting across the table from Austin at breakfast had been miserable. And the day had gone downhill from there.

Further research at the library and then at the newspaper office had turned up nothing more about her parents. Now they were headed for Gold Coin, and she still couldn't talk to Austin—she couldn't even look at him.

Why, why, *why?* Bad enough she'd thrown herself at him, but then to say what she'd said. She'd sounded like some kind of truck-stop floozy. A woman who hopped in and out of beds with the careless aplomb of an alley cat. Her face burned even to think about it.

Austin steered the car onto a turnout overlooking a mountain valley. Two and a half hours driving southwest of Colorado Springs had put them into a whole new world. All around them the Rockies were a patchwork of dark green spruce, brighter green pines, yellow-gold aspens and out-crops of gray-and-red boulders. Layers of mountain peaks, many of them bald above the timberline, stretched into the distance. The sky was so blue it seemed enameled.

He shut off the engine.

In the sudden silence, Star shifted uncomfortably on the passenger seat. A psychic cloud filled the car, rumbling and restless, as prickly as a coil of barbed wire between them. She wanted to apologize. She wanted to plead insanity!

She hadn't the faintest idea where to begin.

He pulled the key from the ignition and left the car.

Granite boulders, striated by glittering white quartz, had been pushed to the edge of the turnout. Austin sat on one, facing the valley.

Wondering if he'd chosen this ethereal place for meditation, she waited awhile inside the car. Restless curiosity overcame her and she followed him. The air was as cold as it was clear. Hands jammed in her jacket pockets, she peered over the edge of the turnout. Tenacious pines and aspens clung to the mountainside, growing wherever the rocks trapped a bit of soil. Not a breath of wind disturbed the trees. Far away, water rushed over rocks.

"Are we lost?" she asked.

He stared distantly. "No." A wayward breeze lifted the ends of his long hair. A few crows relayed messages up and down the valley, but other than that, it was quiet enough to inspire poetry.

"Car trouble?"

"Woman trouble." He turned his head.

Heat rose on her cheeks, and she shifted her weight from foot to foot. He was angry about last night. Or more likely, he was disgusted.

Since when did she care what a man thought of her?

Since meeting Austin Tack, that's when. She hated caring, but she couldn't stop. His opinion meant the world to her, and knowing he held her in low esteem left her humiliated.

He resumed studying the view.

Star eased onto a boulder and dangled her sneaker-clad feet over the precipice. "How long are we going to sit here?"

"Embarrassed silence gives off bad vibes. We need to talk about last night."

"You're the one who kicked me out of bed," she snapped. She hunched turtlelike into her jacket. Apologize, you idiot, she told herself. Her tongue tangled, cleaving to the roof of her mouth.

"That's not the way I saw it," he said. "You laid down terms I couldn't accept, so I stated my own."

She swung her feet, knocking the boulder, causing a miniature landslide of dust and pebbles. "You don't like me. Fine." All the wrong words were coming out of her mouth. That wasn't what she'd meant to say. She meant to explain how being with him felt unlike anything else she'd ever experienced. How his touch set her on fire inside and out. How his kiss roused dreams of living happily ever after with a normal life and a family and a home to call her own. How in the strangest way she felt safe with him, and even stranger, it scared her to death.

"I don't like you," he mused softly. "You honestly think that?"

She hunched deeper in her coat, ashamed.

"Finding out about Jerrod Jones knocked you off your feet. I understand. Those memories of yours must be hell to live with. Then to have a major breakthrough in remembering his full name, knowing something terrible happened." He shook his head in wonder. "Rough."

He was doing it again, reaching inside her head and giving voice to her feelings.

"If anyone deserves a little hand-holding and comfort, you do. You're allowed to feel bad or anxious or scared. You're allowed to need a shoulder to cry on."

Now was the time. He knew she was scared, so she might as well admit it.

"I'm no saint, Jones," he said. "I accept what's freely given. Usually. And the truth is—" his dark eyes were compelling pools ''—you're the most beautiful, desirable woman I've ever met.''

Trembling weakness gripped her knees and heat flooded her midsection.

''Your beautiful body isn't enough. I want your beautiful mind and soul, as well. I can't accept the terms you laid down. That's all there is to it.''

Truth, he spoke a simple truth. He wasn't angry, but...he didn't know. ''What if,'' she began cautiously, ''a person did something bad?''

''How bad?''

She wanted to tell him so much, she ached. ''Real bad. Unforgivable bad. *Evil.*''

''Nothing is unforgivable.'' He hopped off the boulder. His boots crunched lightly on loose gravel. He tipped his head so his face was to the sun. His hair caught light and sparkled like gold dust.

She crept off the rock. ''Nothing? You can forgive evil?''

He extended his hands to her, shifting them as if weighing the air cupped in his palms. ''Forgiveness doesn't excuse the evildoer or the evil act. It frees the victim.''

His curled fingers beckoned. As if tugged by invisible cords, she walked into his embrace.

''Do you know what I mean?'' he asked against her hair.

She did. If the face she saw in the mirror was ever to become a whole person, if she was to live unfettered by the past, then first she must forgive herself. Easier said than done. She hugged him, anyway, and pressed her cheek against his strong shoulder.

''We're partners.'' He rubbed her back. ''You can talk to me about anything. Nothing is too bad.''

She wished that were true. ''Can we just forget last night?'' she whispered. ''We're adults, we can act like adults. I can act like one. I'm sorry for what I did. Let's just forget it.''

"Can you do that?" he asked. He pressed a tender kiss to her forehead.

She stared into his velvety eyes. She doubted if she could forget. She doubted if she wanted to. Kissing him had been heaven. She fit perfectly in his arms. Deep-seated instinct claimed he was the only one for her.

She pulled away. Head hanging, she grasped her elbows and stared at her feet. "You're getting a good eyeful of what a flake I am."

"I don't think you're a flake."

She risked a peek at him. His face was calm and non-judgmental. "Truth is, I'm scared. I'm scared I'll find my parents. I'm scared I won't."

"The unknown is always greater than the sum of its parts."

"What dead guy said that?"

His smile rivaled the glory of the panoramic view. "I did. Truth is often ugly, sticky, hurtful, disappointing. But it's never as bad as what you imagine."

She smiled tremulously. "Never?"

"Rarely, then." He offered his hand. After a moment, she took it, and his long capable fingers entwined with hers. "This is your quest. You can continue, you can quit. Always remember, I'm on your side."

THE ROAD DROPPED STEEPLY over the side of a mountain, then flattened into a lazy curve flanked by wide gravel shoulders. Star stared at a signboard mounted on the right-hand shoulder. Her heart dropped into her belly, where it rested hard and cold. Clutching Austin's upper arm, she whispered, "Pull over. Stop the car."

This was it. Jerry Jones had once stood on this road, smiling shyly and squinting into the sun from under the broad brim of his cowboy hat.

The signboard was deeply weathered, the wooden supports splintered and dark with rot near the ground. In layers of brilliant forest green paint against a snowy background, the sign announced Welcome to Gold Coin, Founded 1898. Underneath were the names of restaurants, a bank and a hotel. Along the bottom, it read, Colorado's Largest Natural Steam Vents. Painted next to that was a picture of a conical mountain with steam curling out the sides.

Austin dug through the folder of photo enhancements. He produced the image of the sign.

It was a perfect match, right down to the typeface. Star's father must have been standing only a few feet from where the car was parked.

"They haven't changed their sign in over twenty-five years?" she asked in wonder.

"They've changed it. The lodge emblems are on the other side. Looks like a fairly fresh paint job. Does it bring back any memories?"

"Not memories, exactly. It just..." She frowned, needing the right word to describe how she felt. "It's right, that's all. This is the place."

Austin drove into town.

Gold Coin nestled at the end of a high mountain valley. Main Street snaked steeply up a hill; sidewalks had steps. Old brick buildings dominated the west end of the street, but at the eastern end, the buildings were made of wood. Dirt roads fanned out north and south. Victorian houses with tiny brown yards were dwarfed by a few massive modern homes sporting satellite dishes and natural landscaping. Small signs planted in yards and in windows declared the homeowners' feelings either for or against bringing small-stakes gambling to Gold Coin.

Creepy feet pitter-pattered up and down Star's spine.

If she had to point out a particular building or landmark and say she recognized it, she couldn't do it. But the sense of familiarity was so overwhelming she could barely breathe. She cleared her throat. "I've been here before."

He parked the car diagonally in front of the Pocket Mountain Hotel. The redbrick, turn-of-the-century building had a brass marker declaring its historical-landmark status.

They stepped out of the car.

He pointed northwest to a conical hill. Starkly gray in comparison to the boulder-strewn forests surrounding it, it looked like a giant anthill. "That must be the volcano."

She shaded her eyes against the bright sunshine. Icy air nipped under her jacket collar. It made no sense for the sun to be so bright and yet the air still be so cold. "I don't see any steam coming out."

"Tourist season is over. The vents must be shut off," he said with a grin. He indicated a diner across the street. "Let's grab a cup of coffee and get a feel for the place."

Inside the diner, Star hoped for a jolt of recognition, but the interior did nothing for her. Built long and narrow, it had a high ceiling and pine paneling on the walls. A soda-fountain-type counter ran the length of the restaurant. It had 1950s-style chrome stools topped by red leather cushions. High-backed booths lined one wall. Handwritten signs advertised mashed potatoes and roast beef sandwiches, vegetable soup, and steak and eggs. A few men, wearing blue jeans, flannel shirts and cowboy boots, occupied counter stools.

A woman dressed in a white butcher's apron over her checked shirt and jeans acknowledged them with a nod. "Have a seat anywhere, folks. Be right with you." She bustled down the length of the counter, filling mugs with fresh coffee.

Austin and Star jostled a moment over who got the side facing the door. Star stopped the argument before it began and gave him the observation seat.

A man left the diner. He paused near the door and took a cowboy hat off a deer antler rack. He jammed it on his head, called a gruff "See you later," and walked out.

Star stared at the hat rack. A big gray-white Stetson was perched on top. Baseball caps in a range of colors, sporting feed store and farm equipment logos, hung from lower antler tines.

"Jones?" Austin said.

"It's bad manners to wear a hat indoors." She smiled at him. "I think my daddy told me that." She glanced at the men seated along the counter. Not one wore a hat.

"Are you remembering something?"

Her shoulders twitched in a bemused shrug. "I don't know."

"It's a misnomer to call memory a noun. It isn't a passive thing. It's an active process."

"What do you mean?"

"There are basically two types of remembering. Recall and recognition. Think of your memories as—" he picked up a glass pepper shaker "—these pepper flakes. Billions of individual details packed away in your brain cells. Recall is a conscious effort to search through the flakes to find the right one."

His analogy made her laugh. "It's a wonder anyone can remember anything at all."

"Recall is more difficult than recognition. Recall takes training and practice."

The waitress sauntered up to their booth. "How can I do you folks today?" She plopped menus on the tabletop.

"Just coffee for me. Jones?"

"Coffee is fine," Star said. The menu board caught her eye. "Is the lemon meringue pie really homemade?"

The waitress waggled her fingers. "These hands. My house. Can't do better than that."

"A piece of pie, too, please."

"Okeydoke. You folks just passing through? Looking at the aspens changing color? The change sure came early this year."

"We may stay a few days," Austin replied.

The waitress's face lit up. "Well, now, the Pocket is a fine place. Cheap, too." She chuckled throatily. "Not that you have much choice since it's the only hotel this side of Windham. Be back in a flash."

"So what's the other kind of remembering?" Star asked. "Recognition?"

"That's a more basic type of remembering. It's remembering in the here and now." He picked up the shaker again. "Each flake is a specific detail. But the brain isn't static, it's continually processing information. Recognition comes when some stimulus pokes a memory flake and it lights up."

"I'm not sure I see the difference." It was interesting, though. Austin's depth of knowledge fascinated her.

"I read about an experiment where two groups of subjects were shown a series of a thousand slides. They were only flashed on the screen for two or three seconds. One group was asked to recall the images they'd seen. On average, the most any of the subjects could remember was seven to ten slides. The other group was shown a second series of two thousand slides with the pictures they'd seen before intermingled with new pictures. They were asked to pick out the images they remembered."

"And?"

"For the group overall, recognition was about ninety percent."

The waitress brought their coffee and pie. Austin graced the woman with a smile. She responded with a dazzle-eyed grin that stripped years from her weathered face. With a bounce in her step, she returned to the counter.

Star arched an eyebrow. The man was such a natural flirt, she doubted if he realized the effect he had on women. "I'll recognize things around here and remember what happened to my folks?"

"It's a possibility."

She slid a piece of pie into her mouth. Contrasting tartness and sweet creaminess made her cheeks constrict. It was the best lemon pie she'd ever tasted. "So what do we do? Wander around until something hits me?"

"Our first stop will be the newspaper office. Until we know more, asking questions is a waste of time." He held up a finger and assumed a professor's posture. "A lesson in the fine art of intelligence gathering. Always assemble your background material first. Hard facts tell you what questions to ask and you'll be able to better spot inconsistencies."

"You mean lies?"

"It depends on the liar."

When the waitress returned to refill their coffee cups, Austin asked her about the local newspaper.

"Oh, sure, we got one," she said. "The *Gabbler,* right down at the end of the street. Can't miss it. It's a weekly, but it's been running since, what..." She tapped her broad chin with her fingertips. "Since 1899. Betty Brownley owns it. Her printing press must be on the fritz again. Otherwise she'd be here right about now. You folks interested in local history?"

"Always," Austin said.

"We're just full of it around here." She laughed at her own joke. "Gold Coin started out as a mining town. Folks said the ore was so rich, you just squeeze it and out pops a gold coin, already minted. That was an outright lie, you understand. We never had a paying mine. Con men spread the story so back East investors would pay good money for plots of land. Nothing produced much of anything until they brought in cattle. We've got some of the oldest continuously owned ranches in the state. And speaking of which, the special tonight is rib eye steak." She held her thumb and forefinger two inches apart. "This thick. Dry-cured, guaranteed local beef. Finest in the country."

Star caught a faint flicker of distaste in Austin's eyes. His refusal to touch red meat might mean he'd go hungry in this town. She smiled into her coffee cup.

"I notice gambling is a big issue," Austin said pleasantly.

She grunted in disgust. "To some folks it is. 'Course now, I think we'd be a lot better off if Doyle Sloane would hurry up with that ski lodge. Skiers would do us a sight more good than weekend nickel-droppers. Know what—"

A man interrupted her. "Ha!" He swung around on the counter stool. His thick neck sank into his thicker shoulders. Shaggy tufts of gray hair sprouted from his balding patch. "Doyle ain't building no ski lodge, Sue, and you know it! Not unless we bring in gambling and pay for it ourselves."

Sue flicked at the air as if shooing a fly. "Quit bad-mouthing the mayor. He loves this place as much as you do."

"Mayor," the man grumbled. He beamed a broad grin at Austin and Star. "We oughtta do what smart folks do and elect a cat to be mayor. I got a big old tom who'll do twice the work Sloane does and won't cost half as much." He harrumphed. "Ski lodge. When donkeys fly."

The other men at the counter laughed and made disparaging remarks about the mayor. Star wondered why they had voted for the man if they disliked him so much. Or maybe this was their way of impressing out-of-towners.

"Don't pay any attention to those old geezers," Sue said. "Doyle's a good man."

"Ha!" the heckler interrupted again. "If that ski lodge of his is so grand, why don't Hagan pay for it? He gives Sloane money for everything else. If you ask me, it's nothing but another of his get-rich-quick schemes. Only he'll get rich and the rest of us'll be run out."

"Nobody asked you," Sue snapped.

He hoisted his coffee cup. "Well, I'm asking for more mud." He pointed his chin at Austin. "Where you folks from?"

"Dallas, Texas," Austin replied.

That turned heads up and down the counter.

"See, see?" the man said to no one in particular. "This is what we get if we open up a ski lodge. A town full of Texans."

Everybody laughed. Even Austin, which surprised Star.

Austin placed a hand flat over his heart. "I promise you, sir, if you build a lodge, this Texan won't be strapping sticks on his feet and going downhill real fast." He cocked his head and frowned contemplatively. "Now, a fishing hole, that would be different."

The laughter increased. Before Star quite knew what was happening, Austin was in the thick of the regulars' conversation. Through two cups of coffee, she listened to stories about the Bureau of Land Management, the price of cattle, how growth along the Front Range was affecting the water tables, and Doyle Sloane, the mayor everyone loved to hate.

What amazed her the most was how easily Austin fit in. Here he was with his long hair and wolfish air, talking to a group of crusty cattlemen as if they'd been best friends all their lives. Within thirty minutes everyone was on a first-name basis and Sue was calling Austin "sweetheart."

Star's impatience grew. Surely someone in this place knew about her father. As friendly as they were, they wouldn't lie or turn evasive. She waited for Austin to ask about her parents. He traded fish stories, instead.

Sue returned with the coffeepot. She smiled at Star. "How was that pie?"

"Best I ever ate." The waitress appeared to be in her fifties, conceivably her parents' contemporary. "Do you know a man named Jerrod Scott Jones?"

Sue pooched out her lips and made musing sounds. Finally, she shook her head.

"He was a cowboy who used to work around here."

Austin gave Star a pointed look. He shook his head almost imperceptibly, but the message came through: *Hush.*

"Jones ..." Sue said. "There's Terry Jones over at High Point. He's got a brother living in Pueblo, working at the steel mill." She turned to the men at the counter. "Any of you boys know—?"

"Not Terry," Star said. "Jerry. I think he was around when Rowena Waxman died."

A crash of breaking crockery made Star jump. She leaned over to see behind her. At the end of the counter, a man sat apart from the rest, one hand raised in midair. The cup he'd been holding lay broken on the floor. His pale eyes blazed.

Silence dropped like a wool blanket over the diner.

Star swallowed hard. The stares she received weren't exactly hostile, but they weren't exactly friendly, either. The man who'd dropped the cup looked at her as if she'd chopped up his dog.

He jumped up, snatched a hat off the antler rack and slammed out of the diner.

Sue took a step backward and cocked her head. She fingered her fleshy chin. One by one, the men swiveled their stools and faced the counter.

Sue asked, "What do you know about Rowena?"

Austin shook his head. "We know she died."

"She was murdered," Sue said harshly. She nodded toward the door. "That was Mark Waxman, her dad. He doesn't like reminders. Especially from strangers."

Slumping on the bench, Star closed her eyes. She could have kicked herself. "I didn't mean any harm," she murmured.

"No harm done. He's a bad-tempered old goat in the best of times." Sue clucked her tongue. "I remember Jerry Jones now." She slapped a dish towel at a man. "Bill, you remember him. Young cowboy. Used to work out at Queen's Cross. Disappeared about the same time Rowena did. Shoot, what was it, twenty, thirty years ago?"

"I remember some," Bill said. He tossed a few dollars on the counter. "Can't waste all day jawing. I've got hay to deliver."

As if Bill had given a signal, all the men paid their tabs and collected their hats. They streamed out of the diner, leaving a chill in their wake.

"What did I say?" Star asked. She looked up at the waitress in mute plea.

"Nobody likes talking about Rowena around here. Might keep that in mind if you mean to stick around."

Austin propped his chin on his fist. "Why is that, Sue?"

"It's too darned creepy, that's why." She shuddered. "We get long winters up here. We get snowed in, cut off from the rest of the world. Who likes to think we're stuck in this valley with a killer? He could be a neighbor or a friend."

"Rowena's killer wasn't caught?"

"Nope."

Star ventured a question she wasn't certain she wanted answered. "What did her murder have to do with Jerry Jones?"

Sue leaned closer, her eyes gleaming. "Him and his family disappeared." She snapped her fingers. "Just like that. Vanished. No one could figure it out. That is, until they found Rowena a couple months later and started putting two and two together."

Star swallowed the growing lump in her throat. "The police think Jerry...killed her?"

"He probably did." Shrugging, the waitress turned away. "Why else sneak away in the middle of the night? Innocent folks don't do that. At least, not around here they don't."

Chapter Six

"This is too doggone insane!" Star said. She stomped across the street. "My daddy didn't kill anybody."

Austin caught her elbow, hauling her up short. "The newspaper office is this way." Austin noticed Sue was watching them from the diner window. He figured by sunset, everyone in town would know about their interest in Rowena Waxman's murder.

So much for keeping a low profile.

She balked. "What's the use? It's plain as day to me that this town has already tried and convicted him. All they have to do is catch him. Besides, he's not here."

"You're scaring yourself again, Jones. Stop it."

She jerked as if he'd slapped her. Planting her hands on her hips, she looked up and down the quiet street. His Ford was the only car in sight; all other vehicles were either pickups or utility trucks with four-wheel drive.

"Sue isn't what I'd dub a reliable witness," he said. "She's talking pure speculation." The person who most interested him at the moment was Mark Waxman, Rowena's father. A hunch told him the man would have plenty to say about the Joneses' disappearance.

"I know, I'm sorry." She hugged her shoulders and shivered. "This place is squeezing me. I feel like one of those lost-in-the-desert cartoons. I'm dying of thirst, then all of a sudden I'm smacked by a tidal wave." She thrust a hand through her hair and clenched a fist. Tufts of bright hair gleamed between her fingers. "Everything feels right, but it's wrong, too. I don't know why."

"So let's get a room. You can wait there, rest. I'll go see what I can find at the—"

"I'm going with you." She forced a thin smile. "I reckon I can handle it." She laughed suddenly. "This is like a scary book. I can hardly stand reading it, but I have to know what happens next."

"So let's go turn the page." He hooked his arm with hers, and they headed for the newspaper office.

The *Gold Coin Gabbler* occupied a squat redbrick building at the end of Main Street. Inside, a young woman pushed a broom around the gouged, ink-stained hardwood floor. Looking more than happy to stop what she was doing, she gave them a bright smile and leaned on her broom handle. "Hi! What can I do for you?"

Austin leaned his forearms on the scarred countertop. The place smelled strongly of ink and solvent. The muffled clank of machinery came from behind a plastered wall covered with ancient calendars and framed newspaper copy. It didn't take much stretch of the imagination to see this place as it was a hundred years ago.

"We'd like to talk to Betty Brownley."

The girl leaned her broom against a desk and yelled, "Mom! There's some people here to see you!" She strode to a door and jerked it open. "Mom!"

A tiny woman, her gray hair cropped in a boyish mop, burst through the doorway. She shot the girl an exasperated glare. "Don't need to shout, Sarah. For pity's sake." With the door open, the machinery noise boomed. A gear scratched and ground. "Go on back and keep an eye on Pete. I've had about all the sidewalk supervising I can stomach in one day."

Sarah beamed. "Yes, ma'am!"

"Not that close an eye," Betty tossed over her shoulder. She slapped both work-roughened, grimy hands on the countertop. "I'm Betty Brownley. What can I do for you?"

"I'm Austin Tack, this is Star Jones. You own the newspaper?" he said.

"Owner, editor, reporter, coffeemaker. You name it, that's my title. You from Texas?"

"Yes, ma'am."

"Thought so. Only a true Texan can make his words purr like that." She pushed away from the counter and beckoned for them to come around into the office. "Time for my coffee break. Can I do you?"

"Sure."

Betty rustled up three coffee mugs and filled them from an old-fashioned cylinder coffeemaker. The brew was black as tar. She didn't offer cream or sugar. She settled on a chair and flung her feet atop a desk. Sighing contentedly, she hoisted her mug in salute.

"What doesn't kill me makes me strong, right?" she said. "I ought to be able to pull a train by now."

"You've owned the paper a long time?" Austin asked.

"Pretty much forever. My husband's daddy bought it from Gaylord Peake, the paper's founder. He was the one who named it the *Gabbler*. Have you ever heard of such a thing? Most folks call it the gobbler. Sheesh!" She rolled her eyes. "Anyway, my Baxter inherited it from his daddy, and when he died, I just kept going. It's a living. So what pearls of wisdom can I fling at you today?"

This was Austin's favorite kind of interview. Betty Brownley loved the sound of her own voice and was willing to talk as long as he was willing to listen. "We're interested in an incident that happened back in 1969. The murder of Rowena Waxman."

Betty laughed so suddenly, she spewed coffee. Chuckling, she swabbed at her sweatshirt.

Star bristled, her eyes flashing dangerously. "Why is that funny?"

"It isn't you." Betty waved lazily. A drop of coffee splattered on the desk blotter. "I'm not laughing at you. But I spent most of yesterday listening to that windbag Doyle Sloane and all his big ideas for bringing in gambling. Have to promote this place, he says. We have to make Gold Coin famous to bring in the tourists. Then you come in asking about the only interesting thing that's ever happened around here. It's timing, Miss Jones. Just timing."

"I see." She settled back on the chair.

"So what do you want to know about Rowena?"

"All we know," Austin said, "is that she was killed and the authorities were looking for Jerrod Jones." He checked to see how Star was reacting. She was wired, crackling with tension.

He'd dealt with hundreds of missing-persons cases. His clients had come to him expressing the full gamut of emotions: anger, sorrow, fear, worry, guilt, curiosity, yearning, greed and every variation in between. In some ways, Star was typical of others who sought birth parents. She needed to fill the void of her past and she needed confirmation of her identity.

He also sensed guilt. Again, that was understandable. Many children who'd been abandoned or given up for adoption blamed themselves.

Except hers went deeper. It had to do with the unforgivable bad thing she'd hinted of. There was a dynamic at play here he couldn't quite fathom, and he was worried about her. It depended on how much she recalled about what happened when she was four years old. If it turned out to be a great deal of a bad thing, could she handle it without breaking down completely?

Betty clucked her tongue against her teeth. "I haven't thought about Rowena in a long time. Poor thing. We went to school together." She gave him a coy look. "I'm not telling you how long ago that was."

"How was she killed?"

"Shot." She poked herself between the eyes. "She'd been dumped out in the hills. Animals got to her. We had ferocious rain that summer, and it must have washed her body loose from wherever she'd been buried. It was some kids who found her."

"How long had she been dead before she was found?" .

Betty swung her head slowly from side to side. "That I can't tell you right offhand. My Baxter might have noted it someplace. I can check. Mind me asking why you want to know? Not that I have anything better to do, what with that stupid hunk of junk back there acting up again. But I'm curious."

"Your photograph," Austin said to Star. He leaned forward. "Actually, it isn't Rowena who interests us so much as it is Jerrod Jones."

Star pulled the photograph from her medicine bag. She handed it to Betty.

The woman frowned for a moment, then nearly jumped off the seat. Her jaw unhinged in open disbelief. "Jerry Jones," she said in a voice laced with wonder. "That's him, sure as shooting."

"You knew him?" Star asked.

"Know him? Hell, I took this picture! I had a brand-new Nikon. My Baxter got it for my birthday. I took pictures of everybody in town. I probably went through fifty rolls of film before I got the hang of it. And there's Jerry. Nice young man, real nice. I've never known a man who could blush the way he did. Of course, a lot of those cowboys are shy. They spend far too much time alone. He and his wife had the sweetest little girls. Twins, like peas in a pod." She tapped her chin. "Uh, Mary and . . ."

Her eyes flew wide and she nearly dropped her cup. "Star. Why, as I live and breathe. Star Jones, that's you! I'm such a knucklehead today. Should've made the connection right off. Mary Christmas and Star Bright. His little Christmas presents, he called you.''

Austin leaned forward. ''Star and her sister were abandoned in Dallas, Texas, in April 1969. They've had no contact with their parents since then. We found an article in a Colorado Springs newspaper that connected Jerry to Rowena and Gold Coin. That's what brings us here.''

''Abandoned?'' She shook her head in vehement denial.

Austin brought out a notepad and a pen. ''So what can you remember about the Joneses?''

Her tongue hooked over her upper lip as she studied the photograph. ''Boy, oh, boy, that was a long time ago.... Like I said, they were a nice couple. Churchgoing, pleasant. Real young. Now, when did they show up?'' Her tongue protruded again and she narrowed her eyes. ''I think it was around when my Baxter got the Volkswagen. Good for tootling, he said, but it wasn't. It didn't have a goose's guts. I could run faster up a hill. So that would have been summer of '67, I believe. They hired on over at the Queen's Cross. Jerry was a wrangler. Wanted to be a horse trainer. Racehorses, if I remember correctly. Or was it cutting horses? Whatever. Karen was the house cook.''

''Karen. My mother's name was Karen.'' Star's gaze went sad and faraway. ''Karen.''

''She was a sweet girl. Pretty, too.'' Betty cocked her head and peered closely at Star's face. ''Have to say you favor Jerry. You're tall and towheaded, just like him. They abandoned you?'' She grimaced. ''That's hard to believe.''

From the corner of his eye, Austin watched Star clamp her mouth shut. She wore a wary, stubborn expression.

''When did they leave, ma'am?'' Austin asked.

She fluttered her eyelashes at him. ''Betty, if you please.'' She giggled, sounding young. ''They left in the springtime before Rowena's body was found. I'd have to check my Baxter's notes before I can tell you exactly when.'' She gestured at him with her coffee cup. "I do know it was peculiar."

"Why is that?"

"Well, see, normally I wouldn't have thought much about it. Cowboys come and go. But Mark Waxman had been raising Cain all over town for a week or so because Rowena was missing. At the time, everyone figured she'd run off and gotten married or something. That Sunday, I ran into Michelle Sloane. Usually she drove the Joneses to church in town with her. I asked her where they were, and she said they took off. I can still feel the chill that gave me. That was too many people just up and disappearing. Like I said, peculiar."

"Did anyone else think it was peculiar?"

"Not until those kids found Rowena. What was left of her, anyway."

"Why did anyone think Jerry Jones might know something?"

"Timing, mostly. They all disappeared about the same time." She turned a fond smile on Star. "Some of us were scared the same thing might have happened to your family."

"Was Jerry a suspect in Rowena's murder?"

"He wasn't until the letter came."

Austin and Star both sat forward, staring intently at the newspaperwoman. Betty arched her eyebrows and took a big swig of her coffee.

"What letter was that, Betty?" Austin asked.

"It was mailed from Denver. It came addressed to my Baxter. In it Jerry confessed to murdering Rowena and said he was sorry."

THE EARTH OPENED BENEATH Star's feet and she teetered on the brink of oblivion. A confession? Like dominoes, events and circumstances clicked into place. Her father killed Rowena. He hid her body. He and Karen fled into the night.

They gave their children to a woman and told her to dump them someplace safe. They fled, fugitives from justice...

No! It could have happened that way, but she knew it hadn't.

As if through layers of muffling wool, she heard Betty speak. "Now, you want to talk peculiar, *that* was peculiar."

It's not peculiar, Star screamed inside her head. It's just plain wrong, all wrong! My daddy didn't kill anybody!

"Came to this office, addressed to my Baxter and marked all over with big red Urgents and Personals. Like who else would open the mail around here? I'm a nosy old broad, but I didn't snoop in his mail, for pity's sake!"

As Betty rattled on, Star stopped teetering and regained her bearings. Cold anger seeped through her veins. Not scared anger, not suspicious anger. Righteous anger. She noticed Austin watching her with evident concern. I'm all right, she told him with her eyes.

"Why did it come here?" Austin asked. "Rather than to the police?"

Betty lifted her shoulders and hands in a broad shrug. "So my Baxter would print it and Jerry could publicly apologize. Of course, Baxter didn't. He couldn't. It wouldn't have been right."

"Do you still have the letter?"

"Maybe so, maybe not." She frowned and looked around the messy office. "I probably can dig up a copy from somewhere. I'm pretty sure we turned the original over to the police."

"So what happened? What did the police do?"

"As far as I know, nothing. What could they do? Jerry and Karen had disappeared."

Star clamped her arms over her chest. "My daddy didn't kill Rowena."

Austin and Betty turned to her. She looked from one to the other. "I appreciate your honesty, Mrs. Brownley, I truly do. But my daddy couldn't have written that confession."

"I'm not saying a hundred percent that he did. All I'm saying is, we got the letter, we turned it over to the police, and they started looking for Jerry."

Austin placed a hand on Star's knee and squeezed. "The important thing," he said, "is finding out where your parents may have gone."

"That's as much a mystery to me as it is to you," Betty said firmly. Behind her glasses, her eyes were soft with maternal kindness.

Star sensed pity and she didn't like it. She wanted nothing less than the truth.

"I didn't have much to do with the paper back then." Betty nodded in the direction of the back room. "I've got four daughters. Two were in diapers when this was happening. Still, I'll be more than happy to go through the files and see what kind of information my Baxter saved."

Austin leaned back on his chair and stroked his jaw. "Who do you think killed Rowena, Betty?"

Betty managed to look surprised, but she blushed a little, too. "It's not my place to speculate like that."

"Not publicly, not officially, but you do have ideas. Who were the players?"

Betty dropped her feet to the floor with a thud. She set her coffee mug on the desk. All of a sudden, she looked like a newspaper owner, crafty-eyed and bullish. "Austin, honey, what line of work are you in?"

"I'm a private investigator."

"Uh-huh. And you, Star? What do you do?"

"Right now, I'm unemployed."

She waved a finger between them. "You hired him to find your parents."

"Yes, ma'am." Star laid a hand on the desktop. "I've been looking all my life. My sister and I were separated. She was adopted. It wasn't until this year that I found her." She graced Austin with a wan smile. "We're not trying to cause trouble. I swear. But this means the world to me. I have to find them. I have to know what happened."

"I'd like to know what happened, too." All traces of saucy good humor had left Betty's tone. "We all would. Rowena, she wasn't much of a prize, but no one should die the way she did. Shot and tossed like so much trash. I don't like thinking Jerry Jones had anything to do with it. Hell, I don't like thinking anybody I know did it. Being suspicious about people I've known all my life is the worst thing. But there's no help for it. Plenty of people had good cause to kill her."

"Please help us, ma'am."

"I didn't say I wouldn't. But I am warning you. You won't make friends in this town by opening up old wounds."

"Why would plenty of people have reason to kill her?" Austin asked.

Betty laughed. "Austin, honey, do you really think you can waltz in here and solve a twenty-five-year-old murder?"

"It's not the murder. It's finding Star's parents. Since you received a letter from Jerry confessing, then either he did it—"

"He didn't do it!" Star exclaimed.

"—Or somebody sent it to frame him. To my way of thinking, whoever sent it knew Jerry wasn't coming back to clear his name. Which could also mean that person has an idea where the Joneses went."

"Good point. Except the person who sent it most likely killed Rowena. So you're back to solving the murder." Her chubby cheeks quivered and her mouth twitched. "A private eye and a prodigal daughter. What a pair. I'll do what I can, but if life gets uncomfortable, don't say I didn't warn you." She refilled her coffee mug and offered to freshen their cups, too.

Austin and Star declined.

"Good old Rowena." Betty clucked her tongue. "Nowadays nobody would pay a bit of attention to her. Back then she was quite a piece of work. She was what we used to call, in the good old days, a loose woman."

"She had affairs," Austin said.

"And the bad manners to flaunt them. She wasn't exactly pretty, but she had flash. Men liked her." She held a hand about a foot above her head. "Hair this high, black as coal. Red lipstick, lots of blue eye shadow. Skirts so short her butt hung out. Gossip said she'd go to Denver or the Springs to hit the bars and she'd be wearing a see-through blouse."

"So why did she hang around here?"

"This town?" Her tongue emerged to help her think. "Rumor said she was in love. My feeling is, she liked being a big fish in a little pond. In Gold Coin, she stood out. In the city, she was just another trashy party girl, lost in the crowd." Her gaze softened and went distant. "In spite of everything, I always liked Rowena. She had big dreams. Big ideas. She wasn't afraid of anything or anybody."

"So who wanted to kill her?"

She jutted her chin at Austin. "Do you have a clean sheet of paper ready? Try every married woman within a hundred miles."

"Yourself included?" Austin asked innocently.

Betty laughed and slapped her knee. "Don't put me on your list of likely suspects, honey."

"Can you be more specific, then?"

"Not really. She was mouthy. She embarrassed people. She had affairs with married men. Lord only knew what kind of schemes she cooked up." She gave him a hard look. "Just because I happen to know that plenty of people would have liked to see her dead, doesn't mean I'm going to point fingers."

Austin accepted her statement with an enigmatic smile. He jotted a few notes on his pad. "Okay, so what about the Joneses? I'll take even wild guesses about where they might have gone."

"Sorry, the well is dry, honey. Like I said before, I can go back through my Baxter's notes and see what I can come up with. But it's been a long time. Back then, before computers kept the Big Brother eyeball on everybody, all a person had to do was cross the state line, and, poof, he vanished."

That wasn't the kind of information Star wished to hear. Narrowing her search to Colorado had been a major breakthrough. If her parents had fled to another state, she was back to square one.

Betty's daughter popped through the doorway and announced Pete had finished repairing the press. "I'm going to treat him to a burger, Mom," she cooed. "You know, since he's been so good."

Betty sighed dramatically. "Only thing worse than sons is daughters." She pushed off the chair. "It's been a royal pleasure, but I have to get back to work." She thrust out an ink-stained hand. "Star, it's a wonder meeting you."

Star shook hands with the woman. "Thank you."

"As soon as I get the time, I'll dig through the files for you." She chuckled and shook hands with Austin. "I guess you two will be around for a while."

"Probably a day or two."

"Don't be strangers. You know where to find me. I'm here more hours than I like to admit."

Outside, the temperature had decreased perceptibly and clouds wreathed the mountaintops. With her hands shoved in her back pockets, Star studied the Gold Rush-era buildings lining the street.

"Austin, honey?" she said wryly. "You sure have a winning way with the ladies."

"It's a gift." He rubbed her shoulder. "Are you all right? It got rough for you in there."

"This is so weird. I didn't mean to get mad at her. I really didn't. But there's something wrong and it's driving me crazy not knowing how I know it." She turned toward the mountains, seeking some magnetic pull to point her in the right direction. "I want to go to Queen's Cross. My parents lived there over a year. Somebody might know something."

"Not yet. We'll be here a few days, so let's go see about a room. Then we'll pay a visit to the local police."

His casual statement filled her with dread. She'd grown up at the mercy of faceless bureaucrats and the child welfare agencies. None of which gave her any love for authority or anything connected to a uniform. "We don't need the cops. They won't tell us anything."

"We can't know until we ask."

"I'd prefer to keep the cops out of it, thank you." She strode across the street toward the Pocket Mountain Hotel.

He caught up to her. "If your father was a suspect, then they investigated his background. They'll have his social security number, previous employers, birth date, the works. They may have the names of relatives or friends."

"Oh." She hadn't considered that aspect. "Do you think they'll tell us?" She leaned her backside against an old hitching rail. The wood creaked.

"Depends on how nice we ask."

She rubbed the hitching rail under her palms. Weather and countless straps of leather had worn it as smooth as polished stone. In her mind, she saw patient horses drowsing, hooves cocked and tails lazily swishing. From far away, a gentle voice told her, "Don't tie a knot, baby. It's a loop, see. Once around and a tuck. You try it...." Her eyes burned and she blinked rapidly.

He wasn't a killer. He'd been good and kind and he'd loved her with all his heart.

"Every time I hear Rowena's name, I get this funny feeling inside and my throat kind of chokes up." She peeked at

Austin, judging how he was taking this. "I think I know her. Down deep inside, I know."

"She has something to do with your father?"

She nodded and peeked again. He was calm and steady, giving away nothing of what he felt. "He didn't kill her. I'm sure of it. But the police . . . there's no statute of limitations on murder. If my father was framed, who's going to believe him? If we find him and he goes to jail, it'll be all my fault."

It's all your fault! Do you hear me? Shut up, shut up! Don't you say a single word to the policeman, do you understand? It's all your fault. I'll make them put you in jail if you talk. Do you hear me—

"Jones?"

She started. Austin's brow twisted in an expression of concern. He held her arm so tightly, he was cutting off circulation and the veins in her wrist pulsed with each heartbeat. He supported her entire weight to keep her from tumbling backward over the rail.

"I'm okay." A lie. Guilt and shame crushed her. Her temples throbbed as if iron-shod draft horses pounded through her skull.

He made a skeptical noise. "You just lost all the color in your face. Let's go find a place for you to rest."

"I'm not sick." She drew several deep breaths, fighting the squirming knots tightening up her insides. "It's her."

He led her, unresisting, toward the hotel entrance. "Her who?"

"The woman who took us to Dallas. Don't talk to the police, she said. She was scared. Oh, Lord, but she was scared, and she scared me, too, and I had to lie on the floor behind the seat and not let anybody see me. There was a policeman and I wasn't supposed to talk." She grasped his hand, suddenly feeling as if she were drowning. She barely had enough strength to lift her foot from the sidewalk.

"Can you remember her name?"

Miserable, she shook her head.

"All right, breathe deeply. Come on, breathe for me."

She followed his soft-spoken instructions. Oxygen filled her lungs and cleared her head. The ghosts of her past retreated into their dark closets. A feeling of stupidity replaced her misery.

"Better?" Austin asked.

She nodded.

"Good." He patted her cheek. "You're giving me ideas. So let's go get a room."

In a daze, Star arranged for a room in the Pocket Mountain Hotel. Peripherally, she noticed the old-fashioned oak-and-iron cashier's cage that served as the front desk. Austin held her arm on the way up the squeaky stairs. He opened a door and urged her inside.

"Relax," he said. "I'll get our stuff."

Left alone, she sat for a long time on the edge of the bed. With her face in her hands, she tried hard to make sense of the emotions churning her insides. All her life, she'd gotten flashes of memory. Disturbing tidbits from the past, as elusive, maddening and often as senseless as dreams. At the moment, she felt surrounded by gigantic loudspeakers, blaring and battering her with sound and sensation.

She remembered. She *knew.*

She knew what had happened to her parents and where to find them—all she had to do was remember.

Chapter Seven

"Ever been hypnotized, Jones?" Austin asked conversationally.

He'd brought their baggage into the room, along with bottles of flavored water and a bag of apple-bran muffins. While he'd been busy, Star had regained her bearings.

When she did, she realized her mistake in arranging for one room. One room meant one bed. And what a bed it was. It was a double with a thick mattress nearly lost underneath a towering oak headboard carved with cupids, roses and curlicues. The embroidered cutwork bedspread had a faintly rosy cast, enhanced by a mountain of pink floral-and-white lace pillows. All that fluff floated atop a down comforter as fat as a flock of sheep.

Maroon velvet draperies, luxurious despite their shabbiness, dropped in heavy swags and folds over the big window. Dainty lamps with stained-glass shades and tasseled pulls perched on rosewood bed tables. The romance of the room was enhanced by the presence of the sexiest man Star had ever known.

Her thoughts about Austin Tack wavered between annoyance, admiration and downright eroticism. Every time he focused his darkly beautiful eyes on her, the rest of the world lost meaning. How in the dickens was she supposed to keep her distance in this fit-for-a-honeymoon room?

She should get another room. Except, this was costing nearly sixty dollars a night. She couldn't imagine how long they would stay. She mentally ran through her finances, and kept coming up with depressingly high debits and very low credits.

"Jones?"

"What?"

"I asked you a question. Have you ever been hypnotized?" He peeled the paper off a muffin. Moist crumbs stuck to his fingers and he licked them clean.

"I don't believe in that hocus-pocus stuff."

"Nothing hocus-pocus about it. The mind is a marvelous instrument. What we, in the collective sense, understand about memory could fit on the head of a pin. Theories abound, but very little hard information is available about how the mind stores information."

"Yeah, so?"

"I do know the mind is a limitless reservoir. What goes in, stays in."

"I already told you I remember things." She fished a muffin out of the bag. Bigger than her fist, it was heavy and smelled of cinnamon and apples.

"And I believe it. But because you were so young, details are fuzzy. Remember the pepper flakes? It isn't easy finding the exact one you need."

"I already know that," she said hesitantly, interested, but suspicious. Hypnotism ranked right up there with palm reading or astrology as far as she was concerned.

"I've seen hypnotism work. It might with you."

"You hypnotize people?" Somehow that didn't surprise her. His deep voice and velvety eyes held mesmerizing power.

"I know some relaxation techniques. The subconscious is busy. Even when you're asleep, it's processing information. Total relaxation can slow it down and allow your conscious mind to do some work. You can focus."

She bit into the muffin. It was chewy, but so fresh it practically melted against her tongue. Her stomach growled. Relaxation didn't sound as scary as hypnotism, though she doubted merely thinking soothing thoughts would help her remember. "You won't make me cluck like a chicken or anything, will you?"

He laughed. "Get comfortable. We'll see what we can do." He popped the remainder of his muffin in his mouth and turned to the window. He closed the draperies, plunging the room into wine-tinted twilight gloom.

He removed the pile of pillows from the bed and invited her to stretch out full length with her arms at her sides and her feet together.

"Close your eyes," he instructed.

She did so. Her hearing turned up a notch, and she heard the wind whispering past the window and footsteps echoing from far away. Sensing the vibration, more than hearing, she discerned a mechanical clanking noise, rhythmic as a heartbeat. As Austin took her through a deep-breathing exercise, she grew self-conscious about the unnatural noises coming from her lungs.

Austin squeezed above her knee. "You're stiff as a board, Jones. Loosen up."

"I'm trying." She peeked through one eye. He sat next to her, grinning ruefully.

"The point is to relax." He untied her sneakers and worked them off her feet. "You look like a sacrifice on an altar."

"I am relaxed. What are you doing?"

He caught her foot. "Close your eyes. Think good thoughts." He began massaging her foot. His fingers were strong, but gentle. "Imagine a peaceful place, soothing."

She tried. Instead, she thought about how much this room was costing, and that didn't include the price of meals or gasoline for the car. She'd noticed a gas station in town and the price of a gallon was at least forty cents higher than in

Texas. She saw herself signing over the entire contents of her savings account to Austin and still being in his debt.

Austin worked his fingers between her toes. It felt nice. "Tell me about your good place."

Her mind blanked. "Uh..." She opened her eyes. "This won't work."

"Give it a chance."

"I feel stupid."

He twisted around to face her. Leaning his weight on both hands, he gazed into her eyes. "You're not making an effort."

Struggling onto her elbows, she glared at him. "Am, too. But this is dumb! What do good places have to do with my parents?"

He lowered his eyelids in several slow blinks. "I sense the problem here isn't one of relaxing. What are you afraid of?"

"Nothing."

"Sit up." He waited until she did so. "Now, tell me what you want."

She draped her arms over her knees. "I want to find my parents."

"Now tell me what you're willing to do to find them."

"I already told you." She looked him straight in the eye. "Anything. I'll do anything."

He leaned closer, nearly nose to nose with her. "Liar."

She narrowed her eyes. "I'm not a liar, Tack."

"You're lying to yourself. You're willing to pay me, follow my lead, share a room. But you aren't willing to trust me."

The truth of what he was saying grabbed her by the throat. "I trust you as much as I do anybody."

"Which isn't saying much." He reached past her and turned on a lamp. A warm, yellow-rose glow filled the corner. "Remember I told you about my floating hunches?"

"Uh-huh."

"In order to snag them, you have to believe they're out there. Then you have to trust them."

She shifted uncomfortably and looked away.

"I have a fair idea about what you went through growing up. Foster homes. Uncertainty. A lack of continuity." He cupped her cheek in his hand and his fingers were warm against her skin. "But, Star, you're far stronger than you think."

His use of her given name lent weight to the seriousness of his words. The warmth of his touch spread through her body and centered in her breast. "I don't feel strong. I just feel... scared."

"Scared is okay. What's important is you're a survivor. Think of the thousands of ways you could have gone wrong. Drinking, drugs, promiscuity, crime. Instead, you embarked on this quest. You've assumed the task of righting old wrongs."

"You make me sound noble." She tried for a light tone, but failed.

"You are. You're also deserving. You have a right to know your past. A right to belong, to have a family. You have a right to want what belongs to you."

More than anything, she wanted to trust him and believe. She caught his hand and pulled it to her lap. She clung to him as if he might fly off the bed and disappear. She stared at the differences in their fingers. Where hers were slim and smooth, his were broad and corded with sinew. "What if," she said cautiously, "it was my fault my family split up?"

"How would it be your fault?"

She rolled her head on her neck and twisted her fingers against his. "I reckon... like I did something... bad."

"You were only four years old."

She didn't hear condemnation or disgust in his voice. She still couldn't make herself tell him about her deepest fear. "Well, yeah, but you know how Kurt says Dana and I are mirror images? She's right-handed, I'm a southpaw. She's all calm and sweet, I'm a hothead. She's good as gold...." Unable to carry through on the thought, she allowed her voice to trail away.

He touched her chin, urging her to look at him. "I see. The good twin and the evil twin. Just like a Bette Davis movie."

She pulled away from his hand. "Don't make fun of me, Tack."

"I'm not. But you're carrying the analogy too far. You aren't evil."

"What if I am?" she retorted stubbornly. She'd never in her life had this kind of conversation with anybody. Now the words had been spoken, and they hung like puffs of steam in the air.

"If you are, then you're fooling a dude who hasn't been fooled in a long, long time. Look at me. I've found hundreds of missing persons, done thousands of background searches. I know what I'm doing."

"I trust that much." She swallowed the growing lump in her throat. "It's hard, Tack. When I was little, I got jerked around all the time. Every time I got comfortable, something happened. I'd get close to someone, then bam, I'd never see them again. Everything had a catch. I learned real early to do for myself. I'm not used to... cooperating."

"I understand."

"It's hard asking for help. Hard depending on anyone. It's hard to relax."

"I understand that, too."

"You're about to understand me to death," she grumbled, but felt lighter. She hadn't told him everything, but she'd told him more than she'd ever told anyone else.

The world hadn't collapsed and fallen into the sun.

Austin hadn't recoiled in revulsion.

"Okay, okay, but I'm feeling too antsy for your hocus-pocus stuff." She inhaled deeply and lifted her head. "Let's go talk to the police." She pushed off the bed, then turned on him. "But I'm telling you, if there's even a hint the cops want to haul my father back to this one-horse town for some mountain-man justice, we're out of there. I won't be party to anyone trying to hang him for something he didn't do. Got it?"

"If you say so."

GOLD COIN'S POLICE station sat off by itself on a low hill overlooking the end of Main Street. The only remarkable things about its unassuming gray brick exterior were the towering radio antenna rising forty feet above its roof and the heavy iron bars on the windows. A black-and-white Jeep sporting a Gold Coin police emblem occupied the parking place in front of the door.

Austin and Star entered the building.

Butterflies flitted through Star's belly. As a child, she'd been a habitual runaway. She'd had more than enough experience with the police. Even now, as an adult, the sight of wanted posters, call boards and radios made her want to turn tail and run.

Austin called, "Hello?"

A loud thump was followed by a voice cursing a blue streak. A young man rose from behind a cabinet. He rubbed the top of his head and winced. Star raised a hand to her mouth and winced along with him. From the sound of it, he'd conked himself a good one.

The man stepped into the open. He wore a khaki uniform shirt and a Sam Browne belt. His black hair gleamed with bluish highlights.

"It's a little crowded in here," Austin said, extending his hand.

The officer shook hands. "You're telling me!" He grinned. "So now that you know my problem, what's yours?"

He glanced at Star and did a double take. As did she. He had the bluest eyes she'd ever seen on a man. They were all the more striking in contrast to his dark skin and dark hair. His cheek twitched.

Austin produced an identification card. "Austin Tack, private investigations, licensed out of Dallas, Texas. This is my client, Star Jones. We're looking for some information."

The officer took the ID card, scanned it front and back, then placed it on the counter. "So you're a client. How do you do, Ms. Jones?" He extended a hand. His smile widened.

After they shook hands, she felt his reluctance to release her. Discomfited by his interest, she looked to Austin.

"We're looking for some missing persons."

"No kidding. Don't get much of that around here. Dave Crocker, chief of police." He raised the hinged drop-counter and invited them to come through. "Have a seat if you can find one." He cleared a stack of binders off a wooden chair and offered it to Star.

The office looked more like a junk shop than a police station. Along with the official paraphernalia, there were mounted deer heads and a stuffed trout decorating the walls. An old six-drawer dresser, partially stripped of its finish, occupied one corner. A skinny bookshelf was loaded to overflowing with science fiction and fantasy novels. Chief Crocker seemed too young for his position. His handsome face was unlined; his movements were quick, but a little awkward. He directed his deep-dimpled smile at Star.

Austin moved a fishing tackle box off a stool.

"Who's the missing person?" Crocker sat behind a scarred desk and kicked up his feet. Huge feet, Star noted with amusement, at least a size fourteen.

Austin nodded at Star. "Her parents. She hasn't seen them in over twenty-five years."

Encouraged by the policeman's interest, she said, "My daddy's name was Jerrod Scott Jones, a cowboy who once worked on the Queen's Cross ranch." She brought out her photograph and handed it over.

Crocker trailed his fingers over hers as he accepted the photo. His open interest made her want to squirm. Isn't this just a bucket of crickets? she thought wryly. Come all the way to Colorado to find a cop who's hot to trot.

"My mother's name was Karen." From the corner of her eye she caught a glimpse of Austin's face. He wore a most peculiar, frozen expression.

Austin coughed into his fist. "The Joneses were last seen in Gold Coin in April '69. Some public sources claim their disappearance might be connected to the murder of Rowena Waxman."

Crocker snapped to attention. His bright eyes gleamed. "You have got to be kidding. Rowena Waxman falls into the legend category. Hold on a sec."

He ambled over to a file cabinet and jerked and tugged a drawer until it squealed open. Humming to himself, he riffled through crammed folders. He extracted a brown folder stained by water rings and faded ink. "Yep, here it is. Rowena Waxman, homicide. This case is still open."

Austin stared intently at the folder. Star's mouth went dry. That shabby old file folder was Pandora's box, filled with answers—but could it contain her remaining hope?

Crocker hugged the folder to his chest. "You know I can't show you this, right? The case has been retired, but not closed. Murder is a capital crime. No statute of limitations." He opened it on his desktop and scanned the information. "Hmm, not much here, anyway."

Austin opened his notebook and brought out a pen. "We're interested in biographical information on the Joneses. Full names, birth dates, social security numbers. The names of any relatives and previous employers."

"I can do that." Crocker rattled off the information, including the name of the Joneses' employer before they were hired by the Queen's Cross ranch, then he added the tidbit that efforts had been made to find relatives. No dice. Both Jerry and Karen appeared to have been alone in the world. He gave Star an apologetic grin. "So what does your husband think about you doing this, Ms. Jones?"

For Pete's sake, she thought, he's flirting with me. He had such a sweet, puppy-dog smile, restraining an answering smile proved impossible. "Not married."

"Oh. *Jones.* Yeah, I should have known."

Though Austin gave no outward sign, Star felt his disapproval. He couldn't be jealous, she thought in wonder. Could he?

"So what else do you have there?" Austin's voice was friendly and mild. Once he'd pulled Crocker's attention off Star, he sounded even friendlier.

Crocker chatted gregariously. A small-town police chief lived a dull life, Star supposed. The phone didn't ring; the radio didn't squawk; no one walked through the door. She and Austin must be the most excitement he'd had in days.

As he skimmed through the material in the folder, picking out details, Star began to get a picture of her parents. Lacking family connections, they had each other. Jerry had been twenty-four years old and Karen had been twenty-three when they disappeared. Neither had any record of previous problems with the law. They had lived quietly on the ranch where they worked, coming into Gold Coin only to buy supplies for their employers or to attend church. Whenever the Joneses came into town, either together or alone, they brought their twin daughters with them. There had been some financial problems due to the twins' births. Star and Dana had been born in Denver, Colorado.

"Hmm," Crocker said. "Vanished into thin air, looks like." He turned the few pages in the folder and shook his head. "That's about all there is."

"Who were the investigating officers?" Austin asked.

"Bill Cox, but he died a few years back." He turned a page. "Tucker Grant was the other one. He was with the sheriff's department from over in Windham. I believe he retired—no, wait, he died, too. Sorry."

"What about personal effects?" Austin asked. "Did the Joneses leave anything behind?"

"I can dig around and see. This happened way before my time. I was a little kid when this happened." He gave Star an inquisitive look. "You haven't seen them in twenty-five years?"

"My sister and I were abandoned in Dallas."

He stuck a toothpick in his mouth. His gaze shifted between her and the folder. "They never tried to contact you?"

She didn't want to answer questions, she wanted to ask them. "No, sir."

"That's weird," he mumbled around the toothpick. He searched through the clutter on the desk until he found a clean pad of paper. He started writing. "I sympathize, Ms. Jones. I really do."

Star didn't believe him for a second. He was stuck in this Podunk town, probably bored out of his skull, and solving an old murder would give him enough party talk to last the rest of his life. Sympathy had nothing to do with it.

Crocker handed over a sheet of paper to Austin. "Here's some people who might know something about the Joneses. The person you really want to talk to is Betty Brownley. She owns the *Gabbler*. Betty was born and raised here in Gold Coin. She knows everybody."

Austin showed Star the list: Betty Brownley, Doyle and Michelle Sloane, Isadora Hagan, Stuart and Queenie Hagan.

Crocker explained, "Betty owns the newspaper. Stuart Hagan owns the Queen's Cross ranch where the Joneses worked. Michelle and Isadora are Stuart's sisters and

Queenie is his wife. Doyle is married to Michelle. He's the mayor. Offhand, I can't think of anyone else. Like I said, talk to Betty."

"What about Mark Waxman?" Austin asked.

The police chief laughed. Lamplight caught his eyes, making them sparkle like jewels. Star got the distinct impression contact lenses gave them their rich color. It bothered her for some reason.

"He's Rowena's father. Don't you think he knows something?"

Crocker pointed vaguely south. "He owns a junkyard outside of town. He's an old-time mountain man and a total crackpot. You can talk to him, but lots of luck making sense out of anything he says." He mimed tipping a bottle to his lips. "He's pickled most of the time."

"We appreciate your help," Austin said as he carefully folded the list and stuck it in his shirt pocket.

"Well, looks like you'll be around for a few days. We'll probably see each other again." He looked directly at Star as he spoke, and his tone said, Hope to see *you* again.

Once outside the police station, Star said, "I don't trust him." The sun was long gone, taking with it any trace of heat. She walked fast toward the hotel.

"Why is that?"

"He's pretty darn helpful."

Austin laughed. "We're probably the most exciting thing that's happened to him in years."

"I was thinking the same thing. Glory-hounds are always trouble." She caught his smirk. "You know I'm right, Tack. He's probably calling someone right now to check us out."

"So? I've nothing to hide. Do you?"

She stopped on the sidewalk in front of the hotel and faced him. "You know what I mean." She poked the center of his rock-solid chest. "I'm not finding my parents just so that idiot can make a name for himself by arresting them. So you can just stop being so doggone reasonable.''

He caught her shoulders and kissed her. A lusty, heart-stopping, mind-blanking, thoroughly outrageous kiss. He actually smacked his lips when he pulled away.

She gasped. Her eyes widened. "What in Sam Hill was that for?" Her heart raced.

"You said stop being reasonable." He gave her an unrepentant smile and looped an arm around her shoulders. He headed into the hotel. "It's late, I'm starving, but first I need to make a phone call."

In their room, Austin pulled a small nylon carrying case, about the size of a large telephone book, from his suitcase. It contained a laptop computer. He took it out in the hallway and set the computer on a red velvet-covered bench next to the communal telephone. Still tingling from his kiss, Star watched him with mingled curiosity and wariness.

He typed information into the computer, his fingers flying over the keys. The next step was hooking up the computer to the telephone.

Star looked down the empty hallway. She whispered, "Is that legal?"

He laughed. "I'm not hurting anything." He typed numbers into the computer. It made a buzzing and clicking noise, then faintly screeched. As soon as it fell silent, he stroked a key. The tiny screen flashed.

He reversed the process and unhooked the computer.

"Wait a minute. What did you just do?"

"I called Sparky," he said with a grin. He folded down the screen on the laptop. "She's a magical wizard who lives in a cave. I throw her raw meat and she gives me information."

Star rolled her eyes toward the ceiling. "All right, all right! You can be reasonable now."

He carried the computer into their room. "Sparky is a researcher," he said, chuckling. "I sent her the vital statistics on your parents. She'll run a hard data search from her end. It saves us time.''

He did all that in less than ten minutes? "You trust her?''

"Yes, punkin, I trust her. Now, let's go find some chow.''

A DREAM ABOUT FUR COATS roused Star from sleep. Still-living fur coats that weighted down her shoulders and breathed hotly against her neck. Her eyelids fluttered open. As she fully awakened, the heavy, warm, living weight remained.

Austin.

She lay on her side, spooned against him, with her head resting in the crook of his shoulder. He held his other arm wrapped firmly around her body. His long legs were molded against hers. He cuddled her the way a boy would cling to a teddy bear.

Wasn't this a fine kettle of fish? It wasn't yet dawn, and judging by the deep steadiness of his breathing, he was fast asleep. The smell of him, a curious blend of honey-sweetness and masculine musk, permeated the down-filled comforter.

Indecision kept her still. Should she ease out of his arms and off the bed? That would awaken him. Lying like this was comfortable, though. If she stayed here and he did wake up, she could feign sleep. He would realize he'd invaded her space and do the easing away.

Except this was nice. Real nice. Good intentions aside, she could not rouse enough energy to move.

He shifted. She held her breath and stared wide-eyed into the gray morning light. He slid a leg over her thighs. He tightened his arm, pulling her closer against his belly.

Molten heat turned her bones into languorous mush. Her breasts seemed to swell and they tingled. An almost overwhelming urge gripped her to scoot her backside against the soft fleece of his sweatpants.

He kissed the side of her neck. "Good morning,'' he said huskily, his breath tickling her ear.

He made no move to release her. She made no move away.

He nuzzled the back of her neck where the short hairs were clipped. A frisson raced the length of her body, building heat in waves, leaving her joints weak and her thoughts swirling.

Let nature take its course, a wicked little voice piped from the back of her mind.

"You smell good," he murmured.

She thrust her legs straight and pushed at his arm. "Hey! Get over on your own side!"

"I am on my own side," he whispered.

She slapped the mattress in front of her. He was right. Sometime in the night, she'd gone crawling straight into his arms. Heat climbed from her throat and burned her cheeks.

She flung back the covers and scrambled out of bed. She smacked her knee on a low table. White pain rocketed through her leg to her hip. She hopped one-legged, holding her sore knee.

Austin propped himself on an elbow. "You're giving me a complex, Jones. I'm not used to women running away." He raised himself to get a better view of her legs. "Especially when they look as good as you do in the morning."

"I bet." She tested her weight. The hot spot faded. She turned on a light. He flinched and closed his eyes. The sight of his muscular shoulders and chiseled pectorals took her breath away. She didn't want to run from him. She wanted that safe feeling warming her soul and his gentle voice telling her she was pretty.

When he opened his eyes, their gazes met and locked. There was nothing enigmatic or mysterious about his expression now. He wanted her.

Her reasons for keeping him at bay grew fuzzy.

Waves of desire turned into a maelstrom of confusion. Sharing a room—definitely a mistake. She escaped into the bathroom.

She'd just tugged on her jeans when Austin rapped on the door. ''I'll be out in a minute!'' She wrestled with the zipper.

''Open the door.''

Unusual urgency in his voice made her comply. ''What is it?''

He waved a sheet of paper. ''We had a visitor in the night. This was under the door.'' He read it aloud.

A friendly warning. Rowena Waxman is dead and buried. Let sleeping dogs lie or the same will be said about you.

Chapter Eight

What kind of cop are you, anyway? Star thought. Dave Crocker had yet to score a single brownie point with her this morning.

First, the police station had been closed. That was when Star and Austin had discovered that Crocker was the police department in its entirety. After knocking on the door and peeking in all the windows at the station, they'd returned to the hotel and looked up Crocker's home number. He'd agreed to meet them at the station. It had taken him an hour to arrive. Crumbs from his breakfast had dotted his shirt.

After all that, he had the audacity to treat the threatening note as a joke.

Star was not impressed.

"You're Texans," Crocker said as if that explained everything. "Some people around here have weird senses of humor." He tossed the note atop the mess in his in-box. "I wouldn't worry about it."

"In my business, I worry about everything," Austin said.

"This isn't Dallas. It's not even Windham. Do you know how many violent crimes I've handled in the past year?" He made a goose egg with his thumb and forefinger. "Zip. My biggest problems are drunks, trespassers and lost tourists. The high school calls when kids are absent so I can make sure they aren't playing hooky." He beamed a don't-worry-your-little-head smile at Star. "Ninety percent of the locals were born and raised right here. Most of the ranches are run by families that have been here for generations."

Worthless, Star thought. He lived in a fantasy world, a regular Mayberry, where he was Barney Fife. She didn't want to talk to him anymore. She caught Austin's eye and indicated the door with a quick shake of her head.

"Thanks for your time, Crocker," Austin said.

Star muttered, "Thanks loads." She pushed open the door.

Crocker slapped his hands on his desk. "I'm not blowing you off. I'm telling you the way it is. Somebody's playing a joke on you, that's all. Nothing but a joke."

"CROCKER'S THE JOKE," Star said as she dug down to the bottom of her duffel bag. Her fingers closed over the holster of her pistol. She hesitated. She'd been carrying a firearm for years and she had a permit, but even so, guns were trouble. "He's no more qualified to be a cop than I am."

She noticed Austin holding a gun case and a shoulder harness. She cocked an eyebrow. "I didn't know you were packing heat. I thought you preached nonviolence."

"No sense getting silly about it," he said without a trace of apology. "Did you bring yours?"

"Uh-huh." That he was arming himself heightened her nervousness. She pulled the pistol out of the duffel. "Sure hope we don't have to use these." She threaded her belt through the holster.

Austin shrugged into his holster harness. His smile turned thoughtful. "We could be making a mistake in not telling Crocker about your memories. Or about the woman who took you to Dallas."

She laughed wryly. Buckling her belt, she told him, "For all we know he's the killer's first cousin. I don't trust him. Besides, a yahoo who'd laugh about a death threat isn't going to take my memories real serious, either." She scooped up her little .32-caliber automatic. It was a piece of junk compared to the Smith & Wesson .38 snub-nosed revolver Austin slid into his shoulder holster, but its familiar weight made her feel less like an easy target. She fitted the gun into the holster and tugged down her baggy sweatshirt to conceal it.

"Look at it this way," he said. "The note proves Rowena's killer is still around. And still worried."

"Oh, goody," she said, making no attempt to hide the sarcasm. "When we run into him, maybe he'll tell us where my folks went before he opens fire."

"Always the optimist. I like that." He pulled on his black leather jacket. "Let's go have a chat with the Sloanes."

Star followed him out of the hotel. As far as she could see, they were the only guests. Its emptiness gave her the creeps. This whole town gave her a case of the raging willies. Logic said this was a busy time of year with the local ranchers readying their stock for winter. Logic had nothing to do with the feeling of dread that increased with every breath she took. "Do you think the Sloanes will talk to us?"

"We'll find out."

The Sloane residence was easy to find. It was the largest house within the town limits, a curious mix of Rocky Mountain contemporary, with towering levels dressed in dark-stained cedar, and Victorian, with curlicues in gingerbread trim around the windows and on the ornate, pale pink front door. The driveway was guarded by a pair of stone lions mounted atop the end posts of an arched pink sandstone wall. A sign, edged in glittering gold, informed them this was the place to find Sloane Construction, Developments and Real Estate Sales. Star couldn't decide if the house was ugly enough to be interesting, or just plain ugly.

The doorbell rang with a deep, drawn-out chime. A man answered the door.

He was well over six feet tall, with blocky muscular shoulders. His belly strained the buttonholes on his shirt and draped over his belt. A striped tie squeezed his fleshy neck. His brass blond hair had a glossy, artificial look that reminded Star of television preachers.

"Howdy," he said in a big, booming voice. He smiled as if he'd wag his tail if he had one.

"Mr. Doyle Sloane?" Austin asked.

"That's me, and aren't you lucky you caught me. I was on my way out. Business. Don't let this sleepy-looking paradise fool you. Gold Coin is a hotbed of opportunity. Are you folks looking for the perfect place to live? Heaven on earth? You sure came to the right place."

"Actually, Mr. Sloane, we're here to discuss other matters. I'm Austin Tack from Dallas, Texas. This is Star Jones. We'd like to talk—"

"Holy moly!" He threw back his leonine head and roared with laughter. He gestured effusively for them to enter. "You're the pair raising Cain all around town. Come in, come in."

Warily, Star followed Austin into the house.

The interior was as eclectic and overdone as the exterior. In the open foyer, antique tables vied for space with enameled black cabinets containing collections of figurines and gewgaws. The walls were covered with somebody's idea of a gallery. One wall held framed photographs of buildings; another was covered with photos of livestock; and yet another was lined with shelving supporting an array of trophies, loving cups and silver platters.

Sloane poked Star with his elbow. He nearly knocked her off her feet. "Quite a showplace, isn't it? If you're interested in building a new home, you ought to talk to my decorator."

Star rubbed her sore arm. "I'll do that."

He invited them to his office. On the way, he yelled for the housekeeper to bring coffee.

The office was a tycoon's dream: walnut paneling, Oriental carpet, potted rubber trees, burgundy leather chairs and bookshelves filled with gilt-edged volumes. Star began to feel as if she'd stepped onto a movie set. All it lacked was Orson Welles smoking a big cigar.

"So you want to know about Rowena Waxman," Sloane said. He sat behind a massive mahogany desk with a finish so deep, items on the top seemed to float. "That's a mystery. I keep telling my old lady, instead of all that dumb poetry she keeps scribbling, she ought to write a book about the murder. That might be worth something."

His open disrespect for his wife rubbed Star the wrong way. She didn't like this man. "Actually, we're looking for my parents. Jerry and Karen Jones."

"Parents?" He squinted at her. "Star Jones... I'll be dipped and lacquered! The twins!" He bellowed laughter and slapped the desk.

A Hispanic woman entered the room. She carried a large silver tray holding a coffee carafe and cups. After leaving it on the sideboard, she exited as unobtrusively as she'd entered.

"Well, now, little lady. Why don't you do us the honors of pouring coffee?"

Before she had a chance to express her displeasure, he turned his attention to Austin. "The Jones twins were really something. Cute as buttons. Couldn't tell them apart to save my life. So I didn't even try."

Star plopped a cup of coffee in front of him.

"Thank you, honey. You sure turned into a pretty little gal." He gave her an up-and-down look that made her skin crawl.

Next one is on your lap, she thought hatefully. As she gave a cup to Austin, his dark eyes sparkled with merriment. She turned her back to Sloane, and mouthed at Austin, "This better be worth it."

"So why are you looking here for your parents?" Sloane asked. He waggled his fingers. "Hand me that sugar, honey."

Again merriment flashed in Austin's eyes. He propped a foot on his knee and laced his fingers over his chest. He looked nice and comfortable. He'd hear about this later—but good.

"Star hasn't seen her parents since they left Gold Coin," Austin said. He gave a condensed version of how Star and Dana had been left at the orphanage. He omitted the part about the mysterious woman who'd taken them to Dallas.

Sipping coffee, Star wandered around the room and studied gilt-framed photographs of buildings. If these were Sloane's projects, then the man was as versatile as he was obnoxious. The photographs depicted everything from single-family homes to hunting lodges to barns.

"Isn't that something?" Sloane said, shaking his head. His hair didn't move. "You haven't seen them since? I guess that about settles it, then."

"Settles what?" Austin asked.

"Who killed Rowena."

"My daddy did not kill her," Star said.

As if he didn't hear her, Sloane went on. "Dumping those cute little girls, there can only be one reason. Guilty as sin."

Anger flared, hot and furious. Sloane was about to get the entire coffeepot in his lap—

Heels clicked on the polished wood floor. A woman called, "Honey? I got your paper ordered, but they didn't have—" a woman opened the office door "—that sand color, so I'm going with..." She stopped short. "Oh, excuse me."

Sloane waved a hand. "You aren't going to believe this."

Star stared at the woman. She was short and plump with a softly wrinkled face framed by wispy mouse gray curls. A pair of blue-framed glasses were too large for her petite features.

Her voice ping-ponged inside Star's head, bouncing off memories and lighting them up like a pinball game.

Stretching out a hand, Star took a wobbly step toward her. "I know you," she breathed. "You're Miss Mike."

"STAR BRIGHT!" Michelle Hagan Sloane laughed giddily. "This is just unbelievable. I can't—my goodness, you're beautiful! How long has it been?"

Interesting, very interesting, Austin thought. He held not the slightest doubt that Star recognized Michelle. Nor did he doubt that Michelle was pleased to see Star. She was a slight woman, somewhat faded and nondescript, her hair and skin blending in shades of gray, her clothing drab. She looked different from the plain but confident-appearing woman pictured in the foyer with all the prize livestock and horses. Yet, Star recognized her.

He wondered if Michelle was the woman who'd driven the twins to Dallas.

"I see you know each other." Sloane sounded petulant. His lower lip jutted. He tapped his fingers in an irritated drumroll on the desktop. "I am just amazed you recognize my old lady, Star. But you don't remember me at all, huh?"

Michelle lifted her chin in a triumphant gesture. "Why should she recognize you, dear? We weren't married at the time. You just flitted in and out. Star and I spent loads of time together. Do you remember, honey? Isadora—Miss Ike? My sister and I, we're twins, too. Of course, you can't tell by looking at us. We aren't identical like you and Mary Christmas."

"Miss Ike," Star said tightly.

"You and Mary were like night and day. She was Little Miss Princess. What sweet manners that child had. And you! We practically had to chain you up to keep you from following your father everywhere. You always wore little overalls and a little hat. If you had your way, you'd have lived on top of a horse. You were fearless, just fearless. Your poor mama had her hands full with you, that's for certain."

Sloane cleared his throat loudly. "Honey, I'm certain Star isn't interested in hearing you wax nostalgic. She's got important business here in Gold Coin."

Star shot him a filthy look, guaranteed to shrivel a more sensitive man. "You have that backward, Mr. Sloane. I'm busting to know everything Miss Mike has to tell me."

Cringing, Michelle gave a tremulous smile. "I do have a habit of babbling. Please, Star, be seated. Tell me how your parents are. Whatever happened to them? It was the strangest thing, the way they up and left us."

Sloane huffed incredulously. "What's strange? Jerry knocked off Rowena. He disappeared to save his hide. Star showing up proves it. Jerry dumped his kids in an orphanage. Like dropping off puppies at a pound. Tell her, Star."

An angry flush mottled Star's cheeks. Her fingers curled over the back of a chair and her knuckles turned white. Austin wanted to escort her out of here, away from Sloane's boorish hurtfulness. But she was a grown-up and could handle herself. Though, he suspected, if he weren't here right now, she wouldn't have lasted three minutes in Doyle Sloane's presence.

"Tell me it isn't true," Michelle said. "Not Jerry—"

Star glared daggers at Sloane. "That's why I'm here, Miss Mike. I'm trying to find my parents."

"You sure won't find them in Gold Coin," Sloane stated. "You ought to be looking in Mexico. Jerry and Karen both spoke Spanish like Mexicans. Remember, honey?"

"I don't remember that," Michelle said absently. She looked on the verge of tears as she regarded Star. "How long has it been since you've seen or heard from them?"

"April 1969."

Michelle sank onto a chair. "Oh, that is so sad. Do you know where Mary is now?"

"She lives in Dallas. She just got married. I was hoping you could give me a clue about where my parents went."

Sloane snapped his fingers. "Disappeared like spooks in the night. Hate to burst your bubble, little girl, but it might be best if you don't find them. They were no damned good, anyway. A pair of drifters, no education, no money."

Michelle rose and grasped Star's hand. "I think we're due for some fresh coffee. Would you give me a hand in the kitchen, dear?"

If Sloane noticed the blatancy of his wife's attempt to get Star alone, he gave no sign. He said, "Juliana made some of her cinnamon rolls. Why don't you bring out a big plateful?"

"Certainly, dear." Michelle led Star out of the room.

As soon as the door shut behind them, Sloane let out a tremendous belch and pounded his chest with a fist. "Women! Getting all dewy-eyed about ancient history." He shook a big finger at Austin. "If I were you, Mr. Tack, I'd take that little girl back to Texas and get her a hobby or something. This snooping around in the past is sure to mean nothing but trouble."

"The choice is hers," Austin said.

"My philosophy is, never give a girl a choice. Females are happiest when you tell them, flat out, honey, do this or do that. It makes them feel secure."

"I'll remember that," Austin said agreeably. Sloane's bulbous nose fascinated him. Rosacea, possibly caused by an excess of alcohol, had turned the flesh a mottled red, like a bull's-eye. "What can you tell me about the Joneses?"

"Not a whole lot." Sloane hooked his hands behind his neck and leaned back on his chair. The chair frame squealed in protest. "I know they both worked for my brother-in-law. We weren't related at the time. I married the old lady in 1970. But me and Stuart were always just like this." He showed Austin tightly crossed fingers.

"Did you ever speak to them?"

The big man shrugged. "I don't like having too much contact with hired help. Hurts relations, you know what I mean?"

"What about the circumstances of their leaving the ranch? Do you remember anything about that?"

"I didn't have a whole lot of time to worry about it. I was working a big job for Stuart." He swiveled on his chair and pointed to a series of framed photographs. "They've got a natural hot spring behind the house. I turned it into a spa. One of the trickiest jobs I ever did."

While Sloane spoke with the tender fondness of a lover about the construction job, Austin observed and listened. Sloane was a hustler, a blowhard and a money-grubber; he possessed the sensitivity of a bull in a herd of a heifers. He seemed proudest of the fact that he was Stuart Hagan's best friend and brother-in-law. Eventually, Austin came to the conclusion that Sloane had little to offer about the Joneses.

During a lull in the developer's self-aggrandizement, Austin asked, "Did you know Rowena Waxman?"

Sloane barked laughter. "You are trying to solve the murder!" He dashed a hand across his eyes. "Yeah, it was a regular soap opera. The town whore and five thousand suspects."

"Did you know her, sir?"

He made a crude gesture with his fist and leered knowingly. "Everybody knew Rowena. Know what I mean?"

"Ah, yes." Revulsion curled through Austin's belly. Sloane's red nose looked more and more like a target.

Sloane glanced at the door. He lowered his voice a few decibels. "Me and Rowena went round and round a few times. Truth is, she was a pretty package, but no prize inside. Drank too much. I don't care for women who drink. No class."

"This was before you and Mrs. Sloane were married?"

"Rowena got herself killed months before me and the old lady hooked up." He shot a glance, more mischievous than guilty, at the door again. "Me, I like variety. Have to be careful nowadays, what with all the diseases floating around. But the old lady understands."

I bet, Austin thought. He smiled in encouragement. "So you think Jerry killed Rowena."

"Who the hell knows?" The expression on his broad, homely face said, Who the hell cares?

"WHAT A HORRIBLE MAN!" Star looked ready to spit. Arms crossed, slouched on the car seat, she glared at the side mirror, watching the Sloane residence recede behind them. "He ought to be hog-tied, dipped in batter and deep-fried!"

"It takes all kinds," Austin said.

"You liked him?" she asked, openly appalled.

"Not in the least." He pulled away from the monstrosity where the Sloanes lived. "So what did Michelle have to say?"

"Not very much." She shivered and hugged herself. "That was the weirdest thing. As soon as she talked, I knew who she was. She even smells the same." She patted at her face as if she held a fat powder puff. "Lilacs, she smells like lilacs. She used to read to us. Poetry and Peter Rabbit."

"Do you think Michelle is the woman who took you to Dallas?"

"I don't think so." The intensely frightened voice of the woman who had escorted them to the orphanage was fixed in stone in Star's memory, but her face was a blur. "Michelle told me my folks had wages coming to them. My daddy was in the middle of a project with Isadora on building a training arena. There weren't any fights. She has no idea why they left. They had no reason to leave."

"Where was Michelle when they took off?" He turned onto Main Street.

"Visiting a girlfriend in Colorado Springs. Her friend had a baby a month early. She said everything was right as rain with my parents when she left."

"So who was at the ranch?"

"Michelle said that's the strangest thing of all. Mr. Hagan had gone to Denver for a stock auction and Mrs. Hagan was ill. She suffers migraines and my mother always took care of her. Devoted, that's what she said. But when Michelle got home, Mrs. Hagan was alone and so sick, she had to go to the hospital."

"Michelle doesn't believe your parents would voluntarily leave a sick woman." He parked the car in front of the hotel.

A storm was building. The puffy clouds from the day before had built into a solid gray mass that wreathed the mountaintops. Interior lighting gleamed yellow through the aged glass fronting the hotel lobby.

Eyeing the threatening sky, she said, "*I* don't believe it."

"Was anyone else at the ranch?"

"Michelle says most everybody was moving cattle. It was just my family and Mrs. Hagan."

Austin made a musing sound. "Did she say anything about Rowena?"

"I didn't ask." She watched him pull the key from the ignition, then caught his hand. "I'm scared, Tack. Something bad happened. Real bad. It's building up inside me. I feel like my heart's going to explode."

His features softened and he slid his arm around her shoulders. She scooted across the bench seat and huddled against his side. He stroked her hair.

"Can you be more specific, punkin? What's bad?"

She shook her head, making his leather jacket squeak. Her memories were phantoms in the closet, bogeymen and bug-eyed monsters, scaring her to death and leaving her without defenses.

Austin's sweet-wild scent curled around her. She felt better, saner, almost immediately.

"When you don't know what you're doing," he said, "the best course of action is any action."

She raised her face enough to see him. "You're talking in circles again."

"I mean, let's get out of the cold. I need to check with Sparky and see if she came up with anything. Then we'll see if Betty dug anything interesting out of the newspaper files." He pressed a tender kiss on her forehead. "You'll be all right. We'll get to the bottom of this, and no matter what happens, you'll survive. I believe in you."

She forced a smile. "That makes one of us, Tack."

"It's enough." He squeezed her tightly before letting her go.

They entered the hotel and stopped at the front desk. From inside the cage, the clerk looked up from a novel and smiled helpfully. Austin asked if he had any messages. The woman told them no.

On the way up the stairs, Star said, "I thought it was just me, but these stairs do lean." The right side of the staircase was at least an inch higher than the left. It gave her a disconcerting, off-balanced feeling.

"I believe that's called quaint charm." Austin turned down the hallway toward their room. He stopped short.

A cowboy waited outside their room. He sat stiffly on a parlor chair, holding his hat on his lap. The nape of Austin's neck prickled. When the cowboy stood, Austin adjusted his pace so he was squarely between the man and Star. He casually unzipped his jacket, freeing access to his revolver.

"Mr. Austin Tack?" the cowboy said.

"Yes, sir." Austin sized up the man. He was lean, with big hands scarred by rope burns and wire cuts. Taking him without resorting to deadly force wouldn't be easy, but it could be done.

"Uh, I work for the Queen's Cross." He pulled his hat brim through his fingers. His leathery face darkened and his Adam's apple bobbed. "Mr. Stuart Hagan's my boss. You know him?"

"I know of him." He felt Star go rigid behind him. "What can I do for you?"

"I have a message from him to you." He looked at the window, the ceiling, the walls above Austin's head, and finally settled on studying his battered boots. His ruddy cheeks turned crimson. "He says, if you got any ideas about setting foot on the Cross, just forget it. If he catches you on his property, he'll see you arrested for trespass."

"He can't do that!" Star exclaimed. "I have to talk—"

Austin placed a restraining hand on her arm.

"I'm just telling you what he told me," the cowboy mumbled. He jammed his hat on his head. "Trust me, he means every word. Ma'am, sir, good day." He strode away as if escaping a vile smell.

Star slammed the side of her fist against the wall. The knock echoed. "That proves it! Stuart Hagan killed Rowena and framed my father."

"IT DOESN'T PROVE ANYTHING," Star grumbled sarcastically. How did Austin stay so calm about all this? This entire town appeared to be conspiring against her search, and all the private eye did was tell her to take it easy.

Stretched out across the bed, with an armful of pillows under her chin, she met Austin with a glare when he walked into the room.

"Hmm," he said.

"What?" She shoved the pillows away and sat upright with her legs folded. "Does Sparky know where my parents are?"

"Just the opposite."

"I don't understand."

"As far as Sparky's sources are concerned, your parents don't exist." He sat on the bed and rested his elbow on his knee and his chin on his fist. "She's run prelims with credit companies and phone directories. So far, zip. It's way, way too soon to say Sparky can't find them, but it could take weeks or even months to receive answers to all her inquiries."

Impatience gnawed at her. "I can hardly stand this place another minute and you're telling me it's going to take weeks?"

He narrowed his eyes and studied her so closely she began to itch. She glanced down at her sweatshirt.

"What?" she demanded.

"You're positive it wasn't Michelle who took you and Dana to Dallas?"

"I'm not sure of anything, except I don't think she was lying to me. But you know what? She's a lot younger than she looks. She was only nineteen when my parents disappeared."

Austin arched an eyebrow.

"I thought she was in her sixties at least. Living with that yahoo..." The mere thought of Doyle Sloane made her shudder. The man was pure slime. "Poor thing, I feel for her. He treats her like dirt. I guess he's always treated her like dirt."

"No doubt. He told me he'd had an affair with Rowena."

She winced in disgust. Her pity for Michelle went up another notch. "Do you think he killed her?"

"It's too soon to draw conclusions." He placed a hand on her knee. "We need to visit Queen's Cross."

"How are we supposed to get to the ranch?" Her big mouth was the reason Stuart Hagan knew what they were doing in Gold Coin. She ground her teeth. She vowed to play everything close to the vest from now on. And to pay closer attention to the way Austin handled people. So far his instincts had been unerring in knowing what to mention to whom.

"The best way is to ask permission."

She darted a look askance at him. "Why didn't I think of that?"

"Michelle Hagan Sloane was tickled to death at seeing you. Her sister might react the same way."

"Isadora? What if she doesn't?"

"Then we'll find another way. I'm not above a little creativity, are you?"

With great trepidation, she called the Queen's Cross ranch. Without identifying herself, she asked to speak to Isadora Hagan. Her heart raced. Michelle had been ecstatic, but Isadora could have the completely opposite reaction to Star's presence.

Star wished Dana were here. A natural-born saleswoman, her twin was a whiz at charming people.

A loud, gruff voice boomed over the telephone lines. "Isadora here. What do you want?"

"Uh . . ." Star's mind went blank.

"Who's there? Who is this? Come on, talk up. I don't have all day."

A memory burst free. A woman shouting, "You idiot! Just because you're a crook, doesn't mean you have to put up a crooked pole. Use the plumb line, you knucklehead!" Star's tiny fingers encased by a big, rough hand. A toothy smile and the rich, healthy smell of horses. "Gotta show those clowns who's boss. . . ."

Isadora Hagan always gave as good as she got and never took any guff from anybody. She had been—still was?—proud of being the biggest, bossiest, orneriest woman in the state of Colorado.

"Miss Hagan? This is Star Jones." Words spilled from her mouth in a nervous rush. "Jerry and Karen Jones are my parents. Dana—I mean, Mary, is my twin sister. I need to talk to you." She sounded like a babbling idiot. Only Austin's gentle smile of encouragement kept her from hanging up in humiliated frustration.

A silence, so deep it seemed as if the world beyond the hotel hallway had disappeared, filled the telephone.

"Star Bright!" The woman practically screamed.

Star flinched away from the phone.

"As I live and breathe, Star Bright. My God, little girl, how the hell are you? I heard rumors you were in town and I didn't believe it. My God!"

Star flashed a disbelieving smile at Austin. He gave her a thumbs-up. She barely had time to think before Isadora was ordering her to write down the address of the Tower Top restaurant in Windham and making her promise she'd be there on the dot at eight o'clock, because reservations were required and Isadora was never late for anything for any reason.

They were in.

Chapter Nine

Austin and Star walked into the *Gabbler* office in time to meet Betty Brownley as she emerged from the back room. Her hands and arms were coated to the elbow with black gunk. It dripped, leaving a trail of splotches behind her.

Betty cried, "You're the private eye, honey! What are my chances of burning down this joint for the insurance and not getting caught?"

Trying not to smile at her frustration, Austin rested his forearms on the tall service counter. "Arson is a tough crime to prove. Fifty-fifty, maybe."

"Good! Those are my kind of odds. If that darned, stupid, clattertrap press explodes in the next day or two, don't be surprised." She snatched up a rag and wiped her hands. She succeeded in doing little more than pushing the gunk around on her skin. "I can't even leave this operation to my kids. All of them are too smart to want it."

"I don't know what to tell you, Betty."

"Don't say anything. This is business as usual." She crossed the room briskly and kicked a small cardboard liquor box. "Here's what you're looking for. I pulled everything I could find about Rowena." Her smile turned apologetic. "Not much here, I'm afraid. My Baxter was better at reporting town meetings than crimes. But you're welcome to it. As long as you do me a favor."

"Anything." He exchanged a grin with Star.

"Top shelf of that cabinet there. Get me the super-duper hand cleanser."

He fetched the cleanser, then asked, "What can you tell us about Stuart Hagan?"

"I could tell you volumes. Only half would be lies. Why?"

Austin told the newspaper owner about the cowboy who'd delivered the rancher's warning. Betty exhibited no surprise.

"That sounds just like him." She used a fresh rag to wipe the cleanser and most of the gunk off her hands and arms. "Old Stuart, he's one of a kind, that's for sure. You already know he owns the Queen's Cross. What most don't know, and no one would ever guess by looking at him, is he's one of the richest men in the state. But he knows, and he likes it that hardly anybody has the guts to stand up to him."

Austin noticed Star intently listening. Her large blue eyes were dark with emotion. She appeared to have lost weight in the last few days, pounds she could ill afford, and her skin was stretched over her cheekbones, giving her a haunted, hungry look.

"Do you think he had something to do with my parents disappearing?" Star asked. More caution than usual colored her question.

"Maybe. The man has a hair-trigger temper and a shotgun mouth. He might have blown up at Jerry and said something." Her eyes narrowed shrewdly. "But what you're really asking is, did Stuart kill Rowena and blame it on your father. I'd have to say no."

"Why is that?" Austin asked.

Betty tossed the blackened rag into a trash can. "Because Stuart doesn't truck with women like Rowena. He's all moral fiber and righteousness. A hundred years ago, he'd have made a hell of a good hangin' judge. As for him warning you away from his property, that's just Stuart. He'd do the same thing if he'd heard you were selling encyclopedias.''

Betty's explanation didn't set well with Austin. He thought she was being honest, but that didn't mean she knew the truth. As he carried the box of papers back to the hotel, he considered everything they'd learned so far.

Precious little.

A hunch pulled at him, though. A hunch he wanted to bury and ignore. The nagging inner voice was telling him that the Joneses had never left Gold Coin. The only difference between Rowena and the Joneses was that a summer storm hadn't washed their bodies from their graves.

He suspected those same thoughts were eating away at Star.

As she held open the hotel door for him, her melancholy clung to her like perfume. It was as if the very air of this mountain valley were poisoning her. He ached for her, imagining the sheer hell of emerging remembrance and the strain it placed on her psyche. Unless she said otherwise, though, the only thing he could do for her was continue.

Once inside the room, he set the box on the bed. Star prowled the room, eyeing the box as if it contained a coiled rattlesnake.

"Hate to say it," she said, "but I don't think Betty knows what she's talking about."

Austin began pulling photocopies of printed articles and handwritten notes out of the box. The *Gabbler*'s copy machine had picked up some of the printing press's quirks. The copies were smeared and smudged. Also included were a few photographs. Sticky notes pasted to them indicated what they were and when they were taken. He studied one taken of the site where Rowena's body had been found. Betty's note said the location was seven miles north of town, about a mile away from any road.

"Well?" Star asked irritably.

"I doubt if she's lying to us." He patted his sidearm. "But notice, I'm not taking her assurances to heart. Hagan probably left us that little lovegram this morning. When we didn't take the hint, he sent the cowboy."

"Oh, boy." She dropped onto the bed. "Can't wait to see what his next message will be." She picked up an article. "He could have killed her, then scared my parents into running. With all that meanness and money, maybe he threatened me and Dana. That would explain why they sent us to the orphanage." She looked up with shining, hopeful eyes. "They sent us away to save our hides."

"Which doesn't explain why they didn't return for you." As soon as the words were out of his mouth, he could have kicked himself. The sparkle left her eyes and her shoulders slumped. He grasped her hand. Her skin was cold. "Something either is or it isn't. Making uninformed guesses confuses matters."

She pulled away from him and sorted through the stacks of papers. His attempts to get her to talk to him about what she felt elicited only monosyllabic replies.

He felt like a failure. He'd brought her this far, built up her hopes, and run her face-first into a blank wall. At the moment, even platitudes failed him.

You wanted a challenge, he reminded himself glumly.

"Tack?" she squeaked and thrust a sheet of paper at him. "It's the confession."

Betty had made a copy of a copy, and the writing was so faint that parts of letters were missing. He read it carefully. It was dated August 28, 1969.

I, Jerrod Scott Jones, am sorry for shooting Rowena Waxman and burying her body. It was a honest mistake and thier ain't no way to say sorry except I am sorry. Please, Mr. Brownley, print this full page on the *Gabbler* so everyone can see I am sorry I did it.

Jerrod Scott Jones

Something about the note struck a chord of familiarity with Austin. Stroking his jaw, he tried to figure out what it was.

Wide-eyed and pale, Star fumbled with her medicine bag. A fragile piece of fringe snapped off in her fingers. She flung it impatiently on the bed where it lay like a discarded mouse's tail. She freed the sheet of cracked blue paper and opened the love letter on the bed.

She breathed so hard, he feared she might hyperventilate.

"Calm down—" Seeing the letter again stopped him cold.

The handwriting on both missives was identical.

Austin shook his head and rubbed his eyes. No mistake. The crabbed, childish scrawl matched. The writer had even used the same misspelling on both pages: "thier" instead of "there."

"Oh, no. Oh, no." Her chin trembled. "He couldn't have…oh, no…" She recoiled from the papers and pressed her fists to her belly. "He couldn't have—"

"He didn't." He looked back and forth from the love letter to the confession and back to the love letter. "Your father didn't write this. He didn't write either of them."

Rocking on her hips, clutching her belly, she stared at him as if he'd sprouted another head.

"Truth is in the tasting," he said.

"Who quoted that?" she murmured.

"Betty Crocker." He carefully turned the love letter around so she could read it. "First off, my apology for not giving this letter of yours the full attention it deserved. Second, I don't think your father *or* your mother wrote it."

"How do you know that?" Some of the strain eased from her face. She sat straighter.

"They were teenagers when they married. I'll go so far as to say they were high school sweethearts who were completely devoted to each other. They had twins together, they worked together, they went to church and lived quietly together. Strife and high drama stand out in anybody's memory. If your parents had been having trouble, someone would have mentioned it.''

She eyed him suspiciously. The color returned to her face. ''What's that got to do with the price of bait?''

He touched the love letter with a fingertip. ''Pookie knows trouble is brewing with Snuggle Bear. Look at this line. 'You know you love me.' And this, 'I'm the only one for you. We both know it. You have to admit it.' If Snuggles loved Pookie, there wouldn't be any reason for those particular statements. The entire letter expresses doubt. This isn't a love letter, it's a plea of pure desperation. People in secure relationships don't write this kind of letter.''

Her forehead crinkled as she caressed her medicine bag. ''I always did think it sounded kind of funny. But they could have been private about their troubles. I know lots of folks who put on good faces for the neighbors.''

''The timing is way off. Let's suppose your father did kill Rowena.''

She bristled like a cat.

''I said, *suppose,* for the sake of argument. He kills her, buries her, packs up his family and splits. He gives you and Dana to a woman who takes you to Dallas. Jerry and Karen go to Denver. He gets remorseful and writes an apology to the *Gabbler.* That's how it had to have happened if your father did it.'' Before she could protest, he held up a hand. ''None of which makes any sense.''

''You're doggone straight about that, Tack. But... why doesn't it make sense?''

He took a moment to sort his thoughts. To help him think, he rustled up his notepad and a pen. He wrote a large number one on the paper. ''Why would your father have anything to do with Rowena? Better yet, why would Rowena have anything to do with him? If your father liked to honky-tonk, someone would have mentioned it. If your father chased women like Rowena, someone would have mentioned that, too." He wrote, No motive.

"Next, your mother would have had to agree to pack up and leave behind a sick woman who was her responsibility. The only way that could have happened would have been if your father told her he killed Rowena. If he went to the bother of burying her, why would he tell anybody?" He wrote number two, and after it, Karen Jones as accomplice.

"The next question we'd have to answer would be, why leave at all? Because he was scared? If he had it in him to commit murder and conceal the body, then why assume anyone would find Rowena or connect him to the crime?" He continued making notes.

"The biggest question is abandoning you and Dana. We haven't picked up a single shred of evidence that your parents were anything other than completely devoted to you. We can assume he panicked. But would your mother? I've dealt with plenty of child abandonment cases. In all of them, the signs were strong. Abuse, a history of neglect, medical problems. None of those signs are apparent in this case."

Star nodded eagerly.

"So let's skip to the confession. Rowena's body was discovered in early August. She'd obviously been murdered. But until this letter arrived, no one suspected your father. So why would he send a confession? Guilt? Remorse? A desire to get caught? Possible, but unlikely. If he felt that badly or if he thought his arrest was inevitable, he'd have turned himself in. Or, suppose your mother wrote this confession and signed his name because she blamed him for losing her children. If she hurt that much, she'd have turned him in."

He showed her his list. "I'd accept one, possibly two of these scenarios. But all of them?" He swung his head in denial. "It doesn't fit with the facts."

"So Pookie is the killer."

"That makes more sense." He turned to a fresh sheet of paper. "Pookie gets into an argument with Rowena and kills her. Buries the body. Goes on about his or her business. The Joneses disappear. Other than a few like Betty thinking it's odd, no one cares. *Until* Rowena's body is discovered. Now the killer has a problem. The cops look for killers. Ergo, Pookie gives them a prime suspect."

"But that doesn't explain why my parents disappeared."

He didn't like the nagging voice in his head explaining the situation for him. Pookie killing the Joneses along with Rowena explained things very neatly. He called himself a coward, but he couldn't bring himself to extinguish the light in her eyes by speaking his thoughts aloud.

He picked up the love letter. "This explains it. You were four years old. You weren't driving around the mountains, picking up other people's mail."

She squinted at the letter. When she finally spoke, she sounded dazed. "It was one of the Hagans. I was right, then, my folks did witness the killing and—"

A knock on the door made her jump.

Austin folded his fingers over the butt of his revolver. "Are we expecting company?"

Star licked her lips. "Around here, it's getting so I expect about anything."

He glided to the door. Standing off to the side, his right hand free and ready to act, he called, "Who is it?"

"Sherry, from the front desk," came a cheery reply. "I have a package for Miss Jones."

Austin cocked an eyebrow. "Think we're getting a horse's head?" he asked, sotto voce.

"Or maybe a little finger wrapped up in a bow." Star jerked her sweatshirt over her gun holster and scooped up the love letter and confession. She dropped them in the box along with Austin's notepad and covered them with the rest of the papers Betty had provided.

She tossed Austin his jacket. He slipped it on, concealing his gun, and opened the door.

Sherry flashed him a broad smile. She held forth a small package wrapped in green-and-white foil, decorated with metallic green curly ribbon. She said, "I have a message for you, too, Mr. Tack." She fished in her jacket pocket and brought out a hotel memo sheet. "Have a nice day."

Austin closed the door. He examined the package carefully before handing it over.

"Too small for a horse head," Star said nervously, and opened the enclosed envelope. It contained a note from Dave Crocker. Though relieved, she frowned and shifted her gaze to the package.

"Crocker," she explained.

Austin dug around in his suitcase and came up with his little computer. "What does he want?"

Star snapped up her head. That peevish tone of voice wasn't at all what she'd ever expected to hear from the private eye. Could he, Mr. Cool personified, possibly be jealous? "He says not everyone in town is prejudiced against Texans." She glanced at the note again, and had to fight a smile. "He also wants to know if I'd have dinner with him tonight."

"We've got plans." He exited the room without so much as a backward glance.

A laugh popped from her throat. He was jealous! The idea of anyone being jealous about that hick cop... jealous about her... A hunch floated past and she snagged it: Austin cared. He truly, genuinely, cared about her. Thinking it gave her a funny, squishy feeling.

This was scary. She suddenly believed he was serious with his kisses and sweet talk. But why? He was handsome as a movie star. Hundreds of women would kill to gain his attention. Intelligent, generous, warm, gentle, confident— what could he possibly see in her?

That question was impossible to answer, but she sure cared too doggone much to give him even a moment's discomfort. She aimed the gift-wrapped box at the trash can and tossed it. It hit the mark with a clang.

Two points, she thought, and crumpled the note.

Austin soon returned. He plugged the computer into the wall socket, did a few magical things with his fingers, then looked up at her. "I've got a report from Sparky." He was all business, his expression closed and unreadable.

Was he angry? Mad at her? Agony rose in her breast. "Good news?"

"Just news." His eyes darted as he scanned the report. "Sparky found an old judgment brought against your parents."

"What does that mean?"

"It means somebody sued them and won. They owed a debt to the hospital where you and Dana were born. Apparently, your birth ran up a large hospital bill and your father had been paying on credit. The last payment made was April 1, 1969. After your folks were eight months in arrears, the bill was turned over to a collection agency. The agency got a judgment."

"So they were paying regular up until they disappeared, then just stopped." She didn't like where her thoughts kept traveling. Contrary to what Austin had told her before about the majority of missing persons being missing because they wanted it that way, none of what they were learning sounded as if her parents had vanished voluntarily.

The terrible things she'd been denying crowded her, clamoring for attention. She tamped them down as best she could. Effort made her head ache. "What else does Sparky have to say?"

"Nothing more right now."

Ask him, she told herself. Ask what you know is true. She drew a deep breath, steeling herself, but she couldn't make herself do it.

She wasn't ready yet to consider out loud whether her parents might be dead.

AUSTIN COULDN'T STAND IT. He kept his ear cocked toward the running shower in the little bathroom as he fished the gift-wrapped package out of the trash. He carefully peeled cellophane tape off one end. He slid back the wrapping paper until he could see the package contained Pocket Mountain milk-chocolate fudge.

A white-hot pain arced across his ribs. His forehead tightened and his jaw muscles clenched. Obviously, Crocker couldn't take a hint. "And dinner, too," he muttered.

He froze, staring in amazement at his fingers crushing the candy box. He, who had devoted his adult life to rising above the failings of spirit represented by avarice, envy and anger, was jealous.

He dropped the box back in the trash can and laughed at himself.

The words of Proust occurred to him: There is nothing like desire for preventing the things we say from having any resemblance to the things in our minds.

Rationalizing what he felt or objectively analyzing it eluded him completely. He was in love with Star and that was that. How or when or why it happened didn't matter. The essence of her penetrated his entire being, making it impossible to imagine life without her. For the first time in a long time, he felt incomplete. It was disconcerting, to say the least.

IT WAS SNOWING when Austin and Star left the hotel. She turned her face toward the clouds. Snowflakes caught on her eyelashes and hair. "I'm going to freeze my buns off." She shrugged her jacket tighter across her shoulders.

"We can go back inside—"

"I don't have another coat." She sighed. "I'll be all right." She hurried to the car.

They headed for Windham.

The road to Windham climbed steadily, hugging the side of the mountains. Although the snow wasn't sticking to the road surface, Austin drove carefully, conscious of the narrow shoulders, and possible patches of ice. The windshield wipers slopped clumps of wet snow around the glass.

"I know what we can do," Star said. She sat at an angle so her feet were squarely under the heater vent.

"What's that?"

"Handwriting. We'll look at all the suspects' writing. We'll check the Sloanes and the Hagans. One of them has to be Pookie."

"Uh-huh."

"It'll work," she said hotly. "We know Pookie is the killer."

"Actually, we're fairly certain Pookie wrote the confession letter. We don't *know* anything else." He hated bursting her bubble. "Handwriting analysis is a job for experts. If we're going to catch a killer, it'll take court-approved experts. To do that we'll need exemplars."

"What's that?"

"Samples big enough for comparison. Two or three full pages at the very least."

Her brow rose and lowered, and she made musing noises. He imagined she was considering the logistics of obtaining useful exemplars from unwilling suspects.

"The only good way to do it is the legal route," he said. "Let's find a contact in the Colorado Bureau of Investigation and get an expert's opinion on whether the Pookie letter and confession are a match. If they are, it might be enough to reactivate the investigation."

"It sounds too complicated."

"Not nearly as complicated as sweet-talking the Sloanes and the Hagans into giving us exemplars."

"Oh." The corners of her mouth twitched. "I reckon breaking into their houses and looking for samples is out of the question."

"Unfortunately. Do you remember where you found the Pookie letter?"

He was very curious about where a four-year-old would have picked up the love letter. No one would have given it to her. She could have picked it up because the paper was attractive, or because it fit in with some childish game. The tone of it was so embarrassing, it was difficult to imagine anyone leaving it lying around on a table or desk.

Twin red reflections through the windshield alerted him and he applied the brakes. The ghostly shape of a bull elk materialized along the side of the road. As large as a horse, its magnificent antlers curving in a deep U supported easily by its shaggy neck, it stared at the approaching headlights. Snow swirled around its shoulders like a mantle.

"Look at the rack on him," Star whispered.

Even in the dim glow of the dashboard lights, her eyes sparkled. Her beauty arrowed straight to Austin's heart. He slowed the car to a crawl.

"Isn't he something?" She leaned forward, both hands on the dashboard. "I could reach out and touch him."

"He's something, all right."

The elk disappeared like a puff of a smoke.

Catching a spark of headlights in the rearview mirror, Austin sped up. Snow was starting to stick in feathery patches to the road and ice was forming, so he kept his speed below thirty. "Don't see much like that in Texas."

Star hugged her elbows. "It makes me shiver. It's like something stepped out of a fairy tale."

Her voice was breathy and excited. The air inside the car vibrated with her pleasure. He chuckled. "You may be more like Dana than you think."

She frowned for a moment, before laughing, too. "Her fairy-tale books and such. Yeah, I reckon she knows all about magic deer and enchanted forests."

The headlights behind them caught his attention. They approached way too fast for road conditions. He didn't know this road well enough to increase his speed. Even if it weren't snowing, large wildlife lurking by the roadside made high speeds downright stupid. He'd seen the kind of damage a deer could do to a car—an elk could cause a catastrophe. He negotiated a sharp curve that snaked alongside the mountain. His tires slipped a little on an icy patch.

Star twisted on the seat. "He's going pretty doggone quick. Think he's drunk?"

As it drew closer, Austin determined by the height and shape of the headlights that it was a pickup or other heavy utility vehicle. It caught up to them on the next curve and all but kissed his bumper. The glare of its headlights illuminated the Ford's interior.

"What in Sam Hill is he doing?" Star demanded. She nervously fingered the chest strap of her seat belt.

Hairs rose on the nape of his neck. That joker was playing a dangerous game of mountaintop chicken. Praying no elk chose to cross the road, he goosed the accelerator.

As soon as Austin sped up, so did the truck.

This time it did smack the bumper. The jolt rocked him on the seat. Star grunted and grabbed wildly for the dashboard. He fought the wheel, aiming for a straight course along the centerline. Star braced herself, clinging to the dashboard. Austin had only seconds to consider his options. Were it another car, he'd slow down, forcing the car behind either to slow down, too, or go around. But that truck was heavy enough to push them off the increasingly slippery road.

"Hold on, Jones, this could get ugly." He gunned the engine.

The Ford leapt forward like a racehorse out of the chute. Both hands on the wheel, focused straight ahead, Austin negotiated curves that seemed to climb forever.

After a momentary lag, the truck began gaining.

The driver was either drunk or on a suicide mission.

Star unzipped her jacket and wrenched up her sweater, freeing her pistol. A soft metallic click announced the safety was off, and a louder, more serious clack sounded when she chambered a round.

"Don't shoot, punkin," he said mildly.

"That fool's fixin' to run us off the road!" She rolled down her window and the rush of icy air sucked the wind from Austin's lungs.

His headlights caught a turnout. It looked narrow, barely wide enough for a full-size car. How steeply the side of the mountain dropped off, he did not know; how many trees were there to break a car's descent, he did not know, either. All he knew for certain was that a homicidal maniac playing catch me-kiss me with his rear bumper was a prime candidate for disaster.

He took his foot off the accelerator, letting the ascent slow his speed. The truck struck his bumper again. Metal screeched. Praying he didn't hit ice, he fought the wheel. Again the truck hit him, and through the open window he heard the big engine roaring. He focused on the turnout.

"Lock on your safety, punkin," he said. "And brace yourself."

He kept slowing. The truck was forced to slow, too. As if the driver was growing angry, each successive impact was harder. The Ford's taillights shattered.

At the turnout, he was still going over twenty-five miles per hour—too fast. No help for it. He cut the wheel sharply and slammed on the brakes. The truck hit the left rear quarter panel, lifting the Ford's rear end. For a moment, Austin felt certain they'd been launched into space. He braked so hard his ankle ached and his hands burned on the

wheel. The truck scraped past, shearing off the side mirror.
The Ford struck something solid and metal crunched. Austin's seat belt locked, slamming the air from his lungs. His
head snapped against the neck rest with teeth-jolting force.

Up ahead, brake lights flared. Tires squealed.

Austin clutched the steering wheel and choked down the
sour taste of adrenaline in his mouth. Star panted heavily.
She held her .32 with both hands.

Backup lights brightened like devil's eyes.

"Ah, hell, he's coming back for us!" Austin exclaimed
and shoved the transmission into reverse. "Shoot at him,
Jones. Just shoot at him."

Chapter Ten

Austin slowed his breathing and concentrated. Their attacker's intent was clear as springwater—knock them off the turnout and down the mountainside. Since he was driving a seventies-model Blazer, he was big enough to do it.

The Blazer's engine was gunned threateningly, full of power and heavy enough to be king of this hill. The rear end was mud-splattered and streaked with snow, so the license plate was obscured. The backup lights cut through the darkness, turning the falling snow red. Austin tried reverse. The Ford's engine roared, and spinning tires flung gravel. Whatever Austin had hit had grabbed the front of the car, holding them fast.

"Get us out of here, Tack," Star said, staring wide-eyed at the Blazer. "He's going to knock us off the mountain."

Austin shifted into drive and tried going forward. Nothing. He tried rocking the car. Nothing. The way the car teetered told him the front wheels weren't getting any traction.

The Blazer jumped at them.

Austin pushed away from the door and locked his arms over his head.

The collision jolted the Ford sideways. Shattered glass peppered Austin's head and arms, pelting his leather jacket like buckshot. The seat belt slammed against his shoulder and hips.

Star cried out in pain.

Austin fumbled with his seat belt catch, but it refused to budge. The Blazer lumbered away, ghostly in the swirling snow, growling.

"Hell with this," Star muttered. She shoved open the passenger door.

Austin tore frantically at his seat belt catch. It was jammed tight. "Get back here!" he shouted as she scrambled out of the car. Visions of the Blazer driver armed with a shotgun or worse danced through his mind. "Star!"

The Blazer's backup lights flared again. The spare tire mounted on the back had prevented too much damage to its rear end. It could conceivably keep pounding at them like a pile driver until it finally pushed the Ford off the turnout.

Austin gave up on the seat belt and unzipped his jacket. Watching the Blazer, he freed his revolver. He used the butt to clear the remaining glass from the side window.

Star fired. *Crack! Crack! Crack!*

The acrid stink of gunpowder blew into the Ford.

The backup lights winked out, leaving the normal taillight glow. The big engine gunned and the wheels spun.

Crack! Star fired again.

The Blazer careered wildly up the road.

Austin leaned as best as he could out the window and aimed for a rear tire. Restricted by the seat belt, he twisted his arms for a decent shot, but the Blazer rounded a curve and got away.

Star fired once more, but there wasn't a chance she hit anything except the mountain.

Austin killed the engine. The world was very quiet, except for wet snow whispering against the car and the rasping of Star's excited breathing. The gunpowder stink faded, but he could smell the rankness of his own fear.

Keeping an eye out for the Blazer's return, he worked at the seat belt until it finally gave. His chest and shoulder ached from pounding against the straps. His next car, he swore, would have air bags. "Hey, punkin," he called. "Are you all right?"

She ducked and looked inside the car. Her eyes blazed fury. "Listen to you! Cool as an ice-cream cone!"

The driver's-side door was caved in. He didn't bother fighting with it and scooted across the bench seat. Star backed up, shifting her wild-eyed glare between him and the road. Snow coated her hair and shoulders. A thin trickle of blood oozed from her right temple.

"You're bleeding," he said.

She touched her face, then studied her fingertips by the wan light from the car interior. "It's nothing. What about you?" She shoved her gun in her holster. Very slowly, she turned her head, and even more slowly, her body turned so she faced away from the road. From their point of view, the drop-off was a chasm into a black eternity.

He touched her shoulder. She groaned and wheeled into his embrace, hugging him tightly and burying her cold face against his neck.

"He tried to kill us," she moaned. "Are you all right? Tell me you're all right!"

"It's okay," he murmured against her hair. He hugged her with all his strength until his fear drained away and his heart stopped pounding.

He leaned back so he could see her. Her bloodied face made his heart hurt. Cold anger burned his gut. "There's only one reason that joker tried to kill us. He knows you can finger him for murder."

She blinked rapidly. "Are you thinking...I know who killed Rowena?"

"I'm sure of it. One way or another, we're going to make you remember."

IT WAS ABOUT EIGHT miles back to Gold Coin, mostly downhill. After an hour of walking, Star was so cold she couldn't even muster enough energy to wipe the snow off her face. Her hands and feet were numb. Her thighs burned. Her knees throbbed with every step. Each gust of wind cut through her like a knife.

Austin didn't complain, so neither did she.

"Are you all right?" Austin asked. "Need to stop a minute?"

She kept putting one foot in front of the other. "Best not. Might not get started again." She tightened her fists inside her jacket pockets. Her skin ached; her joints were frozen.

What Austin had said weighed heavily on her mind. She had witnessed Rowena's murder. She knew it now with the weird certainty with which she felt so many things about the past. Still, details eluded her, clinging to the far reaches of her mind and refusing to coalesce into something coherent. Worse yet, the sense of having done a bad thing was stronger than it had ever been. She kept hearing that woman's voice, telling her to shut up, not to talk to the police, that it was all her fault.

"What about you?" she asked.

"I'm fine." He turned on his flashlight, sweeping the road with the beam. The snow was about an inch deep now. His boots crunched wetly with every step. He turned the light on her. "Take my coat."

His concern did funny things to her insides. "I'm not taking your coat and that's that." She looked away. "If you want to share a little warmth, I don't mind."

He wrapped his arm around her shoulders. Their strides matched. "A car should be along anytime now."

She prayed it wouldn't be the Blazer. "I think that was Stuart Hagan," she said. "I bet he's Pookie."

"Possibly. Rowena might have gone to Queen's Cross to force him to choose between her and his wife."

"Rather than argue, he shot her. I'd remember something, if I could see his face. Or better yet, hear his voice. Why is that, do you reckon? Faces don't make much impression, but hearing their voices takes me right back in time."

They saw the lights before they heard the engine. Star stopped dead in her tracks and stared down the mountain. The approaching vehicle was about a mile away, the lights flickering through the thick trees. She fingered the butt of her .32. Austin unzipped his jacket.

"Good guy or bad guy," he said. "Do we chance it?"

She wasn't in the mood to chance anything. "Not on your life, Tack." She edged off the road and made her way by feel to the facing cliff. Boulders offered cover. She crouched and made herself part of the rocks. Her knees burned, her icy hands felt as if they were about to fall off, but the idea of the Blazer making another run at them made it easy to ignore the pain. Austin crouched beside her. She knew without having to see that his revolver was in his hand.

The lights disappeared around a bend, but the engine noise grew louder. Star eased the safety on her pistol into the off position.

It was a Jeep Cherokee marked with police emblems.

Austin sprang from concealment and ran to the center of the road. He shone the flashlight at the back of the Cherokee, flicking the light on and off. The vehicle stopped and backed up.

For all they knew, Crocker was in Hagan's employ—after all, he'd laughed about the threatening note. He could be here to finish them off and toss their bodies into a ravine where they would never be found. Even though every instinct screamed to run, she made herself trust Austin.

Star holstered her pistol and tugged her jacket over it.

Dave Crocker rolled down his window. "What the heck happened to you?"

"We had a little accident, chief," Austin said. "Mind giving us a lift? We'll tell you all about it."

Between the snow and the darkness, there wasn't much to see at the turnout, but Crocker insisted on looking at Austin's car, anyway. A thick furring of snow made hills and valleys over the caved-in driver's door and mangled rear bumper. The front axle was stuck on an outcrop of granite, and the front wheels were a few inches off the ground. Crocker wiped away snow and shone his nine-cell flashlight beam on the crumpled metal.

"You say a Blazer did this?" he asked, and looked to Austin for confirmation.

Star watched the men from inside Crocker's Jeep. By holding her hands against the heater vent, she'd thawed them to the pins-and-needles stage. She kept a close eye on the police chief.

"An old Blazer," Austin said. "A seventies model, I think, but I can't be positive. It was too dirty to read the license plate."

Crocker rubbed the back of his neck. He looked thoroughly confused and younger than ever. "That narrows it down to about half the vehicles in the county. What about color?"

Austin pressed a fingertip to the damage on his car. "We'll look at this in the daylight and figure it out."

Crocker agreed. He drove them back to Gold Coin.

Ensconced before the old-fashioned potbellied stove in the Gold Coin police station, Star tried hard to control her shivering so as not to spill scalding-hot coffee all over her lap—or worse, dribble it down her chin.

Crocker kept shaking his head as he wrote up the accident report. His incredulity came through loud and clear. Twice he muttered words to the effect that the good folks of Gold Coin just didn't do that sort of thing.

"Neither of you saw the driver?" he asked.

Star gingerly fingered her knee. The soreness, she'd discovered, came not from walking downhill. Both her knees were deeply bruised. She must have banged them on the dashboard without realizing it.

"With any luck, he has a bullet hole in him," Star said, trying to keep from snapping. "Are you going out to Queen's Cross?"

Crocker looked surprised, and perhaps a little frightened. "No."

"It was Hagan! He threatened us. He sent that cowboy to try to run us out of town. You might think he's a joke, but I don't. He tried to shove us off the mountain. The man's a cold-blooded killer!"

His eyes glittered with irritation. "Are you willing to positively state Stuart Hagan is the person who ran you off the road? You can identify him?"

He knew doggone well she couldn't. Just as she knew doggone well that Crocker was out of his league, despite his trying to pretend he wasn't. She looked to Austin for help. He'd gone cool and blank.

"Gold Coin isn't much of a town, but the law is the law." Crocker folded his arms over his chest and lifted his chin. "I'm not rousing Hagan out of bed without a darned good reason to do so. You're sure not giving me a reason."

STAR SAT ON THE BED and glumly studied her bruised knees. She knew who'd killed Rowena—why couldn't she remember? A face, a name, any detail, no matter how small. The holes in her memory were making her crazy.

The bathroom door opened and a cloud of steam billowed into the room. Austin strode out, wearing only a towel wrapped around his waist.

Star's heart lurched. The hotel was old-fashioned, but the towels weren't. They came from the same place where thousands of other motels and hotels purchased their linens. It was white, none too fluffy, and barely big enough to take it out of the hand-towel category. Austin had to clutch the rectangle of fabric to keep it from slipping off his lean hips.

His long, muscular legs were incredible.

He glanced at her, his eyes skimming her face. "Sorry." He rummaged through his belongings and came up with a pair of briefs.

She decided she hated hotels. She'd bathed with too many tiny bars of soap and dried off with too many small towels. She'd drunk from too many cups belonging to other people; opened too many doors with other people's keys.

"Jones?" Austin asked. He sounded worried. "Are you still shaking about the Blazer?"

"Towels" popped out of her mouth.

Looking puzzled, he tightened his grip on the towel around his waist.

"I was thinking about towels." And him, and the future, and a permanent place to set down roots and be part of a community... "I want my own towels. Big ones. Soft as velvet, in lots of pretty colors. Plum and emerald and royal blue."

"Cool."

"And I want a real bed, too." She thought for a moment. "Brass, it has to be brass with curlicues."

"Double cool." He grinned, and his dark eyes sparkled with mischievous light.

She sounded like a nitwit. She laid her forehead against her knees. A low-down, yellow skunk had tried to kill them, and she was prattling on about bed and bath furnishings. "This is dumb."

"Sometimes the little things in life mean more than the big ones."

"Like almost getting killed?" Her body twitched in remembrance.

The mattress sagged as he sat beside her. "We're safe now."

It occurred to her he might be scared, too. He might even need a little comforting. She lifted her head. "I'm not scared anymore. I'm mad. I can't decide who I'm more mad at, the guy who tried to kill us or Crocker."

"Why Crocker?"

"Because he's an idiot. He doesn't know what he's doing. I bet you a year's worth of Sunday dinners he's never investigated a major crime." The scent of his shower-warmed skin wafted to her nose. She loved the smell of his oddly arousing honey undertone.

He cocked his head, questioning.

She wasn't used to giving or receiving comfort. She searched for more appropriate words, or at least something better than complaints about Crocker. Unable to think of a single thing to say, she touched his shoulder. His skin was damp.

"That was sure a close call, though." She eased wet strands of hair off his neck. "Good thing those rocks were there to catch the car." Sheesh, real comforting. Think of something, she ordered herself. "I mean, it could have been worse."

"True."

"It was cold, too." She brushed the underside of his jaw. Stubble rasped her fingers. "I thought I'd never get warm again."

"We're okay now." He placed his hand over hers. His gaze unwavering as he watched her eyes, he kissed her fingertips, one by one. He kissed her palm, his lips silky and gently teasing.

A shudder rippled through her knees and thighs.

"We need some sleep," he said. "We have a lot to do tomorrow." He nibbled a sweet path along the tender flesh of her inner wrist.

"I don't know if I can." What he was doing to her made thinking impossible. Inch by tantalizing inch he kissed his way up her arm. When he touched inside her elbow with his moist lips and warm breath, she couldn't stop a quavering sigh. Skin all over her body ached with hunger for his touch.

"I love your eyes," he said, his voice deep and slow. "They hide nothing."

She looked away.

He cupped her chin and brought her face around. "There's nothing you need to hide from me, punkin." He moved his face closer so his mouth was only a finger's width from hers. He paused.

She answered his unspoken question by lowering her eyelids and kissing him. His mouth was fresh and damp, his kiss deep and soulful, touching her heart. He slid his hand down her throat, around her neck and to her back.

Desire burned her, weakened her limbs. Her body ached with wanting. Enveloped by his strong arms, she floated down to the soft mattress. She entwined her fingers in his damp, heavy hair.

He raised his head. His eyes were luminous, dark and hot, gleaming with desire. "This is getting out of hand. Want me to stop?"

He didn't want her, she thought in horror. He didn't like this. He—

Fierce and swift, she squashed the voice of her insecurities, and focused on his tender expression. She bit down on her tongue to keep from saying anything stupid. If she tried to say anything, she knew sure as sunrise it would be stupid.

She had to do something. He kept waiting, watching. Not knowing what else to do, she groped blindly at his hip, found the damp towel and tugged it off his body. She tossed it clumsily off the bed.

"If you say so," he said with a melting smile, and captured her mouth with his.

THE NEXT MORNING as Star brushed her teeth, Austin rapped his knuckles against the bathroom door. "Hurry up, punkin. We're running late."

And you're the reason why, she thought, and giggled.

She rinsed her mouth and glimpsed her reflection in the mirror over the sink. There it was again, that dreamily mindless smile. Merely imagining how it got there sent tremors through her thighs and left her with wobbly knees. She had to grasp the sink for support as she relived how his kisses had branded her head to toe, and every place in between. No one had ever made love to her the way he had. No one ever would again.

When she opened the door, Austin was waiting, holding her jacket. "Are you all right?" he asked.

Her gaze fell on the bed. Forget brass beds, she wanted one just like this one, towering headboard, cupids, frilly pillows and all—as long as Austin Tack was included. "I'm fine."

"Are you sure?"

How did he do it? she wondered. He looked exactly the same as he had yesterday. He acted the same and sounded the same. She felt absolutely certain their lovemaking was marked all over her face for all the world to see. "Sure I'm sure." If he could play it cool, so could she. She reached for her jacket.

He stepped over and helped her slide her arms into the sleeves. As he adjusted her collar, his knuckles brushed her neck. He whispered, "You've got me twisted up like spiderwebs in a tornado."

Pleased he wasn't so cool, after all, she grinned. Snuggling against him, she rubbed her cheek against his hand. "I'd smooth out the tangles for you, but we're late." She felt a shudder rack his body, and he tightened his grip on her shoulders.

Nope, he wasn't Mr. Cool at all. That pleased her immensely.

Downstairs, as they passed through the lobby, the desk clerk called, "Miss Jones! There you are." She spoke into a telephone. "Can you hold just a moment, ma'am?" She covered the mouthpiece with her hand. "Miss Jones, you have a phone call. Can you talk, or shall I take a message for you?"

"Might be Crocker," Austin said.

Star took the call.

Isadora's brassy alto boomed over the line. "What the hell happened to you, little girl? I waited and waited for hours last night."

"Oh! Isadora, I'm so sorry. I should have called, but by the time we got back to town it was late...." The excuses were weak as a liar's oath. "I should have called. I'm sorry. We had a problem."

"What kind of problem?"

Uncertain how much to say, Star looked at Austin. "What do I tell her?" she mouthed.

"Whatever you want," he said.

Star felt good about Isadora, good about the memories the woman roused, but she was a Hagan and one of the Hagans could be a killer. "We had an accident with the car," she said cautiously.

"You hurt? Not used to snow, I betcha. Those fool blow-by storms don't look like much, but they can be tricky."

"We're all right. I'd still like to meet you. Can we get together?"

Isadora barked a hearty laugh. "You bet we will! You come on out to the ranch this afternoon. Say around four. Supper's at six sharp."

"Your brother told me to stay away from the ranch."

"He did what? Hell with my brother. The Cross is half-mine, and if he don't like company, pah! You be here. I won't accept excuses. I'm dying to see you." Isadora's confidence vibrated over the telephone wires.

Star snatched up a pen and paper to take down directions to the ranch. After she hung up, she waved the paper at Austin. "We've got an invitation to Queen's Cross. Talk about walking into the lion's den." She clucked her tongue. Stuart Hagan was acquiring demonlike status in her mind—was Isadora big enough to stand up to him? She didn't know. "Well? What do you think?"

"I think the opportunity is too good to pass up. Right now, let's go see what Crocker has to say."

Crocker drove them up to the turnout. Star rode in the back seat, savoring memories of last night. Until Austin, she'd never known how much she liked kissing. Light kisses, wet kisses, nibbles, licks—she loved them all.

Austin touched her knee. She started.

"Crocker arranged for a tow truck to meet us at the car."

She caught Crocker eyeing her in the rearview mirror. She'd missed something. "What about it?" she asked.

"The tow truck driver is Mark Waxman." Austin's face and voice gave away nothing of what he felt. "The chief here says Waxman has ideas about who killed his daughter."

"They're all wrong," Crocker said. "The old man's crazy as a sheep in a snowbank. I can't stop him from talking your ears off, but I thought I'd warn you. When I first took the job, he wanted me to reopen the case. He said he had proof about the killer. He doesn't."

"What about my parents?" she asked. "Do you think he knows anything about them?"

Crocker lifted his shoulders. "He's never said anything to me about your folks."

Star was surprised Waxman had said anything at all to the police chief.

At the turnout, Star tried to quell the sick feeling churning her stomach. The sky had cleared and the sun beat down on the snow. The glare was so harsh it was painful on the eyes. All the snow had melted off Austin's Ford, exposing the damage. The turnout itself was barely big enough for the car, and except for the rocks they'd hit, there was nothing between the turnout and a hundred-foot drop into a rocky canyon.

Crocker and Austin examined the car. The entire driver's door was caved in; the door wouldn't open. The mangled rear bumper hung by a single bolt, and only thin shards of plastic remained of the taillights.

"Brown," Austin announced. He cupped a sheet of paper in both hands. "He was hitting us mostly with the spare-tire mount, but here's some brown paint."

Crocker sighed as he opened an evidence bag. "I'll have to send it to the state cops for lab work. It'll take weeks to have this analyzed."

"You don't think attempted murder is worth it?" Star asked sarcastically.

Crocker actually cringed and assumed a shamed-puppy smile. "I'm just saying how long it'll take. This is a serious matter, and it'll take time to investigate."

"So check out Stuart Hagan's vehicles. Does he own a brown Blazer?"

Heat crept over Crocker's handsome face. He kept his eyes lowered.

"You'll know the right one when you find it. I put bullet holes in it."

"Hagan owns a lot of vehicles. He's even got his own airplane. I'll give him a call and—"

"So he can ditch it?" It struck her that Crocker might be afraid of the rancher. Disgusted, she turned away.

She heard an approaching truck. Within a minute, she spotted a tow truck lumbering up the steep, curving road. If Dave Crocker thought Mark Waxman was crazy and full of bull, then that was all the more reason for Star to pay extra attention to whatever the old man had to say.

Waxman maneuvered his truck into position. Head down, his face hidden by the broad bill of his cap, he wordlessly set to work. Star recognized him from the diner. She wanted to tell him she was sorry for blurting out her question about Rowena. Austin joined him, helping with the cables.

Crocker sidled next to Star. He watched the operation. "We keep getting off on the wrong foot, Miss...Star," he said softly.

She fought the urge to grimace.

"Did you get my package and card?"

"Uh-huh."

He lifted his hat and smoothed his hand over his hair. She noticed how sun glinted on his brilliant eyes. He did wear contact lenses. She wondered if he stood in his underwear and posed before the mirror in the mornings, flexing his muscles and thinking he was hot stuff.

"I, uh, really would like a chance to start over."

She wanted to say something cutting, knock him down a few pegs. But prudence held her tongue. Like or dislike, they needed Crocker for whatever little bit of good he could do. "How about letting me take a look-see at the file on Rowena's murder?"

He groaned. "I can't do that."

"You could at least take me seriously."

"I've already given you everything I have on your parents." He glowered at the wreck. "My hands are tied as far as this is concerned. I don't have any proof to start an investigation."

Star could not believe her ears. Either this man was corrupt and living inside a powerful man's pocket, or he was incredibly stupid and naive.

"How about dinner at my place tomorrow? I'm a good cook, if I do say so myself."

It was all she could do to keep from laughing. "I've got too much to do."

He folded his arms over his chest. "Maybe we can make it a business thing. I could bring the case file." His voice rose hopefully. "You've got time for that, right?"

She practically salivated at the thought of seeing the case file with her own eyes. Perhaps, too, her visit to Queen's Cross ranch would rouse enough memories for her to lay some real proof on Crocker's plate. Or, at the very least, she fully intended to snoop around and see if she could find a brown Blazer customized with bullet holes. He'd have to do something about Stuart Hagan then. She forced a smile.

"Well, if it's business, then bring the file on over to the hotel."

His entire face lit up. Good golly, she thought, the man could do toothpaste commercials. All of a sudden, he looked too pretty, too Hollywood-fake. It was as if he'd been hired because he looked good in the uniform.

"Your room?" he asked.

She saw her mistake immediately. This clown was reading what he wanted into her suggestion. The mere thought of him making a pass at her turned her stomach.

"I mean, the hotel restaurant or lobby. You can show me the file."

His smile faded, and the pull of his brow turned peevish. He darted hateful looks at Austin. "I can't flash that kind of stuff around in public. Just come to my place. We'll have a nice supper and talk about your case."

She desperately wanted to see the file; she just as desperately didn't want to encourage Crocker's amorous idiocy. She tossed her own glares at Austin. This was all his fault. Before last night, she'd have gone to Crocker's place and done whatever was necessary to get the information she needed.

She wondered what would happen if she accepted the invitation, then showed up at Crocker's place with Austin. Crocker would probably burn the file before their eyes.

Apparently reading her dilemma as indecision, Crocker lowered his voice. "I'll fix you a filet mignon that'll knock your socks off."

Austin called for the police chief to give them a hand.

Gears ground as Waxman started the winch. Metal groaned and creaked. Austin stood near the Ford and guided Waxman with hand signals. The Ford's front end lifted off the rocks. Waxman left it dangling. He slouched over to do an inspection of the undercarriage.

"Axle's busted," he announced. "Have to haul it in to the shop."

Star wondered how much this was going to cost her. Her cash reserves were sinking perilously low.

"How long for repairs?" Austin asked.

"If you don't care what it looks like," Waxman said around a toothpick jutting from the side of his mouth, "day or two. If you want it pretty, maybe a week."

"Pretty doesn't matter."

"You're in luck, then. I got me a junker in the lot. Same model, with a blown engine, but a good chassis. If you don't care that it's green, I can give you a door and quarter panel, too." He spat into the dirt. The toothpick defied gravity and remained twiddling from the corner of his mouth.

Austin faced the old man squarely. "Do you mind giving Star and me a lift back to your shop, Mr. Waxman?"

Crocker took a startled step. "I'll ride you back to Gold Coin."

Waxman looked Austin up and down, his red-rimmed eyes shrewd, but undecided. He looked over Star, as well. Lifting her chin, she met his eyes, and in them recognized a kindred soul. Waxman sought justice, too, public opinion be damned. He turned toward his truck. "Hop in," he said. "I'll give you a ride."

The police chief looked none too pleased.

Star squeezed in between the two men on the bench seat with her long legs awkwardly crammed next to the transmission console. With the Ford in tow, Waxman drove down the mountain road. Star had a million questions to ask, but she kept her mouth shut. She'd upset him that day in the diner. She had no intention of doing it again.

"I've been hearing about you all over town," Waxman finally said. He glanced in the rearview mirror at the battered Ford. "I'd say some folks are worried you might find a few things best left buried."

"I'd say you're right," Austin said.

Sunlight caught the silver bristles on Waxman's chin and cheeks. "You're acting like it's all a big mystery, and it ain't.

I know who killed my girl and I know why. But no one listens to me and they ain't gonna listen to you, either.''

"So who did it, Mr. Waxman?"

He pointed at a metal sign planted by the roadside. It was a Property For Sale sign, offered by the Sloane real estate corporation. "Doyle Sloane, devil take him. He shot my little girl like a dog."

Chapter Eleven

Mark Waxman shifted his rheumy-eyed glower between Austin and Star. "Rowena loved Doyle Sloane." He spoke the name as if it were made of vinegar.

They sat inside Mark Waxman's double-wide trailer. Star had been inside trashy places before; she'd lived in a few. She'd never seen anything like this. Several metal trash cans overflowed with garbage, beer cans and spaghetti sauce jars. The few pieces of furniture were buried under newspapers, men's magazines and auto parts. Three large, soggy dogs lay in corners, filling the trailer with the stink of wet fur.

From her perch atop a rickety bar stool, Star reached out to pet the nearest dog.

Waxman spoke sharply. "Leave 'em be! Wolf hybrids. Can't trust 'em for nothing."

"Wolves?" she asked. They looked like scruffy husky-shepherds to her.

"Wolf dogs. Got eight of 'em running around the place. Folks think they're cute when they're pups." He made a disgusted sound and spat into a trash can. "They're not so cute grown-up, so city folks dump 'em in the mountains. Let 'em run free. Pah! Make good junkyard mutts, though." He ruffled the stiff mane of the nearest wolf dog and the animal opened one yellow eye. "These three are so old, they're worthless. Still can't trust 'em, old or not. Got teeth like a bear trap. Take off your arm in a heartbeat.''

Star's revulsion faded. Waxman was filthy and bitter, but under the cruddy exterior beat a heart generous enough to take in discarded pets. She exchanged a look with Austin and saw respect in his dark eyes.

Austin said, "So you think Rowena and Sloane were having an affair?"

"Uh-huh." He spat again. He lost the toothpick that time and immediately plucked another from a greasy tin holder. "She latched on to him soon as he showed up. He ain't local. Don't know squat about ranching or mountain living. Acts like he invented Gold Coin. Hear him talk, he built it from the ground up."

Sloane having an affair with Rowena made him a likely suspect, but Star couldn't see what it had to do with her parents. Waxman hadn't mentioned her parents once, and she wondered if he'd even known them. She could feel another dead end building up, brick by brick.

"Having an affair makes it easy to suspect him," Austin said in his gentle, neutral voice. "But you know more, Mr. Waxman."

"Uh-huh. Ain't no one gonna listen, though. Sloane is Hagan's pet, is what he is. Won't no one touch him. Not the law around here, anyway."

"I'm listening, sir."

Waxman laughed. "You look like a hippie, but you got some manners, son. I like that. Is it true what gossip says? You're a private eye?"

"Yes, sir."

"Guess you about seen it all, then?"

"I'm surprised on occasion. So why Sloane?"

Admiration filled Star. It didn't seem to matter to whom Austin spoke. He had a gift for saying the right things at the right times, and winning confidences in the process. The old man actually seemed to be enjoying this conversation.

"Like I said, Rowena set her sights on Sloane. He had all she wanted. Lots of ambition, gonna be rich, knew the right people. I never could get it into her head that she wasn't the right kind of people for him. Know what I mean? He got himself Michelle Hagan. Not 'cause she was anything to look at. Girl always looked like a sack of flour. But being a Hagan made her downright pretty. That's what Sloane wanted. All that Hagan money."

"Rowena didn't like Sloane courting Michelle."

"That's it!" Waxman slammed a fist on the debris-covered counter. Dishes rattled in the sink. "I'm gonna get him, she'd say to me. Stomp around here, throwing things, smashing plates. Lovin' him one second and hatin' him the next. The night she disappeared, she says she was gonna fix his wagon once and for all. Took outta here like she was on the devil's mission." He looked toward a grimy window and for once his shifting eyes were still.

His sadness touched Star. He knew what his daughter had been, and yet, he mourned her still.

"When you say fix his wagon," Austin said, "what do you mean, exactly?"

"Don't know, exactly. Pretty sure she was..." His voice dropped to a mumble.

Austin leaned forward. "Pardon?"

"Blackmail!" Waxman choked on the word. "She was blackmailing him. Sloane got himself engaged to Michelle sometime around Christmas. That's when my girl started acting crazy and all. Sucking up to Hagan was one thing, but marrying his sister was another. Sloane wasn't gonna spoil that for nothing. Sure not for the likes of Rowena."

"So she extorted money from him in exchange for not ruining his relationship with Michelle."

"Uh-huh." He hopped off the stool and shuffled to the rear of the trailer. His chunky work boots made the trailer creak and groan. The wolf dogs lifted their heads, but when he bypassed the kitchen area, they returned to sleep.

"This is making sense," Star whispered. "Rowena must have gone to the ranch to confront Michelle. She wasn't there, but Sloane was."

"At least, Michelle said she wasn't there."

His nonchalant comment made her flinch. "You can't possibly be thinking Michelle killed Rowena."

Austin shrugged.

Waxman returned with a tattered shoe box, held together with silver duct tape and tied shut with string. "The cops thought I was crazy. Still do. They're the crazy ones." He untied the string and removed the top. "They laughed at me." He brought out a red savings passbook. "Proof's right there."

Star stood next to Austin so she could see what the passbook contained. It was so old, the entries were handwritten and stamp dated. The account had been opened in January 1969 with a deposit of five hundred dollars. The deposits in varying amounts continued on a weekly basis until April. Star totted the figures in her head: $3,050.

"Cash from Sloane so she wouldn't blab to Michelle." Waxman nodded firmly.

"And the police didn't consider this evidence." Austin examined the passbook carefully. "Curious."

"Nah. Said she earned it from tips at her job as a cocktail waitress. Ha! My girl had two allergies. Ugly men and hard work. Ain't no way she pulled in that kind of money." Reluctantly, he pushed the box closer to Austin. "I know what you're thinking. She was sleeping around. Cops said the same thing. Uh-uh. Weren't no other men after she met Sloane. No way. She loved him as much as she hated him, and that's the solemn truth."

Austin poked through the box. It contained ticket stubs, a pair of fuzzy dice, a cheap plastic kewpie doll and a gold-colored bracelet set with green stones.

"This is her sweetheart box. Gifts from Sloane. Used to be a packet of letters, too. Only they disappeared when my girl did."

Austin and Star jerked to attention. "Letters?" they asked as one.

"Uh-huh. Ain't never read them, but I saw 'em once when she was crying and carrying on, drinking and feeling sorry for herself. Had 'em wrapped up in a ribbon. Suppose they was love letters from Sloane."

Star swallowed the sudden moisture in her mouth. Through her sweatshirt, she fingered the outlines of her medicine bag. Of course. Rowena had taken her collection of letters to confront Michelle—and Sloane stopped her.

Austin asked, "Do the nicknames Pookie or Snuggle Bear mean anything to you, sir?"

The old man pulled at his bristly chin. Finally, he said, "Don't think so." He grasped the sweetheart box. "So what you thinking? I'm a crazy old man, booze pickled and mean spirited?"

"No, sir, I don't think you're crazy at all."

"I went after Sloane once. That man lies like a snake on a rock. No one believed me over him. All it got me was ninety days in the county lockup." His pale eyes blazed. "But one of these days I'll get me some proof folks will listen to. Then by damned, his head will be mine."

WAXMAN LOANED A JEEP to Austin and Star. "No charge," he growled when she offered to pay. He promised to have the Ford running in a day or two.

The Jeep was at least thirty years old, and if it had ever had shock absorbers, they'd long since lost their usefulness. By the time they turned onto Main Street, Star was inspecting her teeth with her tongue, searching for knocked loose fillings. When Austin shut off the engine, her ears kept humming from the scratchy, screeching, gear-grinding noise.

"I ought to get one of these," Austin said, patting the rusted, bare metal dashboard. "This is fun."

"You are so odd," Star said, and swung her legs out of the Jeep. It had no doors. Her cheeks burned from the freezing wind. "So, is he right about Sloane?"

Austin raised his shoulders in a noncommittal shrug. "The letters bug me. If Sloane wrote the letters, then he was the one afraid of losing Rowena, not the other way around."

"Maybe she wrote them, and he made the mistake of giving them back. No." She shook her head hard. "He had to have written them, because he wrote the confession, too. Do you reckon Mr. Waxman is wrong about who dumped who?"

His brow furrowed in deep thought, Austin didn't answer. Intent on not missing a word he might say, she almost struck him when he stopped short in the hotel lobby.

Doyle Sloane sat in the guest parlor, drinking coffee and reading the *Rocky Mountain News*. When he saw them, he put aside the coffee and newspaper, and rose. He beamed a broad smile their way. It didn't touch his eyes.

"I've been looking for you," he said in his booming voice. "We've got the dining room to ourselves. Coffee is my treat."

Before either Star or Austin could decline, he strode toward the hotel restaurant and began bellowing orders at the waiter.

"Are you going to ask him if he killed Rowena?" Star cocked an eyebrow in challenge.

"Next to knowing when to seize an opportunity, the most important thing in life is to know when to forgo an advantage," he replied. "So said Disraeli, and he was quite correct." He made a sweeping gesture toward the restaurant. "We'll play it by ear. After you, punkin."

One of these days, she determined, she'd have to find out where, when and why he'd learned all those quotes.

She took a seat as far from Sloane as she could get. The man's slimy presence made her want to scrub with lye soap and burn her clothes. Poor Michelle, she couldn't help thinking. Living with Sloane must be pure misery. Did Michelle suspect her husband was a murderer? Or was suspecting him of philandering enough?

"You two are causing quite a stir in this little burg," Sloane said. After the waiter poured coffee and laid out a plate piled with Danish pastries, Sloane ordered him to leave the pot and make himself scarce. He smiled at Star. His teeth made her think of the story of Little Red Riding Hood. "I sympathize. I do. But you know by now that your folks aren't anywhere around, Star."

Her back muscles tensed. Sloane wasn't making a social call. The longer she looked at his big, fake smile and TV-preacher hair, the more he looked like a murderer.

"I don't know anything, *yet*," she said through gritted teeth.

Sloane flinched and his eyes narrowed. "You've grown into an attractive woman, Star. If you'd do some work on that hick accent of yours, you could probably be in the movies."

Austin cradled his coffee cup. Head lowered, he appeared to be divining the future in the rising steam. Keep cool, his posture told her. Don't let him rattle you.

Sloane tore a big chunk off a Danish. "Yeah, there's probably a whole lot of things you could be doing. A lot more interesting than poking around in the past."

"What's your point, Mr. Sloane?" Austin asked.

"No fiddle-fooling around with you, eh, Mr. Tack? All right, straight to the point, then, man-o to man-o. You're stirring up trouble and I don't like it."

I bet you don't, Star thought.

"Gold Coin's in trouble. You Texans understand boom and bust. So you know what I'm saying. What with the environmentalists raising Cain about cattle damaging the range lands and the antimeat people saying eating beef's akin to eating cyanide, we're losing ranchers right and left. And it's going to get a lot worse before it gets better. The only thing that'll save Gold Coin is tourism. God knows, I work my tail off. But it's hard. We're thirty miles off the main road. We don't have the history of Cripple Creek or the glamour of Vail or Aspen. Nobody's bothered trying to develop ski areas. Except me, and do you have any idea what it costs just to build one lift? Even old Pocket Mountain has let us down. We've still got plenty of hot springs, but the big ones from the mountain have all but dried up."

"I sympathize, sir," Austin said, "but what has that got to do with our finding Star's parents?"

"Public relations!" Sloane exclaimed as if the point were so obvious it shocked him. "That damned Betty Brownley is eating up all this murder nonsense. You two have got her thinking she actually knows something about journalism. She's bragging to me that the *Gabbler* is going to have more than just social gossip and weather reports in the next issue. How's this going to look? Yeah, bring your tourist dollars, folks, just watch out for mad-dog killers on the loose." He shook a thick finger at Austin. "It's like herding turkeys to get the people around here to do anything. For years now I've been trying to get them to vote for limited-stakes gambling. I just about get them convinced, then you show up."

Star sat back on her chair. "How in Sam Hill are you laying the blame on us? We don't care if you gamble or not. Or about ski lifts or tourists or hot springs. I just want to know where my parents went."

He slammed both hands on the tabletop. "They aren't here!"

If he wanted to intimidate her, he failed. She met his glare with all the heat she could muster.

Sloane settled back on his chair. He popped some Danish into his mouth and chewed sullenly. He began nodding and kept nodding as he pulled a fat wallet from inside his suit jacket. "You're throwing a wrench in the works. I've got an election coming up and important things to do. But I don't moan and groan about problems. That's not my way. I fix them." He opened the wallet and eyed the contents. "So let's be realistic. How much will it take for you to go away?"

A muscle jumped in Austin's cheek, but otherwise he didn't react. Star found it easy to picture Sloane twenty-five years ago, trying to buy off Rowena. She wanted more than anything to ask him flat out if he was a killer. She managed to refrain, barely.

"I don't want your money, Sloane."

He pulled a sheaf of bills from the wallet and fanned them. "A thousand bucks?"

"Go to hell."

"Five thousand?"

She laughed in disgust. "I'm not leaving until I find out what happened to my parents."

"Ten thousand." He stopped smiling. His eyes were mean little shards of flint.

Austin dropped a spoon in his coffee cup and stirred it around, making the china clink. Watching it, rather than Sloane, he said, "Mark Waxman claims you killed his daughter, Mr. Sloane. I have reason to believe her murderer knows where the Joneses went." He slowly raised his eyes. They were merciless.

Sloane's big mouth snapped shut.

"What do you think about that, Mr. Sloane?"

"Waxman is crazy. And I don't like what you're implying."

"Which is?" His voice was deadly soft. "You already told me you'd had an affair with her. Was she blackmailing you? Were you waving your wallet around so she wouldn't jeopardize your marriage to Michelle?"

Goose bumps rose on Star's arms. Austin might preach nonviolence, but at the moment he looked like a cold-blooded jungle cat on the prowl. And Sloane was his prey.

Sloane shredded the Danish between his fumbling fingers. "Rowena Waxman was nothing but a two-bit whore. Whoever killed her did this town a favor. But I didn't do it. Furthermore, I don't give a damn who did. Get the hell out of my town."

"Or what, Mr. Sloane? Another round of king of the hill?"

Drawing his head warily aside, Sloane murmured, "King . . . ?"

Austin pushed away from the table. Standing next to Star, he looked down at the big man. "All we need is a direction, sir. Point it out and we'll be happy to take it. Otherwise, we'll be seeing you around. Good luck with your gambling issue." He headed for the door.

He stopped short in the doorway. Star nearly hit his back.

Looking over his shoulder at Sloane, he said, "By the way, do the names Pookie and Snuggle Bear mean anything to you?"

In rapt amazement, Star watched the color drain from Sloane's face. The whites showed all the way around his pupils and his mouth hung slack.

He abruptly grabbed a napkin and dabbed at his fleshy lips and chin. His jowls quivered. Pure, seething hatred blared from his eyes.

Austin and Star walked out.

"I THINK WE CAN ELIMINATE Michelle as the woman who took you and Dana to Dallas," Austin said. He was perched on the bed in their room, studying a topographical map of the area around Gold Coin.

He'd been busy this afternoon, communicating with Sparky via computer, ordering background investigations on Doyle Sloane and Stuart Hagan. He'd asked Betty

Brownley for everything in the newspaper files concerning the Hagans and the Sloanes. She'd been more than happy to oblige and had sent her daughter, lugging a huge box filled with papers, to the hotel. Star wondered if Betty envisioned a Pulitzer in the making.

Standing before the bathroom mirror, Star said, "I pretty much eliminated her, anyway. But why do you say so?"

"In order for her to take you to Dallas, she would have to have known about the murder. I can't imagine her marrying Sloane if she thinks he's a killer."

Star gestured at him with a makeup brush. They needed to leave soon in order not to be late to Queen's Cross. "Women can do the doggone dumbest things in the name of love."

He looked up, his eyes sparkling. "How dumb?"

Star refused to look at his eyes—if she did, they'd never get out of this hotel room. "Doesn't matter, anyway. I'll never forget that woman's voice. It wasn't Michelle." She returned to the problem of trying to disguise the small cut and big bruise on her forehead with her pitiful supply of cosmetics. All the powder was doing was making her look sunburned. She tossed the brush into her bag and leaned over to scrub her face.

"My impression is, Sloane kept a string of girlfriends," Austin said. "He probably still does. He could have coerced one of them into taking you girls to the orphanage."

The implication of what he was saying struck her like a blow. With her face covered with lather, Star froze. Austin's touch startled her. She rinsed her face and straightened. In the mirror, his face was solemn. His fingertips brushed her back.

Words to ask what she most feared knowing hovered on her tongue. The facts seemed so simple, almost tidy. If Sloane murdered Rowena, then arranged for a woman to take Star and Dana to Dallas, then it must mean her parents had been murdered, too.

Shut up, shut up! It's all your fault.... The woman's voice rang in her head, harsh and hateful with accusation.

Austin handed her a towel. She woodenly dabbed her dripping face. Ask him, she ordered herself. Say it out loud and get it over with.

He watched her in the mirror. She felt his empathy wrapping about her like a warm woolen blanket. And still fear held her silent. The stakes were too high. What if her parents were dead and what if it was her fault? If she ever saw a glimmer of revulsion or censure on Austin's face, or heard it in his voice, she'd die.

"Are you ready to go?" he asked.

"I reckon," she choked out.

"Whatever happens at Queen's Cross, remember, I'm there for you. You're strong. You can handle it."

She hoped so.

Riding to the ranch in the Jeep was an experience. The ragged canvas top let in more wind than it kept out. The open doorways and rotten muffler made conversation impossible. Every crack in the road felt like the Grand Canyon; every bump was Mount Everest. There were no seat belts, so Star had to choose between keeping her hands warm in her pockets or holding on for dear life.

The weather had cleared. Not a trace of clouds or haze marred the crystalline sky. Once past the arched, wrought-iron gateway, the road to Queen's Cross was so beautiful it almost made her forget her discomfort. Jays and magpies flashed through the Ponderosa pines and aspens. Leaves had covered the ground in a carpet of brightest gold. Small herds of fat Angus cattle, their black coats gleaming in the lowering sun, grazed the brown high-country grasses between patches of snow.

When they topped a hill and saw the ranch house, remembrance hit her with stunning force. Nestled in a flat, sweeping valley, the main house was built long and low with white stucco walls and a red tile roof. A windbreak of blue spruce trees caused a flash in her mind: *Ollie ollie oxen free!* The sharp tang of running sap and sticky needles clinging to her hair. Soft giggles of little girls playing hide-and-seek under the drooping boughs. The double doors on the house, decorated with a big ring knocker, daring her to give it a good pounding.

Austin pulled around the lazy loop of the driveway and parked next to a battered pickup truck. "Star?"

"I remember this place," she whispered. "When it snowed, we used to sled down that hill over yonder. And there was a glider on the veranda. It squeaked, and we could make it sound like a cat yowling." She turned wide eyes on him.

Conflicting emotions made focusing difficult. Part of her was so scared, she trembled; part of her was awash in nostalgia. Austin kept a firm hold on her arm as they walked up to the front door.

He rang the bell.

A woman answered. As tall as Star, she was far heavier, with thick shoulders and a barrel chest. Her red flannel shirt was tucked into blue denims that fit tightly on solid hips. Her face was broad and square, her skin leathery and deeply etched from the sun. She wore her brown hair in two long plaits that dangled over her shoulders.

"I'll be danged," she said in a gruff, amused voice. "Except for that hair, you're the spitting image of your daddy."

This had to be Isadora Hagan. "Miss Ike?" Star asked cautiously.

"You do remember me!" She threw back her head and laughed. She waggled a finger. "I'm telling you right now, though, that Ike-and-Mike crap went out twenty years ago." Her big shoulders hitched. "You really do remember me, huh? And you must be the private eye. Austin Tack, is it?" She grabbed Austin's hand with such force he stumbled half a step. She pumped his hand vigorously.

An image formed in Star's mind. Clopping boots and wood scraping the floor. A rack near the door for big hats and oilskin coats. The soft grit of spilled flour under bare feet. A clear, overly serious child's voice reciting...sing-song...

Star scrunched her face and rubbed her temples with her fingertips. She wanted this memory to clarify so badly her head ached.

"Come in out of the cold, little girl. Come in!"

Nothing had changed. Star knew it the instant she walked into the house. The wide foyer still had a polished tile floor and framed photographs hanging on the walls depicting prizewinning bulls and quarter horses.

As if reading Star's mind, Isadora laughed. "Not much has changed, eh? You can blame us all. I don't pay a damn bit of attention what the house looks like, and Stuart's wife, Queenie, is stuck back in 1943 or thereabouts. She barely changes her clothes, much less the decorating." She looped an arm around Star's shoulders. "Cocktails in the parlor, my girl!"

The parlor was actually the formal living room. Except for a vaguely uncomfortable sense of trespassing, Star gathered little impression from the room. It was huge, with a central fireplace made of brick with a copper hood, and hunting trophies crowding the walls. A curved bank of windows offered a panoramic view of the mountains.

Isadora shoved a cut-crystal glass in Star's hand. It contained an inch of amber liquid. Isadora gave an identical drink to Austin, then hoisted her own. "To the good old days." She tossed back her drink with the careless aplomb of a hard-core drinker.

Star pretended to sip for politeness' sake. The smell of whiskey made her nose twitch.

"I don't remember this room," Star said.

Isadora refilled her glass. "Not surprising. No children allowed. Not that it stopped you much from exploring. You were a pistol, Star Bright, always in and out of everything." She laughed suddenly and slapped her thigh. "I remember one time, you got into Queenie's jewelry chest. Tarted up Mary like a little Christmas tree. Good God, I thought Stuart was gonna have a stroke right then and there when you little girls come tottering out wearing fifty grand worth of diamonds."

"Mr. Hagan didn't like us very much, did he?"

Isadora shrugged lazily. "He doesn't like nothing. Old sourpuss. I swear, he was born ninety years old and no sense of humor. He sure liked your mama's cooking, though. We've never had a cook before or since who can turn out biscuits the way she did." She dropped onto a leather club chair and sobered, eyeing Star. "I hear your accident last night was no accident. Is that true?"

Austin skirted a bearskin rug. He set his glass on the fireplace wall. "We were run off the road."

"Did you see who did it?"

"No, ma'am."

"It was a brown Blazer," Star said. "An old one. I reckon someone doesn't want me finding out where my parents went."

"Peculiar." Isadora sipped her drink. "Why would that be?"

Star looked to Austin. She wanted to confide in Isadora. The rancher was a powerful woman with powerful connections. They needed a friend like her—but she was a Hagan. Austin gave no clue as to what he was thinking. Since he didn't answer, Star took it as a sign to proceed.

"Because someone is scared I'll find out who murdered Rowena Waxman."

"Are you gonna do that?"

"That's not why I came here." She looked to Austin again. Hands behind his back, he stared dreamily into the fireplace.

"When Jerry and Karen hightailed it out of here, it was like they disappeared off the face of the earth." Isadora snapped her fingers. "Vanished. No one's heard nothing since. At least, not until you showed up. What do you know for certain?"

"I'm surprised Michelle hasn't filled you in."

Isadora snorted. "Michelle wouldn't tell me if my hair was on fire. So go on, what do you know?"

Again, Star looked to Austin. As motionless as the stuffed animal heads on the walls, he looked deep in his own thoughts. Absorbing vibes or examining the meaning of ashes, she supposed. She told Isadora what had happened to her and Dana. Encouraged by Isadora's acceptance, Star also told her about the woman who'd taken the twins to Dallas.

"And ain't seen hide nor hair since," Isadora said, subdued. "Any ideas about the woman?"

"I'll know her when I hear her," Star said. "I'll never forget her voice."

"Never say never, honey, you were awful young. Just a mite. You couldn't have been more than four or five. Shoot, I barely remember what I had for breakfast, much less what happened when I was a kid." She scooped up the whiskey decanter. "You ready for another?"

"No, thanks." She fingered her medicine bag, tracing the familiar, comforting edges through her sweater. "Dana—I mean, Mary—she forgot. She even forgot about me. But I remember."

"Hmm." Isadora freshened her drink. If the whiskey had any effect, she didn't show it.

"Were you friends with my parents? Did you talk with them?" Star sat on an ottoman and toyed with the heavy crystal holding her untouched drink.

"Oh, yeah! Your daddy and me—" she showed crossed fingers "—were like that. He was a young pup, but he had a way with horses. See, me, I'm outnumbered around here.

Cows, cows and more cows. Yuck! I hate cows. Horses are my life. Jerry, well, I swear he was a regular Dr. Doolittle when it came to horses.''

Star glimpsed movement from the corner of her eye. Austin caught it, too, and turned around to face a pair of French doors.

A woman peered into the living room. Frail and bent, her cloud of snowy hair quivering as if kissed by a breeze, she peered fearfully at Star.

Isadora sat forward and boomed, "Queenie! Come on in and say hello. You ain't gonna believe who this is."

Queenie clutched her chest. Her face was pasty except for hot spots of color on her cheeks. "I know who it is! Get out!" Her voice rose to a quavering shriek. "Get out of my house or I'll call the law! Out!"

Star couldn't breathe. She couldn't move. The crystal glass dropped from her suddenly numb fingers and hit the thick rug, splashing whiskey on her jeans leg.

The voice! Queenie Hagan was the woman who had driven her and Dana to Dallas.

Chapter Twelve

Austin snagged Star's arm and clutched a handful of her cotton sweater. She kept running until the fabric stretched as far as it could. Caught up short, her feet slipped on the polished hardwood. Austin stepped under her weight and kept her from crashing to the floor. She squirmed and twisted, flailing her arms wildly.

"Stop!" Star yelled. "Where's my daddy and mama? What did you do to them? You know! Stop!"

"Get away! Get away!" Queenie shrieked. Arms clamped over her head, she shuffled down a long hallway.

Austin locked his arms around Star's belly and swung her off her feet. "Calm down. It's okay, calm down." Clasping her body to his chest, he felt her thundering heart and raspy breathing.

Queenie slipped through a doorway. She slammed the door shut. A lock thunked. Her panicky wail was muffled through the wood. Star tried to lunge at the door, but Austin tightened his grip. As thin as she was, she was strong. Her muscles quivered and strained, and it took all his strength to hold her.

Still holding a drink, Isadora sauntered toward them. The hallway, which ran along the back of the house, was faced on one side with a wall of glass. It overlooked a landscaped garden and buildings set against a backdrop of striated granite cliffs. Isadora paused to look out at the view. Her face was gray, her mouth taut.

Stretching out a hand to Isadora, Star cried, "It's her, Miss Ike! She's the one. Make her come back. She has to talk to me, please. Miss Ike, *please!*"

The rancher sipped her drink and eyed Star over the rim of the glass.

"Stop it now," Austin whispered in Star's ear. She whipped her head around and it shocked him to see her eyes brimming with tears. Her chin quivered. "It's okay, punkin, calm down. You have to stop this."

She stopped fighting him. A heavy sigh escaped her and she sagged in his arms.

"I didn't invite you out here to give you fits, Star Bright. You just scared the hell out of Queenie, and she's a sick woman."

"I'm sorry, I don't mean to scare her," Star said in a shaky, small voice. "But she's the one. She left us at the orphanage. I know it's her. She drove a big old car and made us lie down on the floor in the back and told us to be quiet." Her eyes darted wildly. "Please, Miss Ike, make her talk to me. She knows what happened to my parents. Please!"

Isadora leaned her shoulder against the glass wall and pressed her glass to her cheek. "Queenie's ill with heart problems and blood sugar and migraines. She can barely drive into town, much less go gallivanting around Texas. Sorry, hon, you're mistaken."

Austin caught a whisper of uncertainty in Isadora's voice and saw it in her eyes. Despite the woman's calm, she was badly shaken. He relaxed his hold on Star. To his relief, she made no sudden moves toward the door where Queenie had disappeared. He placed his hands on her shoulders. She trembled.

Lifting her chin, Star drew in several deep breaths. Shrugging away from him, she said in an aside, "I'm calm, okay?" She turned her attention to Isadora. "I'm not mistaken, Miss Ike. I know what I know. I've heard that voice in my head for over twenty-five years. It's Queenie. You have to believe me. Please make her talk to me. I'm begging you.''

A man slammed through the French doors from the living room. At least six feet four inches tall, he was built like a bear. An enraged bear. Crimson faced, he stomped down the hallway. Gingery hair, liberally streaked with white, fluttered with every step. His pale eyes blazed and muscles strained his shirtsleeves. Cords stood out on his thick neck and veins rose on his temples.

"What the hell is going on here?" he roared.

Star stumbled backward, lodging her body against Austin's chest. She gasped. Austin stepped around her, putting her protectively behind him. His nostrils flared and his skin prickled.

Isadora shifted her stance. Her mouth twisted in a sneer. "Thought you were up at the north camp, Stu."

"I was out in the garage. Teresa said Queenie's having a spell." His wild-eyed gaze searched the long hallway before landing on Star and Austin. "What the hell are you doing here?''

"These are my guests." Isadora grinned tightly. She appeared to relish her brother's fury.

A spate of obscenities spewed from his mouth. *"You!"* he growled, shaking a ham-size fist at Star and Austin. "I know who you are. I told you to stay the hell off my property—"

"It's my property, too," Isadora said. "If you can't be civil, then leave.''

"Civil?" Spinning on his boot heel, he yelled, "I'll show you civil!" He stomped away.

"Uh-oh," Isadora said, and put her glass on a small table. "He's either calling the law or fetching his shotgun. Guess we ought to cut this little party short. Sorry, I thought he was gone.''

Austin heard the lie. Isadora was up to something. It might be family hostilities and business as usual, or something darker. Perhaps Isadora suspected her brother and sister-in-law had something to do with Rowena's murder.

Star violently shook her head. "I have to talk to Queenie. Please."

"I can probably keep him from shooting you, but he'll still be a royal pain. You have to go." She cocked her head, listening. Satisfaction gleamed in her eyes. "You better go now. I'll come visit you later."

BACK AT THE HOTEL, Star sat on the middle of the bed, with her face in her hands. "I'm sorry," she said for the umpteenth time. "I lost my head. I'm sorry."

Standing at the window, Austin said, "There's nothing to be sorry about."

"I blew it!" she cried. "Chasing an old lady. Screaming like an idiot, acting like a fool...but it's her. What am I going to do?"

"I believe you." He turned from the window. Garbed as he was in a black fisherman's sweater, with the rosy-hued lamplight turning the edges of his hair to molten gold, he looked otherworldly and very wise.

His calm presence soothed her, the psychic equivalent of smoothing ruffled fur.

"Reckon I'm losing my mind." She sighed and clutched two fistfuls of hair. "She knows what happened. How do I make her talk?"

"You know, too, punkin."

She lifted her head. "What do you mean?"

He approached the bed, silent, his step as determined as his expression. He placed both hands on the bed, bringing them eye to eye. "You *know* what happened. The time is ripe for you to bring it out of the darkness."

A convulsive shudder rocked her from head to toe. "What do you mean?"

"You'll do anything to find your parents."

Chilled by the dark depths of his eyes, she swallowed hard. "You know I'll do anything. I swear, anything at all."

"Take off your britches."

A protest rose in her throat, but she squashed it. He was dead serious, and this had nothing to do with playing cute.

She removed her shoes, gun belt and jeans. Austin closed the draperies and turned off all the lights except for the single bulb in the bathroom. He left the bathroom door open a few inches. He took off his boots and stripped down to his briefs, then double-checked that the door was locked before he sat on the bed, propped by the pillows.

He shoved down the comforter and patted the bed. "Sit between my legs."

Stiff with apprehension, she did so. He invited her to flip the comforter over their legs for warmth. She leaned her back against his chest. He took her hands into his and rested them at her sides.

"I want you to relax, Star. Sit, listen to the darkness, get comfortable. We don't have time to deal with your control issues, so we'll sidestep them for now."

"Control issues? What's that mean?"

He rested his cheek against her hair. "You were abandoned at a young age. Foster homes didn't give you the nurturing you needed. You've assumed a protective shell. By remaining in control at all times, you can't be hurt. You're controlling the memories, too, keeping them locked away so they can't hurt you. It's time to unlock the door."

"You're saying I'm crazy?"

"The opposite." His warm breath caressed her ear. "You're keeping yourself from going crazy."

"I'm not a control freak. I don't go around ordering everybody to do things my way."

"That isn't what I mean," he soothed. "Suffice to say, from one rotten-childhood survivor to another, I happen to think you are one of a hell of woman." He massaged her palms with his thumbs.

The unexpected compliment arrowed straight to her heart.

"There were many roads you could have taken. Alcohol, drugs, promiscuity, petty crime. You could have married abusive men to replay childhood scenarios and try to fix them. You could have been a victim. Instead, you got tough."

He meant it, just as he meant most things he said. The knots in her belly loosened.

"I need you to trust me enough to stop being tough. Open your heart and your mind. I need you to listen and believe. I'll never hurt you. Do you trust me enough to believe it?"

She wanted to so much, she ached. "Yes."

"That's my girl. Comfortable?"

Surprisingly enough, she was. "Uh-huh."

"What I want you to do is match my breathing. Concentrate, feel the rhythm. Don't worry if it feels unnatural at first. Just concentrate."

She closed her eyes. Awareness made her tingle. His chest was hard against her back, like the firm feel of a good mattress. The comforter was weighty and warm. Austin breathed deeply, slowly. His chest rose with each inhale and relaxed with each exhalation. She waited a beat for his next inhale. She rose with him, drawing air deep into her lungs.

It seemed to take forever before she found his rhythm. Her lungs protested against her conscious efforts. Muscles in her chest refused to relax. By sheer force of will, she made herself breathe in time with him. In, out, draw the air deeply so she could actually feel her diaphragm working, feel her ribs expanding and contracting. Feeling so much inside her own skin, actually examining her inner workings, grew interesting.

"You're doing good," Austin said, barely above a whisper. "How do you feel?"

"Fine." The darkness and shared warmth under the comforter were making her sleepy.

"Good, good. Are your eyes open or closed?"

"Closed." Ghostly flickers and wavy lines danced inside her eyelids.

"Let's take a little walk inside our heads. Picture a meadow in the summertime. The temperature is seventy-five degrees and the sun is high and bright. The sun beats down hot on your skin, but when you pass through the shade it almost feels cold. It's a nice feeling, hot, cold, bright, shady, the grass cool and springy under your feet...."

His voice was silky, seeming to come from everywhere and nowhere. She actually saw the meadow. The grass was green as emeralds and star-dotted with tiny flowers in white, pink and yellow. Birds twittered and chirped. A light breeze made the leaves rattle.

"It's a safe place, Star. Butterflies have shimmery wings, and the birds come so close you can sprinkle their tails with salt. It's the safest place in the world. You can sleep on the grass if you'd like. Bathe in the stream. Eat berries until your lips and tongue turn purple. Safe and cozy..."

Under his spell, she floated, enjoying the scenery in her head.

"It's safe to remember here, Star. Safe to examine your subconscious. Your subconscious is a book holding your memories. Look at the book. Rub the pages between your fingers. If you get tired or upset, you can close the book. It's yours, it'll always be there, whenever you're ready to open it and take a look at the past."

She saw it. A heavy tome, open across her knees. Sunlight reflected off the ivory pages. The print was sturdy and black.

"Are you ready to look?"

"Yes."

"Then let's go to the page when you last saw your parents."

She turned a page in her mind. "It's the Grand Lady," she said. "Oh, she's beautiful, wearing a crown, and her dress is as long as forever."

"What is the Grand Lady doing?"

"Just looking at me. I'm doing something I'm not supposed to be doing. It's a cave, I think." She frowned, trying to pull the images together so they made sense. "No, not a cave, a box."

"Describe it."

"Um, it's got smooth sides." Her fingers moved sluggishly as she tried to recall the texture of the walls. "Wood...it's wood, all polished and smelling like lemons."

"What aren't you supposed to be doing?"

"The cave is off-limits. It's the boss's and off limits, no children allowed. If I get caught, I'll have to sit in the corner. Mary never has to sit in the corner. Mary is always good. She always does whatever she's told and she never sasses. The corner is white and it's boring, there's nothing to see."

"But you went to the off-limits place, anyway."

"Uh-huh."

"What are you doing?"

"Reading a story about the Grand Lady. I like stories about her. She's the queen of the whole world and she's magic." Her throat suddenly constricted. "It's the giant," she whispered. "I can hear his boots. Clomp, clomp, clomp. He'll catch me and I'll have to sit in the corner again."

"Star? It's a safe place, punkin. A beautiful meadow where nothing can hurt you. If you're scared, close the book."

"I don't want to. I want to keep going."

"Can you see the giant, then? What is he doing?"

"He's mad. There's a lady and she's wearing fancy shoes. They're red and shiny and they've got little gold taps on the toes and heels. She's mad, too."

"Can they see you?"

"Uh-uh." She began to rock. Austin folded his arms over her breast. His fingers spread, covering her biceps, keeping her safe. "I can see them. She's saying, it's true, it's true, I got the proof right here." White light flared in her brain and she jumped. She smelled gunpowder.

"What is it? What do you see? Star? What's on the page?"

"She fell down." She rocked harder; Austin rocked with her. "She's on the floor and she's looking at me. Her eyes are wide open and she's looking at me. There's—oh, god, there's blood on her face and it's running like rivers."

"She can see you? Does she talk to you?"

"Uh-uh, uh-uh. The giant, the giant..."

"What about the giant? What is he doing?"

"Making them burn. In the fireplace under the Grand Lady. All the proof is burning up. The Grand Lady, she's watching it burn."

"Oh, yes, punkin, you're doing great. Nothing to be scared of. Just turn the page. Can you see what's there?"

She turned the page in her mind. There, as clearly as a movie show, she watched the giant scoop up the lady. Long black hair drooped over the giant's arm. Drops of blood splattered on the rug, mixing with the blues, greens and reds of the flowered pattern. Boots clopped away, thudding muffled on the rug and sharp on the wood. A door opened and rain-dampened air blew inside, making her shiver. Gunpowder stink hung in the air, mixing with the smell of burning wood. She saw her child's hand pick up a piece of paper. It was blue and it smelled like flowers. The lady had called it proof.

"Keep talking, go on," Austin urged.

She told him about leaving the cave and running, calling for Mama. She was scared, so scared, and her heart felt like it was trying to fly away and her mouth tasted bad. Mama, she kept screaming, the giant hurt the lady. She found

Mama in Miz Hagan's room. It was dark and stank of medicine, and Mama told her to be quiet and not yell, but she kept yelling, anyway, and made her come, but the giant was gone and so was the lady. Then Mama was on her knees and feeling the rug. She held up her fingers and they were glistening red.

She shivered violently and opened her eyes. The meadow was gone, the book was gone, all she saw was darkness cut by a thin shaft of light through the bathroom doorway.

"Star?"

She twisted in his arms until she could see his face. She blinked and blinked and finally focused on the gleam in his eyes.

He stroked her back and hair. It wasn't until he touched her cheek that she realized she was weeping. Tears streamed in silent rivers. Tears of grief and loss and final acceptance.

"They're dead," she whispered, and clutched his shoulder. "Daddy and Mama are dead. The giant killed them."

Holding her tightly, he murmured, "Oh, baby, I'm so sorry." He pressed hot, tender kisses to her wet cheeks and burning eyelids. "I'm so sorry."

"Mama made me stay with Miz Hagan. Mary was crying." The memories swamped her, threatened to drown her with a clarity so sharp her head throbbed. "Miz Hagan was crying. My fault, it was all my fault for being where I wasn't supposed to be. I made Mama go see. I took her by the hand and made her look." Overcome by sobs, she buried her face against the thick curls on his chest.

Between her tears and Austin's soft voice, she relived the night of so long ago. She remembered Mary huddled on the chair, crying steadily, and Queenie Hagan telling them to be quiet and stay in the room. She ran to the window and looked out at the yard toward the cottage. She saw her parents outside, under the tall security light that illuminated the garden and path to the cottage. It had been raining, and puddles caught the yellow light.

"Do you know if your parents called the police?" Austin asked.

"I don't know," she sobbed. "I wanted to go to them, but Queenie wouldn't let me. She wouldn't let us out of the room. Mary kept crying and crying. I was mad, furious. I wanted my daddy."

"Then the giant came back?"

She nodded against his chest, now hot and damp from her tears. "Queenie kept pulling me away from the window. I wanted to see. I wanted out of there, but there was a lock on the door. I couldn't open it." She jerked suddenly and stared unseeing into the darkness.

"Shh, shh, Star, it's okay. You're safe here with me."

"Mary fell asleep. I kept waiting for my mother to come back. Queenie made me sit on a chair, but I kept getting up." She touched her cheek. "She knocked me upside the head. Then she left. I kicked the door and hit it with my hands. I woke up Mary and she started crying again. I ran to the window. There was a big old chair. I dragged it and pushed it and got it to the window. I stood on it and tried to open the latch. I couldn't do it. I kept hitting the glass and screaming to raise the dead."

"Shh, shh," he murmured. "Slow down, take a breath. Slow down."

She gulped in air; her chest hurt as if she'd run ten miles, top speed. "That's when I saw the giant again. He was dragging my daddy. I could see him going in and out of the shadows, walking backward, dragging daddy by the arms. I screamed and screamed and screamed." She gripped his shoulder so hard, her fingers cramped.

He placed his hand flat between her breasts. "Slow down. Breathe. Take a good, deep breath."

It took a long time for her to regain control. Finally, her throat loosened and air came easier. "Queenie came back. That's when she took us away. She made us lie down on the floorboards behind the seat. She was crying. Mary was crying. I kept screaming and yelling, but she wouldn't stop. She said it was all my fault. I was a bigmouthed brat and none of it would have happened if I hadn't acted bad.''

Tears gained the upper hand again, and she sobbed until there was nothing left inside.

She remembered.

FOR A LONG TIME Austin sat in the darkness, holding Star while she wept twenty-five years of grief and fear. Mingled admiration and sorrow filled him. In hindsight, he supposed when he'd first offered to help her, he'd hoped to find her parents alive and well. The victims of poor judgment or harsh circumstances, but willing to make amends with their daughters. It had been a hope he'd known better than to feel.

He understood what had happened now. Playing where she wasn't supposed to have been, Star had witnessed Rowena's murder. The killer had burned the Pookie/Snuggle Bear letters, then taken the body away to bury it. Star had run to her mother. Karen found the blood, but no sign of the body or the killer. So, naturally, she told her husband. They'd been unwilling to believe someone had died based on the words of a hysterical preschooler, so they did the most sensible thing: they waited for someone in charge to arrive and tell them what to do. That someone was the killer, who was probably covered with dirt and blood from burying Rowena. He thought he'd gotten away with it, but the Joneses informed him otherwise. So he killed them, too, and made them disappear. Then Queenie, either because she'd been ordered to do so, or because she had a flash of conscience and realized the twins were in mortal danger, took them away.

Star hiccuped softly and sniffed. He groped on the side table and found a box of tissues. He pulled a bunch free and gave them to her. She murmured her thanks in a raw, husky voice.

The way she'd survived spoke well of her great inner strength. Love for her warmed his blood. He kissed the top of her head.

"How are you doing?"

She lifted her head. "I'm okay." She sounded as if she meant it. "What do we do now?"

Therein lay the rub. Even if they could figure out who the giant was—two solid contenders were Stuart Hagan and Doyle Sloane—they didn't have the kind of evidence that would stand up in a court of law. The only way they could prove the murders had been committed would be to find the bodies. Since they hadn't surfaced in twenty-five years, they probably never would.

She idly stroked his shoulder and neck. "All these years, I thought I'd done something evil. I kept hearing Queenie tell me it was my fault, and I believed her."

This was the source of her self-doubts and fears of being the evil twin. Queenie might have saved Star's life, but she'd scarred her soul in the process. "It wasn't your fault. You were little more than a baby."

"I reckon in a way it was my fault. I was where I wasn't—"

"No!"

Startled, she jumped.

He caught her chin. "It is *not* your fault. Great evil was done, but not by you. Nothing you did drove the killer to do what he did."

"But I—"

"You did nothing. You saw something that frightened you and so you did what any child would do. You went to your mother. All blame, guilt and responsibility sits squarely upon the shoulders of the killer. Not you. Never, ever you."

She pushed upright. Her hand rested on his thigh. Light from the bathroom silvered the angles of her cheekbones and chin.

He eased damp hair off her hot face. "I mean it, Star, with all my heart. Say it. *It is not my fault.*"

"But I feel—"

"Say it, anyway. Say it often enough, and you'll believe it. Your head knows it's not your fault. Make your heart believe it, too."

The sea tang of her tears drifted to his nose. She whispered, "It's not my fault."

"Keep saying it, punkin. Say it as much as it takes."

She pushed off the bed. Head hanging, she entered the bathroom and closed the door.

Alone in the darkness, he hooked an arm behind his head and frowned. Anger remained within him, cold and awaiting direction. A grave injustice had been committed. Because he loved her, it was his duty to help her right the wrongs. Because he loved her, he'd never give up this quest.

The question was, how? He'd never been directly involved in a case of repressed memories. It was his understanding that the courts were inconsistent in choosing to believe victims who remembered as adults their childhood traumas. Prosecutors were often reluctant to accept such cases because they knew how unreliable memory could be.

They needed hard evidence.

The Pookie letter was evidence. He felt ninety percent positive a handwriting expert would agree Pookie was also the author of the so-called confession from Jerry Jones. Mark Waxman would testify Rowena had letters in her possession.

Except...without proof Jerry was dead, authorities could claim Jerry was Pookie. Waxman hadn't read the letters, and knew nothing about Pookie or Snuggle Bear. The letters were circumstantial at best; at worst, they made Jerry look guilty.

The obvious hit him. He bolted upright and laughed softly. He turned on the lights and brought out his computer. Within minutes, he was writing a memo to Sparky. If his hunch was right, it might not be enough to convict, but it might be enough to reopen the investigation.

Star came out of the bathroom. Her eyes were red rimmed and swollen, but she was calm. She slid onto the bed and draped an arm over his shoulders. She kissed his bare shoulder.

Desire tangled his fingers, and he typed a string of gibberish. As he backspaced to erase the mistakes, she walked her fingers over his hip and across his thigh. He wiped out an entire line of good words before he caught himself.

"You're too good for me, Austin Tack." Her voice was still rough from crying. Her hand grew bold. "What are you doing?"

"Seeing if Sparky is worth all the money I pay her." He resumed typing, though neither fast nor well.

Her expression was incredulous. She pulled away from him. "Paying her?"

Realizing his mistake, he repressed a groan.

"How much do you pay her?"

"Don't worry about it."

"We have a deal! No surprises." She huffed in exasperation. "No telling how much it'll cost to fix your car. This hotel room is costing a fortune. I'm not—"

"Shut up," he snapped, shocking them both. Irritated as much by his anger as by her harping about money, he saved what he'd typed so far and shifted on the bed so he faced her. "Let me say this as plainly as I can. Simple words. I do not want your money."

Eyeing him suspiciously, she fetched her little black logbook. "How much does Sparky cost?" She opened the book and held a pencil poised to write. "We have a deal, and it's not negotiable."

"Everything is negotiable."

"Why? Because we're sleeping together?"

Without thinking, he snatched the book out of her hand. He scanned her small writing. She'd logged every mile traveled and every hour he'd expended on her behalf. He ripped a page out of the book.

"First time I saw you—" He ripped another page.

Her mouth hung slack. Her eyes were huge.

"—My heart about exploded." Another page and another. He tore them to pieces. "I'd never met a woman like you and I knew it. My whole body felt it. Call it chemistry, call it fate. Call it a joke played by angels. Whatever it is, it's real. Right at the moment, I'm sick of pretending it doesn't exist." He tore out a handful of pages, ripping them in half. "I think about you when I'm awake. I dream about you when I sleep. Every time I touch you, my brain turns to mush. Making love to you is nirvana."

Out of pages, he grasped the little book in both hands and ripped it apart at the spine. He tossed the pieces in the air. "Maybe you're just dumber than dirt or maybe I'm the world's biggest jackass. But I love you, anyway. Whether you like it or not, I do not want your money. And quite frankly, punkin, you're not big enough to make me take it. Now, excuse me. I have work to do."

Man, oh, man, but it felt good to get that off his chest. Pounding the keys, he finished the memo to Sparky.

Chapter Thirteen

Austin's declaration of love stunned Star. She sat speechless while he finished working on the computer. When he left the room to make a phone call, she slowly gathered the shredded remains of her logbook.

He loved her?

He knew her secrets, her past and her moods. He'd lived practically in her pocket ever since they left Dallas. Still he claimed to love her.

If he'd quoted some long-dead philosopher or poet, or talked circles in his mystical way, she could discount his words or ignore them as theoretical spouting off. She stared at the bits and pieces of the book. But this... this outburst could have only come straight from his heart.

Austin returned. He crouched to put away his computer.

"That took a long time," she said cautiously. "Phone problems?"

"I called Kurt."

"Kurt Saxon? Why? Did you tell him where we are?"

"Because we need legal advice. And yes." His shoulders hitched in a silent laugh. "He says hey."

She dumped the torn paper in the waste can. If Dana thought Star's search for their parents was neurotic, she'd think trying to solve their murder was downright crazy. She'd worry and fret and demand Star do something sensible that didn't involve killers, guns or getting run off the road. "What did Kurt say?"

"They're back home. In Cancun, your sister fell asleep on the beach and, in his words, looks like a beet-juice-pickled egg. He says not to worry, he has lots of lotion and plenty of time to apply it."

She heard his deadpan teasing in a new way. She saw him in a new way, too, noticing how his hair started dark at the roots, but lightened to tawny gold wherever it had been touched by the sun. How the line of his cheek and jaw looked sculpted by a chisel. How his every movement spoke of quiet, efficient strength.

He loved her.

She hadn't the faintest idea how she was supposed to feel or respond.

"What else did he say?"

His cheeks expanded and he blew a heavy breath. "I'm starving. Let's go downstairs and I'll tell you over dinner."

"Are you fixing to tell me bad news?"

He pulled a face. "Depends. So now that you know what you know, how do you feel?"

Her experiences with love could be summed up in thirty seconds. She didn't know what to feel or how to feel it. He loved her, and somehow he'd wormed his way past the wary bramblebush surrounding her heart. Austin Tack represented loyalty, trust and security. She suddenly wanted those—him—so much, the craving set every nerve tingling. Heat seeped over her face like hot honey. She couldn't bear looking at him; couldn't bear him seeing the naked hunger in her eyes.

"Don't lock down on me, punkin," he said gently. "Remembering what happened to your parents is a major shock, but for your own good, you have to stay on top of it."

Oh. Now her cheeks flamed. She pulled up a knee and rested her face against it. If she survived this day with her sanity intact, she could survive anything.

"Talk to me."

"I don't know what I feel," she said with a sigh. "Kind of empty, like I've set down a sack of concrete and I can breathe again." She looked up. "I always hoped for a good explanation for why they dumped me." Another heartfelt sigh escaped. "I sort of expected this all along."

"I understand."

"I'm all mixed-up. Not knowing was fixing to drive me nuts. So part of me is glad I know. It isn't what I wanted, but I'm kind of glad, anyway. Does that make sense?"

He said it did.

It bemused her to note a hint of relief on his face. Or, perhaps, it was a mirror of the odd relief she felt herself. "Mostly I'm mad. Not hotheaded mad, but..." She searched for the right words.

"You want justice," he offered.

"That's it! One of those son of a guns murdered my parents. Queenie covered up for it. They have to pay." She turned her gaze to the table where their sidearms lay. They looked oddly appropriate on the turn-of-the-century table, against a backdrop of Old West-style flocked wallpaper. It was as if she and Austin were gunslingers, riding into town to wreak havoc on the bad guys.

"It's either Sloane or Hagan. We can't let them get away with it."

He tented his fingers and touched them to his chin. His dark eyes absorbed the light, turning as unreadable as a moonless night. "We can't go charging around the countryside, demanding confessions. Without hard evidence, you won't be able to convince the authorities to investigate. We need a plan."

"Do you have one?" she asked hopefully.

"A glimmer. Let's discuss it over dinner."

When they went downstairs, they found a party of tourists dining in the hotel restaurant. Austin asked the waiter for a corner table. Star caught herself constantly bumping into Austin, or brushing his hand with hers, or rubbing shoulders. Each touch made her body jump as if electrified. His woodsy-wild scent enveloped her, intoxicated and distracted her. How she managed to sit and spread a napkin over her lap without knocking over the table, she didn't know.

"Are you all right?" He glanced at the tourists. They were a young and rowdy bunch, apparently celebrating something. "Do you want to go somewhere else?"

"Only other place is the diner." The Gold Coin gossip mill was so efficient, probably word was well out about her chasing Queenie Hagan. She sipped water. "I'm not up to facing the bunch over there. So what did Kurt say?"

"He gave me a short course in repressed-memory syndrome."

"I don't have a syndrome!" she said hotly.

He patted her hand. "Don't get testy on me. You know Kurt always calls the shots as he sees them. And the reality is, the courts are highly skeptical about the reliability of adult witnesses who remember crimes from childhood."

The waiter appeared and they placed their orders. As soon as he left, Star said, "So I've got a syndrome and you're saying no one will believe me."

"I'm not saying that at all. But finding believers will be difficult. Finding believers willing to do something about it will be more difficult."

She turned her gaze toward the punched-tin ceiling. "So what does Kurt say we should do?"

"*Corpus delicti.* Body of the crime. In this case, we take it literally. We need bodies to prove a crime was committed."

Instead of grief, indignation arose. Her parents deserved better than anonymous graves. She'd make sure they got their proper resting places if she had to die trying. "So we get ourselves outfitted with picks and shovels and start digging?"

"I had in mind looking for corroborating evidence."

"What's that?"

"The Pookie letter, for example. By itself, it means nothing." He held up a hand to count off on his fingers. "But we can couple it with it being in your possession, and the handwriting matching the confession, and Mark Waxman testifying he saw letters in Rowena's possession. Then it's getting closer to evidence."

"Is it enough for a judge to order everyone to make handwriting samples?"

"I asked Kurt about that, too. He has a friend connected to the D.A.'s office in Denver. He'll get in touch with him and see what he has to say."

His caution annoyed her, but she understood what he was saying. Knowing what had happened was one thing; proving it might be a bear.

"We have Waxman's testimony about Rowena. That means little by itself. But a chance exists we can prove Sloane made those payments to her."

"Right."

"I didn't say a good chance." He grinned.

The waiter brought coffee and a basket of bread. The smell of hot bread caused Star's appetite to roar to life. She reached for the basket at the same time Austin did. Their hands collided. So did their eyes. All rational thought winked out of her brain, leaving only bemused wondering about how he'd gotten so lucky with his thick fringe of sooty eyelashes.

"We might be able to corroborate details you remember. The red shoes, for instance. If Rowena's body was found with the shoes and there aren't any published sources saying she was wearing them, it backs up your story." He split a chunk of bread in half and offered her a piece.

She accepted it. "Betty will help, you reckon?"

"The biggest help will be Queenie."

Star snorted in disgust. She'd blown her chances with the rancher's wife, but good. When was she going to learn to slow down and *think!* "She knows my parents were murdered and she knows who did it. That makes her an accomplice. She'll never talk to us."

"Ah, but she may have made a mistake."

Star wondered where he was finding room for optimism. No one who had worked at the orphanage had even seen Queenie. She'd dumped them on the doorstep without so much as a note.

"She talked to a policeman," he said. "Somewhere between here and Dallas, it's possible she got popped for speeding or reckless driving or something. That's what Sparky is working on. It's a long shot finding traffic records that old, but stranger things have happened."

She glanced around to make certain no one hovered close enough to overhear. "So if we can prove she was on the road, then we can make her tell us who the killer is? It has to be Hagan, doesn't it? She's protecting her husband."

"He's my favorite suspect, but Sloane is still in the running. It's not inconceivable that Rowena told him what she intended to do and he met her at the ranch. Our real problem is, memories fade and people forget. What Kurt says, and I agree, is we gather what hard evidence we can find and try to find a friend in authority to reactivate the investigation."

"The cops?" She laughed bitterly. "Like Crocker is going to do anything. He's about as competent as a bug in a fishbowl, and that doesn't cover him being scared to death of Hagan."

"He's not our only option. There's the sheriff's department, the state police and district attorneys. Kurt also suggests we find a psychiatrist for you."

She sat back hard on the chair. "A headshrinker?" she exclaimed. She hadn't realized she'd spoken so loudly until the party of tourists quieted and looked her way. She leaned closer to Austin and spoke through her teeth. "I am not crazy."

"Don't be so touchy. I'm not saying—"

"When I was a kid, I got dragged to every headshrinker, therapist and social worker in town. They called me incorrigible and a delinquent. Big deal, I was a runaway. But they called me crazy because I wanted my parents. I'm not going through that again."

He caught both her hands and pressed them to his chest. "We got dealt the same hand, remember? Stuck in situations we hated, no one willing to take our side, not able to do anything about it. At least, nothing constructive. But we're grown-ups now. What applied when we were kids doesn't apply now."

Subdued by his sensibility, she muttered, "I hate doctors. Especially head doctors."

"I know. But we need to document your memories. We need an expert willing to testify you're a plausible, reliable witness. Prosecuting attorneys are impressed by experts."

"If I have to..." she dragged out.

"I'll be with you every step of the way. You aren't alone in this, punkin. Trust me."

She wished there were some way to avoid seeing a psychiatrist. One of her deepest, darkest fears was of being labeled a hopeless nut and locked away.

"Kurt will go through his file of experts. He knows some people who have dealt with repressed memories."

A cheerful voice suddenly rang. "There you are!" Betty Brownley bustled into the restaurant. She waved greetings to the waiting staff as she pulled a chair from another table, and sat with Austin and Star. "I've been looking for you." She fluttered her eyelashes at Austin. "You're causing quite a stir in the female population, honey. At least ten women were asking me about you. What do I tell them? Available or not?"

He smiled, slow and smug. "Not."

Star's heart gave a little leap.

"Too bad. We could use some fresh blood around here. Anyway, you'll never guess what I found." Her entire face radiated pleasure. "It's one of my Baxter's old note-books." She produced a tattered, yellowed old reporter's book from inside her jacket and presented it to Austin with a flourish. "Interviews! I didn't realize he'd talked to all these people. Now, I haven't read his notes word for word, but who knows? Maybe there's something in here about where your parents might have—"

"They're dead." Star began buttering a chunk of bread.

Betty's mouth snapped shut. She used a knuckle to nudge her eyeglasses higher on her nose.

Star looked at Austin, hoping her big mouth wasn't getting them into more hot water. He cocked an eyebrow, but said nothing.

"Do you want a story for your paper, Ms. Brownley? Here's one. They were murdered and I witnessed it. I saw Rowena's murder, too." It surprised her, how calmly she was able to speak. Her trip through the meadow, reading the book of her past, had cleared her head and her emotions. Determination had replaced her fears and uncertainty.

"You witnessed it?" Betty whispered. She scooted her chair closer to the table and leaned forward. "Who did it?"

Betty's acceptance caught Star off guard. "That part I don't know. I was hiding under a piece of furniture or inside a cabinet. All I saw were legs."

"This was at Queen's Cross? Rowena was there?"

"Yes, ma'am."

The waiter brought their dinner: a steak for Star and broiled fish for Austin. The young man seemed delighted to have Betty eating in the restaurant, but she waved away his offer of a menu and asked for coffee.

Star poked her fork at the steak. "You've heard Mark Waxman claim Doyle Sloane killed his daughter."

"Who hasn't?" Betty scowled.

"Rowena had a packet of love letters. We think she was using them to blackmail Sloane. Her killer burned those letters. Except one. I picked it up. All these years I've been toting it around, thinking it was from my mother to my father."

"You actually saw the murder?"

"I also know who took me and Dana to Dallas. It was Queenie Hagan."

This time, Betty's mouth dropped open. "No," she finally breathed, and one side of her mouth pulled into an incredulous smile. "Queenie's been on her deathbed for something like forty years. I can't recall the last time she left her house."

"She sure left it the night my parents were killed. As soon as I heard her voice, I knew it was her. And she knows I know. Seeing me scared the britches off her."

The newspaper owner turned a shrewd gaze on Austin. "What about you, honey? What do you make of this?"

"All we lack is hard evidence."

"Incredible. What makes you think it's Doyle Sloane?"

"He's got a motive," Austin said. "Waxman claims Rowena loved Sloane and she was furious about his engagement to Michelle. He believes she was blackmailing him. She could have gone to Queen's Cross to confront Michelle or Stuart."

Betty shook her head. "Doyle Sloane's a blowhard, not a killer. He's all bark. No bite to him."

"Wouldn't you agree," Austin said, "he's ambitious and greedy?"

"Well, sure. But so are lots of people. That doesn't make them killers." She shook an ink-stained finger at him. "Public sentiment aside, I like Doyle. I know his faults, but his heart is usually in the right place. He's done a lot for this town. Like he says, talk loud enough and good enough, and action follows."

"Marrying Michelle was a major coup for him," Austin countered. "Would he have allowed the town bad girl to interfere?"

"You make it sound so cut-and-dried, honey. I've known him almost thirty years. It was my Baxter who introduced him to the Hagans in the first place."

"Stuart Hagan is a suspect, too," Austin said.

This time, Betty wasn't so quick to protest. She helped herself to the breadbasket and butter bowl.

"I got the impression there's a lot of tension out at the Queen's Cross. Stuart doesn't appear to enjoy sharing control with Isadora."

"You've got that part right, honey." Betty chewed contemplatively, her gaze distant. "I'm surprised they haven't used a chain saw to cut the house in half."

"Why halves? Doesn't Michelle own an interest in the ranch?"

"Not anymore. I don't know the details, but Stuart and Isadora bought her out years ago." She darted a glance at the tourists and lowered her voice. "I always thought Michelle loved the Cross more than any of them. For Isadora, it's just a place to board her horses, and it's a cash cow for Stuart, but Michelle loved it. When we were schoolgirls, she used to keep art journals. She'd draw plants and animals and mountains. For a couple years, she won prizes at the county fair with her drawings. She loves the land and the mountains."

"Probably gave it up so Sloane can't get his mitts on it," Star muttered.

Betty didn't argue.

"One sister down, only one to go," Austin mused. "Rowena could have screwed up Stuart's plans to get Michelle out of the way. That's a motive."

"And risk losing the Cross?" Betty denied it with a firm head shake. "Can't see it."

"Hagan doesn't strike me as the type to worry about petty little details like getting caught."

"Queenie knows who did it." Star reached under the table and touched Austin's knee. His calmly reasonable presence made this conversation bearable. "She's known all along. I don't know if she's keeping quiet because she's scared, or because it's family. You have to help us, Ms. Brownley."

Betty rubbed her temples with her fingertips. "I hope you aren't thinking I'm going to print any of this, are you?"

"Why not?"

Betty turned to Austin, who didn't appear astonished by the woman's denial. "This is all conjecture, rumor. My paper doesn't operate like that. You don't even have proof Jerry and Karen are dead."

"But I remember!"

"You were only four, Star. How reliable can memories be when you were four years old?"

STAR FINALLY GAVE UP on sleep. Too much wore her mind. They'd spent a long time with Betty in the restaurant. The newspaper owner was a believer, but, like Austin had said, not enough of a believer to do anything.

Star sat up on the bed and wrapped her arms around her knees. The room was cold despite the clanking of an old furnace. Through a parting in the draperies she could see the night was clear and moon-bright.

Along with the enormity of her quest, the truth was sinking in: it wasn't her fault. She wasn't the bad seed or evil. She hadn't driven her parents away or caused the tragedy. She'd lived with her secret guilt so long, however, she was almost reluctant to let it go. She was like a wild animal in a cage, suspiciously eyeing the open door, not quite daring to believe freedom lay only a step away.

"Star? What's wrong?"

Austin's voice startled her; she'd thought he was sound asleep. "Nothing's wrong. I'm just thinking."

He turned on the bedside lamp. She winced away from the sudden glare. He asked, "Want to talk about it?"

"I'm tired of talking."

"Ah, action." He draped an arm over his eyes.

She studied the interesting way his triceps curved in a sinuous line and the juncture of his arm with its diamond of soft, black hair. Armpits weren't supposed to be sexy, but his were. Her fingers itched with the urge to run her nails along his skin and see if he was ticklish. They'd made love earlier, sweet, fulfilling and silent; the scent of desire clung to her still.

"I don't want to wait for some cop to believe my story. Let's kidnap Queenie and make her talk."

Austin laughed. He peeked under his arm. "That's a joke, right?"

It wasn't, but she shrugged, anyway. Queenie would crack. They could tape-record her confession....

"Star."

"What?"

"You need to sleep. We have a lot to do tomorrow."

She didn't want sleep. She wanted to catch a killer. Austin's cool, clear head suddenly annoyed her. It was easy for him to be reasonable, detached and logical. His parents weren't buried like so much refuse in the Rocky Mountains, their good names tainted by murder.

He made a clicking noise with his tongue. He sounded suspiciously mother-hennish, and her annoyance deepened. It wasn't fair to have come so far, to finally know what had happened, and then not be able to do anything because of stupid technicalities. Hard evidence, corroboration— horse hockey! The way she saw it, she had every right to round up the bunch of them—Stuart, Sloane, Queenie and even Michelle—and hold them at gunpoint until one of them cracked.

Austin patted the pillow behind her. "Sleep, punkin."

She eyed Baxter Brownley's notebook lying atop Austin's suitcase. She could take it into the bathroom and read in there.

He sat up. "How about if I rub your back? I guarantee, five minutes of my special massage and you'll sleep like a baby."

Remembered pleasure rippled through her. Heat simmered in her midsection. If he touched her, sleep would be completely impossible.

He smiled crookedly. "Those big blue eyes of yours don't hide much."

She buried her face against her knees. He teased his fingers along her back. Air whooshed from her lungs and caught in her throat. Her nerves seemed to sing in hunger.

"If you don't want a back massage," he purred, "how about something else?" He kissed the nape of her neck.

She melted, losing all feeling in her arms and legs, except for shivering weakness in her thighs. She licked her dry lips. "Uh," she began, then had to clear her throat. "What you said. About you and . . . me . . ."

"About how I love you?" He kissed her again, tickling and tantalizing sensitive skin. "I do love you, Star, and if I may be so bold, I think you love me, too."

She loosened her grip on her knees and turned her head enough to catch his scent. "Is that so? What makes you so sure? Maybe it's just lust or something."

"If it was lust, you wouldn't keep fighting me or yourself. Stop playing the tough girl." He rested his chin on her shoulder. "Admit that you're crazy about me."

A smile fought for freedom. She chewed her lower lip to stop it. "I admit nothing. I don't know how I feel."

"How do you feel about this?" He cupped a breast and flicked her taut nipple with his thumb.

Thunderbolts of desire exploded. Her eyes glazed.

"Or this?" he purred as he stroked both hands down her sides, over her ribs, following the indent of her waist. He grasped her just above her hipbones, squeezing the tenderly erotic sites with his strong fingers.

With a groan, she fell back against him. "Austin Tack, you don't fight fair."

"I didn't know we were fighting." He stroked her thighs, his fingers leaving trails of fire.

This was nuts. When he held her, kissed her, made love to her, nothing else mattered. In his arms, the past lost meaning. The only reality was the feel of him, the sound of his heart and the sweet smell of his skin. Her quandary revealed itself with sudden, painful clarity: until she obtained justice for her parents, she couldn't commit her heart to Austin; and unless he committed himself to her, she couldn't believe he loved her. But she couldn't demand his commitment unless she were free to love him. She didn't want a purely physical relationship with him, yet that was all she had to offer.

She caught his hands. "Stop it."

"What's the matter?" Hurt colored his husky voice.

His pain sliced across her heart. She pushed his hands away and scooted out of his reach. She groped at the foot of the bed for her nightshirt. Finding it, she pulled it over her head.

"Star?"

"I told you before, there's no room in my life for anything except finding my parents."

The bed coverings rustled as he shifted position. "It's all or nothing with you? Black or white."

"You don't understand." She stared fiercely at the door, resisting the urge to spin around and fall into his arms. "It could take months or years to find my parents and bring their killer to justice. I'm telling you right now, until I find them, you'll never be number one in my thoughts. You can't be. So you can't love me. It's not possible."

"Oh, but I can and I do."

"Until when? You get bored? I'm not going back to Texas until I find them. I can't have a life until I find them." Tears rose, tightening her throat and making her chest hurt.

"What do you want from me, Star?"

She wished she knew.

"I'm not going to force you to choose between me and finding your parents' killer."

"You will," she said. "Not now, but eventually. That's what always happens. I have to choose. And the answer is always the same." She turned around and made herself look at him. "I don't know how I feel about you, I truly don't. Being around you jumbles me up inside. I can't think or reason. I do know I don't want to hurt you."

It was as if a mask dropped over his face, turning his expression to stone.

"Right now I feel pretty doggoned hopeless. I'm scared I'll turn out like Mr. Waxman. Mean and bitter and alone, knowing the truth and not able to do anything about it. I know just how he feels because I'm in the same predicament. I can't turn loose of the past." She wanted more than anything to know what he was thinking, but his eyes were unreadable. "You deserve better than me, Austin."

"I know what I deserve," he said, and rose from the bed. He grabbed a blanket and pillow.

"What are you doing?"

"I need some sleep. You can have the bed."

"You know I care about you."

He settled himself on a chair and snuggled into the blanket. He closed his eyes.

She was hurting him. His pain reached out to her, tearing her into pieces. It was killing her. "I can't tell you I love you if you're not number one to me. And you aren't. You can't be. That's not to hurt you, it's just a fact."

"If you say so," he said coolly. "Kill the light. I want some sleep."

Chapter Fourteen

Austin and Star stood on the front porch of the Sloane residence. Austin turned up his collar against a crisp wind. It was clouding up again. In the distance, the mountaintops were wreathed in fog. The temperature was dropping. Their breath was visible and the air was scented with ozone heaviness, announcing possible snow.

Star focused on the door, waiting for someone to answer the doorbell. She hadn't said much to him this morning. For once, he was grateful. He wasn't certain what to say to her.

For all its joys, the hellish thing about love was it left him wide open and vulnerable to pain. And she'd zapped him good last night. He still felt in his heart that she loved him as much as he loved her. *But,* no way did he intend to ever place her in the position to choose between him and finding her parents. That would most likely lead to a pain that no amount of inner strength, meditation or philosophy could help him ease.

Michelle Sloane answered the door. Her expression was at least ten degrees colder than the air.

Austin figured Michelle had a powerful motive to cover up a murder. Mousy and plain, she'd never had a boyfriend until Sloane blew into town and swept her off her feet. He doubted if she thought Sloane loved her more than he loved Stuart's money and influence. Even so, marriage was probably better than enduring the constant stress of Stuart and Isadora's power struggles.

"I'm sorry, Star," Michelle said. "I can't let you in. You made Doyle angry."

"Is he here?" Star asked.

"No, but . . . please, you have to go away."

Star stepped closer to the door. When Michelle started to close it, Star put out her hand. "My parents are dead, Miss Mike."

Michelle gasped and backed away from the door. Her mouth formed a soft O.

"They never left Queen's Cross on their own. They were murdered."

"Wh-what?"

"I was there." Star followed Michelle into the foyer. "I saw Rowena die. When her killer came back to the ranch after burying her, he killed my parents." She walked stiff legged, advancing slowly on the cowering woman. "Queenie Hagan took me and my sister to Dallas. She knows who the killer is. I think you do, too."

"No," Michelle whispered and turned helpless, frightened eyes on Austin.

He shoved down feelings of pity as he stepped inside and closed the door.

"Miss Mike, I'm not crazy. I don't want revenge. I want justice. Do you know where my parents are buried?"

Michelle clapped her hands over her ears and squeezed her eyelids shut. Moaning, she swayed from side to side.

Star raked both hands through her hair. "Baxter Brownley interviewed you about the day my parents disappeared. You told him you knew nothing about it because you were with a friend who was having a baby. You also told him Doyle drove you to Colorado Springs. But Doyle didn't mention it to Mr. Brownley. He said he was working on a construction job. How come he didn't say he'd gone to the city with you?"

"He did take me! I cannot abide driving at night. I would like you to leave, please. If Doyle returns, he'll be very upset to find you here."

"Mrs. Sloane, I understand this is uncomfortable for you," Austin said. "If there were any way to do this without involving you, we'd do so. Does your husband own a brown Blazer?"

"I don't see where that is any of your business," she said halfheartedly. She kneaded the bridge of her nose. The wattles under her chin quivered.

"Does he?"

"What does his Blazer have to do with anything? It's an old piece of junk, anyway. He only uses it to check properties when it snows. Besides, it's gone. It was stolen."

Star sucked in a light gasp. Austin pulled his chin.

"Doyle was quite angry. He's embarrassed to be seen driving it, but still...why are you looking at me like that?" She clutched handfuls of thin hair and wailed, "Go away! Just leave!"

"You didn't hear about the other night?" Star asked, her voice and posture incredulous. "We were about shoved off a mountain. Somebody tried to kill us!"

Austin laid a soothing hand on her shoulder. Her discomfort around people came not from being antisocial, but from hypersensitivity to emotion. The greater Michelle's agitation, the greater was Star's. She struggled for control, her expressive face agonized. Genuine pain shone in her eyes. She jerked away from him and turned her back on the miserable woman.

He focused his attention on Michelle. "Rowena went to Queen's Cross. We don't know exactly why she went there, but it had something to do with your husband. She was murdered and her killer took the body away."

"No!" Michelle wrung her hands. Tears slipped down her cheeks.

"Jerry and Karen confronted the killer when he returned. He killed them, too. Three people, Mrs. Sloane. Two children orphaned. An old man lost his only daughter. The killer hasn't repented. He's trying to shut Star up. He tried to kill her." He noticed the tiny gold cross hanging on a chain around her neck. Betty had told him Michelle never missed a Sunday service. "Great evil has been done. Don't make it worse, Mrs. Sloane. I know you're estranged from your family. Is it because of the murders?"

"I can't believe this."

Her lie was as plain as her tears. She did believe it. Perhaps she'd suspected it all along.

"Help us, Mrs. Sloane. Talk to us about what you know."

"I don't know anything." She faced a wall covered with photographs of her as a girl.

Star made a move forward, but Austin stopped her. He suspected Michelle was remembering how life before Doyle Sloane used to be—how she used to be.

After a long moment, she lifted her eyeglasses and dashed away tears. Each breath made her shudder. "Doyle will be furious."

She led them to her husband's office. Posting herself by a window, she watched outside. Austin guessed she was keeping an eye out for her husband. He wondered who frightened her more, them or Doyle?

"Star, tell her about the place where you were that night."

Pacing the overdone office, she described the wooden cave in the room with the Grand Lady, big fireplace and multicolored carpeting.

"Stuart's office," Michelle said. Though it was early in the morning, she poured a stiff drink, straight bourbon. "You weren't allowed in there. No one is, actually." She sipped and grimaced. Her eyes filled with tears again. "The Grand Lady is Queenie's portrait. It's a life-size oil, hanging over the mantel. She was beautiful once upon a time.

You adored that portrait, Star Bright, and couldn't resist it." A faint smile trembled on her lips. "Stuart would be just outraged whenever he found your coloring books and toys under his desk."

Star stopped pacing. "I remember. I used to make up stories about the Grand Lady. How she was a princess and had adventures."

"I loved you and Mary, but I always liked you best. You were so ornery, always getting into mischief. Fearless. I suspected you rather enjoyed Stuart's rages."

"You didn't?" Austin asked.

Hot color spotted her cheeks. "Stuart frightens me. Even as a boy, he was ferocious. Now Isadora, she's different. She enjoys baiting him. I used to think a good fight with Stuart was part of her daily vitamin requirement." She smiled sheepishly. "I was glad to get away from them. We're— we're estranged. Doyle sees them constantly, but I rarely do."

"Do you know where Stuart was the night the Joneses disappeared?"

"Stuart isn't a murderer."

"Where was he?"

The woman closed her eyes. Austin knew she was in her mid-forties, but her weary expression, rounded shoulders and washed-out skin made her look seventy.

"I think he was in Denver, attending a stock sale. He was furious when he found out Queenie had been left alone. Afterward, she was so ill, she had to be hospitalized." She gazed nervously out the window. "I think Queenie is the only person he's ever loved. She's never been much of a wife. She's never been much of anything. But he never yells at her, never loses his temper. I honestly believe he'd lay down his life for her."

Or vice versa, Austin thought. "Do you know where he stayed in Denver? A hotel? Friends—"

"He's owned an apartment there for years and years. He spends a lot of time in the city, at least one weekend a month."

He tried coaxing details about her brother from her, but she had none. Time and disinterest had washed details from her memory. "What about Doyle? Where was he?"

She drank from the whiskey glass. She gagged and sputtered, but choked it down. She pressed the back of one hand to her mouth. "He did drive me to Elizabeth's home."

"Did he stay with you?"

She shook her head. "He couldn't. He was building the spa for Stuart at the time. Doyle is quite talented. He can build anything." Her words had a desperate ring, as if she needed to convince herself. "When Jerry and Karen disappeared, he was working on the spa for Stuart. It's a masterpiece, constructed around a natural hot spring. I still think it's the best thing he's ever done."

"Do you know if your husband was acquainted with Rowena?"

"Everybody knew Rowena." She stared at the floor.

Austin noticed she wasn't denying her husband's possible guilt. "When was the Blazer stolen?"

She flinched guiltily. "I'm not sure, exactly. Doyle noticed it was gone yesterday. We don't keep it in the garage. It's in a separate shed."

"Did your husband report the theft?"

"Of course. It's old and ugly, but it is insured."

Interesting, Austin mused. Dave Crocker knew they'd been attacked by a person in a brown Blazer. Why hadn't he told them about Sloane? "Do you have a sample of your husband's handwriting, Mrs. Sloane?"

"You're asking ridiculous questions!" She plopped onto the desk chair.

"Are we?"

"You sound like that crazy old Mark Waxman! For years and years he's been telling anyone who'd listen that Doyle killed Rowena. I don't believe it. Not for a second." She stared at her hands. "Even though . . . Doyle had an affair with Rowena."

Star spun around. "You know about that?"

Michelle covered her eyes. "Everyone knows. But that was a long time ago, before we were married. Sleeping with Rowena was practically a rite of passage in Gold Coin. My goodness, if you think that's reason enough to have killed her, then you have quite a lengthy list of suspects to—"

Austin interrupted quietly. "She was killed at Queen's Cross in your brother's office."

"So you say!" Michelle exclaimed. "Why should I believe any of this? Why? Why?"

"Because it's true, Miss Mike!" Star yelled back. "It's true." She brought out her medicine bag and opened it. "Here's the killer." She spread the Pookie letter open on the desk and waited, glaring, until Michelle looked. "This person killed my parents. He buried them and I want to know where. Can we please have a sample of your husband's handwriting?"

Michelle stared at the faded blue paper. Color drained from her face, leaving her looking as if she'd seen a ghost.

"THAT WENT SWELL," Star muttered as she rubbed her temples with her fingertips.

Thinking the interview with Michelle had gone far better than expected, Austin nodded agreement. He steered the Jeep toward the police station.

"I was being sarcastic." She nudged his shoulder. "Why are you looking so smug?"

"We accomplished a lot."

She clamped her arms over her breast. Her eyes sparkled with skepticism. "Michelle getting crocked at nine o'clock in the morning and throwing a stapler at you rates right up there with curing cancer? *Sheesh!* I don't think giving her a nervous breakdown is much of an accomplishment."

That part he wasn't proud of. "Just because she says she doesn't believe us, doesn't mean she doesn't. She recognized the Pookie letter. I'm positive of it. We put a bug the size of Texas in her head. Trust me, she'll be doing some heavy-duty thinking. Also, we can cross her off our list of suspects."

"Uh-uh. If anything, she's gone up a notch—"

"Use your head."

"I am! You heard her. She hated Rowena. And I don't care if she knew about Sloane or not. He humiliated her. I say that's cause enough for killing."

"I agree. Except, try and picture Michelle hauling not one, but three corpses. Picture her cold-bloodedly murdering two people to cover her crime. And for the most interesting picture, imagine why Queenie would have been so afraid of Michelle that she'd drive across the country in order to save you."

She opened her mouth, but nothing emerged. A light frown creased her brow.

"She also has an alibi we can check fairly easily. I doubt if Michelle's friend will mix up the dates concerning her premature baby."

"So why did it go well?" she asked cautiously.

"She's denying what we said, but as Nietzsche said, belief in truth begins with doubting all that has hitherto been believed to be true."

"You mean, she's going to start wondering."

He pulled the Jeep up in front of the police station and shut off the engine. In the sudden silence, he nodded. "Exactly, my dear Jones. When she wonders hard enough, she'll keep adding the twos and coming up with five. She'll want to know why."

"She'll ask Sloane."

"I'm counting on it. If Sloane isn't the killer, I feel confident that he'll complain to Hagan."

"And then they'll all know that I know." She graced him with one of her rare, unselfconscious smiles. With her face pink from the cold and her short hair tousled, she was so beautiful it made him ache. "And the killer will have to make another move and we'll be ready for him."

Sudden fear rose in Austin. They played a dangerous game in the killer's backyard. A deadly game with players out for blood—Star's blood.

Her smile faded. "Why are you looking so odd?"

Why, indeed? It hit him that he was fast approaching forty, and perhaps it wasn't so much a lack of challenges that had him dissatisfied, but that he was tired of being alone. The seed of his discontent had been planted the day he met Star. The more he got to her know her, listened to her husky twang, smelled her fresh soap scent, watched the sun glisten on her pale hair, and discovered the richness of her exuberant though wounded soul, the greater his dissatisfaction grew. He could not imagine life without her—yet he was painting an immense bull's-eye on her back and using her as bait to catch a killer.

"We have another option," he said.

Her eyes acquired bloodthirsty light. "Kidnap Sloane and Hagan and choke a confession—"

"We pull out. Go home. I'll use my contacts to find investigators here in Colorado. We'll get you to a shrink to document your memories. We'll petition the state attorney to reopen the investigation."

Her upper lip lifted. "Are you plumb loco?" She held her thumb and forefinger a fraction of an inch apart. "We're this close to finding the killer. I'm not backing down now."

"This is dangerous."

She bristled like an offended cat. "So? I dare you to quote at me about how being all snug and safe is better than seeing justice done. Go ahead."

"I don't want you hurt." Or dead and lost to him forever.

"I'm not waiting another twenty-five years. I won't do it. We're here, we're close. If you don't have the guts for it, then I'll do it myself." She twisted on the seat and swung her legs out of the Jeep.

He caught her upper arm. "Damn it, Star, I love you. We've got a future together. That's worth more than getting you killed."

Her belligerence faded. Her gaze traveled the cloudy sky, the mountains, the rusted dashboard, and finally settled on the front door of the police station. "You just don't get it," she said quietly. "I don't have a future. As long as they're lost, all I have is now."

He tried to quell the hurt. "My way will work. It'll take more time, but it will work. And you'll be safe."

"Safe doesn't matter." She turned her troubled gaze on him. Her torment was clear and painful to behold. "All those years I thought it was my fault. I thought I'd done something wicked. Now I know different. Thanks to you, I'm even starting to believe it. But doggone it, if I quit, it will be evil. They're my mama and my daddy, and I owe them. I'm not scared about getting hurt. The only thing I care about is finding them. Nothing is going to stop me. Nothing."

He turned her loose. Slumping against the seat, he pulled off his sunglasses and rubbed his eyes.

"Dana's probably right. I'm obsessed. Except, it doesn't feel crazy to me." She rubbed his shoulder. "I don't mean to hurt you, Austin, please believe that. But this is like you quitting the marines to help your daddy. It was your responsibility and you shouldered it like a man."

Low blow, he thought. "It's not worth getting killed over."

"Then what is?"

Her retort struck dead center in his core of beliefs: principles, honor and justice were the highest expression of humanity and should never be compromised, no matter what the cost.

"Don't be thinking I don't care about you. I do." Her voice dropped to barely above a whisper. "I feel closer to you than I do to anybody. But how can I can even think about loving you when I have to do this? Please understand."

Damn it all to hell and back, but he did understand. He jerked the key out of the ignition. "Let's go lay it out for Crocker."

This time she stopped him. Smiling shyly, she caressed his leather jacket sleeve. She pressed a soft kiss on his cheek. "Don't be mad at me. Or hate me. Please. If I say the words, will it make it easier? I *need* you, Austin."

Everything inside went into a slow melt. Food and sex, she'd claimed, were all that drove a man. She'd neglected to mention the power of big blue eyes shining with tentative trust. For that, he'd spit in the devil's eye. He cupped her cold cheek in his hand. Her kiss was sweet and intoxicating.

Maybe they were both crazy, he considered. Ah, but it was a madness he could live with.

They went inside the police station.

They found the chief of police cleaning a deer rifle. The pieces were spread out atop newspapers on his desk. The sharp smell of gun oil filled the tiny station. Crocker smiled broadly at Star.

"You two just can't seem to make friends in this town," Crocker said with a laugh. "Stuart Hagan chewed my ear off for an hour last night. He wants me to arrest you for harassment and trespassing."

Austin cleared a stack of hunting magazines off a chair for Star. "Did he say why?" he asked.

"You're pestering him. He won't stand for it." He examined the bolt mechanism for a few seconds before setting it aside. "How are you today, Star?" He flashed a smug smile at Austin. "Are we still on for dinner?"

Dinner? A bolt of jealousy seared Austin's belly. First candy, now dinner?

"*Austin* and I are looking forward to it," Star said in an unusually sweet voice. Her smile was sticky-sweet, too, but didn't reach her eyes. "Reckon you'll come up with a good reason by then for not telling us about Doyle Sloane's Blazer."

Crocker stammered, his mouth opening and closing, but nothing coherent came out.

"His *brown* Blazer," she added. "It was pretty darned convenient for him to just happen to lose it the same day we got run off the road. When did he report it stolen? Before or after I plugged it full of bullet holes?"

Crocker shook a finger at her. His bright blue eyes blazed. "You can't come traipsing in here, accusing the mayor of hit-and-run!"

"Considering it was attempted murder, I reckon I have the right to make an accusation or two." She glanced up at Austin. "By now you ought to know why we're really here. Have you heard what happened to my parents?"

"You found them?" He picked up the magazine floor plate and began wiping it with an oily rag. His hands trembled.

Betty Brownley had clued them in on how Dave Crocker had become chief of police. Gold Coin used to have a regular police department with as many as five officers. As the population dwindled, the townsfolk had wanted to abolish the police department altogether, but Sloane had convinced the town that it wasn't a proper town without proper law enforcement. Crocker was a status symbol, hired by Sloane, who also had the power to fire him.

"Well, it looks like we got here ahead of the gossip for once," Star continued. "They're dead. Murdered. It happened the same night Rowena was murdered. The same person killed them all.''

Laughing halfheartedly, Crocker scrubbed at the floor plate so hard his knuckles whitened.

"It happened at the same place, too. Out at Queen's Cross ranch. Rowena was shot dead inside Stuart Hagan's office. Now, you tell me why he thinks I'm harassing him.''

The gauntlet was down. Austin wondered if Crocker was man enough to pick it up. He leaned his shoulder against the wall and watched.

To his credit, Crocker stopped laughing and polishing the gun part. "Say what?''

"I witnessed it," Star said. "I was in Stuart Hagan's office the night he, or Doyle Sloane, murdered Rowena. After he buried her and came back to the ranch, he killed my parents. I don't know what he did with the bodies. Buried them, too, I reckon.''

"That's a hell of an accusation to make.''

"But it's true. Do you remember the woman I told you about? The one who drove me and my sister to Dallas? It was Queenie Hagan. And that's why Stuart Hagan doesn't want me anywhere near his ranch. So what are you going to do about it?''

"My inclination is to call you crazy as a June bug." He fiddled with the cleaning supplies on his desk. Worry strained his mouth and eyes.

"We went over all the public sources we could find. We looked at all the pictures that showed up in the newspaper and some that didn't. There're a few things I know that didn't show up. I know Rowena was killed at the ranch. She went there with a packet of letters. Her killer burned them, except for one. I picked it up and I still have it. The handwriting on the letter matches the confession sent to the *Gabbler*." She leaned forward, earnest and angry. "Rowena was wearing red shoes. They were high heels with little gold taps on the toes and heels. Her hair was long and loose.

Not like in the pictures of her where it's all piled up high. When the killer picked her up off the floor, it fell over his arm. I remember that."

Crocker swung his head from side to side. His mouth hung slack, and his eyes narrowed to slits.

"It took me a long time to remember all this, and now that I do, I'm going to get justice one way or another. So what are you going to do about it?"

The chief kept shaking his head.

"If you feel it's outside your expertise, Chief," Austin said, "we're more than happy to take what we have to the state police and the district attorney."

"God Almighty, you're serious."

"Real serious," Star said. "And so's the killer. So you'd better ask Doyle Sloane about that missing Blazer."

The chief had been pushed hard enough for now, Austin determined. He took Star's elbow. "We'll be over at the hotel. When you're finished checking out what Star had to say, pop on over. Coffee will be my treat."

Outside the station, Star said, "That was a bust." She shuddered and grimaced. "Sitting there all slack faced with his eyeballs bugging. He looked like a kid finding a frog in his peanut butter."

"He's like Michelle. He doesn't want to hear it, but he won't be able to unhear it. Don't underestimate him. Even a lousy cop is still a cop at heart."

She made a noise of disgust. "He's pulling in his head like a turtle, waiting for us to blow away."

"If he ignores us, he'll find out we're serious about bringing in the big guns."

"If anyone will ever listen to us," she grumbled, and climbed into the Jeep. She braced for the shake-rattle-and-roll ride.

"Crocker will stew a while. Let's head on over to Waxman's place and find out if the car is ready." He started the engine. "We can ask him about what Rowena was wearing when she disappeared. I have a feeling he remembers. I also want to show him the Pookie letter. Maybe he'll recognize the handwriting, or some detail will mean something.''

He drove out of town. The Jeep offered no protection whatsoever against the freezing wind, and Star hunched deep in her jacket with her hands shoved into her pockets. He concentrated on the rutted dirt road.

She suddenly grabbed his arm and shouted, ''Stop the car!''

He didn't hesitate. At the side of the road, he shut off the engine. She kept clutching his arm so hard he felt her fingers through his heavy jacket. Her face wore that distant, dreamy, utterly sad expression that always alarmed him. It meant she remembered something. He followed her line of sight.

Here, the road curved snakelike through nests of boulders and cracked gullies. Few trees sprouted from the sparse topsoil. He spotted a wisp of steam and, nearby, a tiny forest green marker.

Like a sleepwalker, she climbed out of the Jeep and hiked toward the marker. Austin hurried to follow.

It was a hot spring, cupped by reddish boulders glittering with yellow-and-white soda crystals. The marker warned that the water was not potable. It stank of sulphur, like overcooked hard-boiled eggs. Steam curled off the surface.

''What is it, punkin?''

''The pit.'' She sighed heavily as she stared at the sluggishly bubbling water. ''I wasn't supposed to go near the pit. Little children drowned in the pit.'' She raked back her hair with anxious fingers. ''Then the men came and dug up the pit, made it bigger and blacker.'' Her voice dropped to a whisper. ''I know where they are. That's where he was dragging them. To the pit.''

The sheer, perfect sense of it struck Austin. It must have been hellish work for the killer to dig Rowena's grave in the hard, rocky soil. Then he finds himself with two more bodies and daybreak coming fast. So he notices the hot spring, with the surrounding foundation dug and ready for the workers to pour the concrete. Plus, he no longer has to worry about anyone seeing him do his dirty work. So he buries the bodies in the foundation work, then waits for the concrete pourers to forever entomb them.

Star tore away and stomped in aimless circles. She pounded at her skull with her fists. "What are we going to do? I know where they are! I saw him! Austin, what are we going to do?"

Bright ideas failed him. They sure couldn't show up at Queen's Cross with shovels in hand and expect anyone to let them dig up the spa. They needed a court order. With the scanty evidence they had, there wasn't much chance of getting one.

He caught her arm and pulled her up short. Seeing her on the verge of tears, he hugged her tightly. He stroked her back until she stopped shaking. "Forget the car. We have to call Kurt. This is the kind of problem he lives for."

"What can he do?"

"The only way we can get under that spa is with legal sanction. A court order. It's the *only* way. If we set foot on the ranch without the law backing us, Hagan will shoot us on sight. And Crocker will consider it justified."

They drove back to town. The first thing he noticed when he turned onto Main Street was Crocker's police vehicle parked in front of the hotel. Austin grinned tightly. Only the truth could have made the cop move that fast.

As soon as Austin parked, Crocker stepped out of his Cherokee. Short hairs prickled the nape of Austin's neck when he saw the icy, no-nonsense "cop" expression the chief wore. This was not good.

"Hey," he said mildly.

"Both of you, step away from the vehicle," Crocker called.

Faces appeared in windows lining the street, reminding Austin of a B-grade Western. Keeping his hands well away from his body, he followed Crocker's orders.

Watching them, Crocker sidled to the Jeep and began feeling around under the seats. He pulled aside a ratty, crusty old tarpaulin. Anger glittered in his eyes as he freed his sidearm.

"What in Sam Hill do you think you're doing?" Star demanded. She stood on tiptoe to peer inside the back of the Jeep.

"Shut up!" He pointed his .45 at Austin's head. "Both of you! Up against the car. Both hands on the metal. Feet spread. Move!"

Wondering what was under the tarp, but somehow not surprised at this turn of events, Austin did as ordered. He urged Star with his eyes to do the same. Crocker patted them down and took their weapons. He jerked Austin's right hand up between his shoulder blades. The slap of the cuff was sharp and icy against his wrist.

"You have the right to remain silent...."

Chapter Fifteen

Gold Coin's police station had one jail cell: an eight-by-eight-foot holding cage lacking so much as a window. Inside, Star paced like a tigress, while Austin lounged on the wooden plank shelf that served as a seat and a bed.

"He's not just stupid, he's brain damaged," she muttered, grabbing the cell bars. She glared at the steel door separating them from Crocker's office. "We didn't steal that jewelry. It's a setup!" She raised her voice to a shout. "Hey! Crocker! Get in here! I want my phone call!"

"Save your breath, punkin. He's not here."

"Not here? How do you know that?" She turned her attention to the door lock. It looked deceptively simple with a solid steel faceplate and a large round keyhole. Too bad she never wore bobby pins.

"I heard him leave." He cocked his ear toward the cement-block wall. "And now he's back."

Star listened carefully, but heard only her own angry breathing. Then a door slammed and boots tromped across a wooden floor. "What are you, Tack, half-cat? Hey! Crocker! Get your tail in here! I want—"

The police chief opened the steel door. His handsome face was carved from stone, and his eyes were ice. "Stop that shouting."

"What? I'm disturbing the other prisoners?" She tried to rattle the bars. Useless. "This is a setup, you idiot. That box of rocks was planted by the killer because he knows I know where he buried my parents. You have to let us out of here!"

Gazing somewhere a few inches above her head, he opened the cell door. He jerked his head. When Austin swung his feet to the floor, Crocker snapped, "Stay where you are. Just you, Star."

Crocker was up to something. Cotton, tinged with coppery fear, filled Star's mouth. She balked at the opening. Austin rose to his feet. His eyes turned black and narrow, emanating deadly cold. Crocker fiddled his fingers over his gun butt.

"You've got a visitor, Star. Come on."

"We were set up," she said, inching out of the cell. No telling what passed for justice in this nutty town. "You know it. You're letting them use you—"

"You used me!" He slammed the cell door shut. "Swishing into town with your wild stories, coming on to me." He shook his finger in her face.

It took all her self-restraint to keep from slapping his hand. Or his cheek. She wished she were her twin. Dana would have this half-baked idiot wrapped so tightly around her perfectly manicured finger, he wouldn't know which way was up. As it was, she could barely contain her temper. "Coming on to *you?* Ha! If you believe that, let me tell you about a bridge I have for sale."

"All this time you were nothing but a two-bit thief. A con artist. Robbing an old lady. A *sick* old lady who's never hurt anybody in her life. You ought to be ashamed of yourself."

Talking reason to an alligator would garner better results. She submitted to having her hands cuffed behind her. Austin caught the bars. His knuckles whitened.

Star gave him the bravest smile she could muster. "I'm not scared of him." Crocker led her out of the holding area, and the big steel door clanked shut behind them.

He took her to a small back room. Star barely noticed the steel shelving stacked to overflowing with books, papers and boxes, or the 1950s-era refrigerator humming noisily in the corner. Her gaze locked on Queenie Hagan.

The old lady, swathed inside a fox coat several sizes too large, sat erect on a metal folding chair. "Thank you, David," she said in a surprisingly firm voice. "I won't be but a moment with this young lady."

"If you have any problems, Miz Hagan, give a shout." He left them alone and closed the door.

There was nowhere to sit, nor was there a safe place to lean. So Star stood in the middle of the cramped room and glared down her nose at Queenie. "You did this," she said. "You planted that box of jewelry and called Crocker."

"You'll never be able to prove it. In fact, you'll never be able to prove anything. When it comes down to your word against a Hagan's, well, I fear you haven't a prayer. That, my child, is a fact of life." She coughed delicately into her fist. "I am not a well woman, Star. You're causing me immeasurable stress. I may very well end up in the hospital because of this."

Stunned by Queenie's dry honesty, Star backed up a wary step. "You're an accomplice to murder. We both know it. I *will* prove it."

"I'm afraid that is impossible. You see, the contents of my jewelry box have an insured value of well over $150,000. That, my dear child, makes you and the young man guilty of grand larceny. As far as anyone is concerned, you are a con artist who used the story of your missing parents as a ruse to gain access to our ranch. No one will ever believe anything you have to say."

Loathing made her stomach hurt. "I have proof."

"Do you?" Queenie shook her head. "I harbor no ill will toward you, Star. Truly I don't. But you're trying to destroy my family and I will not allow it. What's done is done. The past makes no difference."

Star struggled a moment against the handcuffs. Queenie stiffened and opened her mouth as if to call for help.

"I am willing to make a bargain with you," Queenie said. Her eyes were faded gray and pained, but determined.

Great fear gripped Star. This old woman's body might be weak, but frail flesh garbed a core of pure steel. Star began to realize who actually ruled Queen's Cross. "No deals."

"I will refrain from pressing charges on the condition you leave this town immediately. You will never return. Nor will you send any agents on your behalf. If I ever hear of you or anyone making inquiries about Rowena Waxman or your parents, I will go through with pressing charges. You and your young man will go to prison."

"I won't let you get away with murder!"

"Do you honestly believe anyone will ever listen to you? Good heavens, you were nothing but a baby. What do babies know? I saved your life once, Star. I am trying to do so again. But if you force me to choose between you and my family, then I am very sorry."

"You're evil," she ground through her teeth.

Queenie shook her head in denial. "Take it or leave it, Star." She was immovable as a mountain. Hopelessness such as she'd never felt before filled Star with such despair that her throat tightened and her eyes turned gritty. She kept hearing Austin: "What would you do to find your parents?" And her reply: "Anything."

If it were only her, she'd fight to the bitter end—prison or no prison. She'd willingly sacrifice her money, reputation, freedom, even her life—but this monster was threatening Austin. Austin, with his gentle hands and confident voice and unshakable belief in her.

She'd been lying to herself . . . lying to Austin.

It struck her with such mind-numbing force that there was nothing to think about, nothing to consider. The inescapable fact was, putting Austin Tack in a cage was the one thing she could never do.

DAVE CROCKER ESCORTED Star and Austin to Waxman's junkyard. Once there, he, with great reluctance, returned their weapons. "I don't know how you squared this with Miz Hagan," he said. "You conned her, but not me. Get your car, get the hell out of Gold Coin. If I see you again, your butts are mine."

Star checked the clip on her .32. He'd confiscated her ammunition. "You're not just a fool, Crocker, you're a damn fool. Those people are getting away with murder and you're helping them do it." She clutched her medicine bag. After releasing them, Crocker had returned it to her—minus the Pookie letter. He claimed he was keeping it for evidence; she reckoned it would get "lost" in the near future.

Austin holstered his revolver. He smiled at the police chief. "Don't forget Rowena's red shoes, man."

Crocker gunned his engine and tore down the graveled road as if the devil were nipping his heels.

Austin began lifting their luggage out of the ratty old Jeep. Wolf dogs watched silently from behind tall chain-link fencing. "Looks like it's time for plan B."

A few snowflakes swirled around his tawny hair. The clouds had dropped so low, the surrounding mountains were shrouded in a gray blanket. Trees whispered in the wind, sounding like malicious gossips not trying too hard to keep their voices down. Star couldn't wait to get out of Colorado. She wanted heat and humidity and flat Texas landscape. She wanted as far away from the arena of her defeat as she could get.

"First stop, Windham. The sheriff ought to be interested in what's going on—"

"No plan B, or C, or anything. It's over." Queenie's frail, thin-skinned, utterly cold face filled her inner vision. The old lady meant what she'd said and she had the power to back it up.

Austin snapped up his head. "It's not over."

"*Is*. No one will ever believe me. Who am I? Hmm? No education, no money, just trash from Texas. Who cares what I remember? We'll never get under that spa. It's over."

"Ah, punkin—"

"Don't!" She threw up her hands to fend him off. "Don't you get it? That crazy old woman means what she says. And she'll do it, too. She's got the money to do anything she wants. We can't fight her. The way it looks now, we are just a couple of con artists, come riding in here with a tall tale so we can get to Queen's Cross and the jewels. Nobody cares about Rowena or my parents. So they win. Let's go home."

"No."

His soft-spoken stubbornness rasped her wounded nerves. "Doggone it, Austin! You were ready to quit this morning."

"Not quit, change tactics. There's a big difference."

"The only difference I give a hoot about is that evil old witch putting you in prison!"

Mark Waxman strode toward them, his steel-toed boots shuffling gravel. A wolf dog followed lazily on his heels.

Shame filled Star. She'd let him down, too. Because of her and her big mouth, Waxman would never find the justice he sought for his daughter's death. Unable to bear his sad eyes, she had to turn away.

"Saw Crocker," Waxman said, and spit as if to rid his mouth of the police chief's name. "What did he want?"

Austin handed over the Jeep's keys and told him the story about the jewels.

The old man never once exhibited surprise. "Queenie, huh?" he murmured, looking down at the dog now flopped at his feet. "Funny how it's always the sickly, timid ones who bite the nastiest. So she's covering for Sloane."

"I think it's her husband rather than Sloane." Austin laid a hand on Star's shoulder. In a calm, almost detached manner, he recounted what Star had witnessed so many years ago, including her belief that the Joneses were buried under the hot-spring spa. He added, "I'm sorry, sir, but unless we can prove a crime was committed, our hands are tied. But we'll be back as soon as we figure out how to get under the spa. You can count on it."

"This calls for a drink." Waxman's face had gone gray. He slumped toward the trailer.

"Pitiful," Star murmured, choking back tears. "Let's get out of here." She grabbed up her duffel bag and slung it over her shoulder. "I can't take any more of this place."

"We haven't finished, Star."

"I'm the boss. I call the shots. We're through." She pressed her fist against her nose. "You did what you said you'd do. We found my parents. It's enough." Each word was like a sword through her heart. But what could she do? Imprisoning Austin was as good as killing him.

"Lay on, Macduff. And damn'd be him that first cries, 'Hold, enough!' "

She didn't need a translation for that one. "Queenie means what she says, doggone it! You'll go to prison. You'll lose your job and everything you worked for. I thought you were brave, not stupid, Tack." She grabbed his elbow and pulled. "Let's get your car and go."

As immovable as a granite boulder, he cocked his head. One side of his mouth twitched in a grin. "I'm the reason you mean to quit?"

She gave up trying to pull him. "I was wrong before. I made my choice, and it's you." She jammed her hands in her pockets and stared at her sneakers. This was love. Even a knothead like her could recognize it. She loved this man with all her heart, and harming him would destroy her world.

He touched her chin and lifted her face. "We've got options, punkin. Trust me on this."

"Can't risk it." Her eyes burned.

"Hey, I'm smarter than the average bear."

She laughed softly. "I know that one. You best remember, old Yogi got an awful lot of boulders dropped on his head. Let's just get out of here."

Waxman came out of the trailer. He was carrying a bottle of whiskey in one hand and a rifle in the other. He'd exchanged his baseball cap for a woolen hunter's cap with earflaps, and wore a bulky shearling coat. His eyes held a frighteningly cold expression, somewhat dead, mostly mad.

Star dropped her duffel. She edged closer to Austin.

Around the ever-present toothpick, he said, "Your folks are under the spa, you say, Miz Star? You sure about that?"

"Pretty sure," she replied weakly, staring at the rifle.

"So if I dig 'em up, it proves Stuart Hagan killed my girl." He focused his icy, bloodshot glare on Austin. "I heard you right, did I?"

"It's a start," Austin said cautiously. "What do you intend to do, sir?"

Waxman swigged whiskey. "Looks like they were right and I was wrong. It wasn't Doyle Sloane. It was Stuart Hagan. Fine, I'll apologize later. Right now, I've got a score to settle. Let's see him buy his way out of this one." He tromped across the driveway and through a wide gate.

"What in Sam Hill is he fixing to do?" She broke into a jog, but when she reached the gate, a gray-and-white wolf hybrid slipped out of the shadows. Its yellow eyes met hers with an unnervingly direct gaze. A silent snarl revealed rows of large, white, sharp teeth. Heart in her throat, she backed away from the gate.

Cupping both hands around his mouth, Austin shouted, "Mr. Waxman!" Only the wind answered.

There was nothing they could do except wait. It wasn't long before they heard the rusty, throaty, clattering roar of heavy machinery belching into life.

"Uh-oh," Austin said. "Hope that's not what I think it is."

Before Star could ask him what he feared, a bulldozer swung into view between the rows of junked cars. Its original yellow paint was mostly worn away, patchy with dirty rust. Huge tires churned gravel and mud into slush.

"Damn," Austin breathed.

Both hands on the big wheel, with the whiskey bottle sticking out of his coat pocket, Waxman steered the massive machine through the gate. Star and Austin ran out of the way as it grumbled onto the driveway. Their shouts for the man to stop went unheeded. He never even glanced their way. All they could do was watch as the bulldozer made slow, majestic, determined progress over a hill and out of sight.

"He's fixing to dig up the bodies," Star said. "Hagan will kill him."

"Yep." Austin ran for the trailer. Star ran after him. He bounded up the rickety metal steps. He ripped open the door, and froze.

Three snarling snouts thrust through the doorway. The wolf hybrids were white muzzled and cloudy eyed. They meant business. No intruders allowed inside. Austin's face paled. Star reached for her gun, then remembered she had no ammunition. The private eye backed slowly down the steps, feeling carefully for footing. As one, the animals withdrew. They never made a sound.

"Phone calls are out." Austin slid a hand over the back of his neck. He stared at the tall chain-link fencing surrounding the junkyards and outbuildings. "How many dogs did he say he had?"

"Eight, I believe." She sighed. "That puts five of them between us and your car." She kicked a rock, sending it skittering against the trailer skirt. She listened, but could no longer hear the bulldozer. She wondered how long it would take Waxman to reach Queen's Cross—how long before Stuart Hagan came out shooting. "Now what?"

He returned to their pile of belongings. He pulled a map of the area from his suitcase. He pinpointed their location.

It was approximately six miles to Gold Coin and around fifteen to seventeen to Queen's Cross. Considering her sore knees, the altitude and the hilly terrain, Star figured it would take at least an hour to run into town. "How long do you reckon it'll take him to reach the ranch?"

"If he sticks to the roads, about two hours, give or take." He trailed a route with his finger. "It looks like this valley is passable for a bulldozer. And here's a road. If he cuts across here, it won't take so long."

Her heart sank. "Hagan will kill him."

"Or he'll kill Hagan. We've got to stop him."

She eyed the flat, ugly sky. It was trying to snow, but not very hard. It would be dark soon. She couldn't recall seeing any homes between the junkyard and the town. "It's going to be a long, cold run." She looked around for a place to stash their belongings out of the weather.

"No time for exercise, punkin."

She looked between him and the expanse of junked cars, piled tires and towering mounds of machine parts that lay between them and the garage which contained his Ford. "I'm not hurting dogs. I just can't do it."

"I never harm an animal if I can avoid it."

She laughed helplessly. "I'm not letting you in there after your car, either! Those critters will eat you for dinner. If there was just one, it'd be different. But there are five of them."

He laid a heavy hand on her shoulder and looked her straight in the eye. "Tell me again how much you care about me."

She opened her mouth to order him to stop fooling around, but "I love you" slipped out. Her cheeks burned. She wanted to look away from his eyes, but they trapped her.

His smile, so warm and intimate it made her shiver, captured her heart and squeezed it. He touched her, forehead to forehead. His sweet breath tickled her nose. "Then trust me."

"How? We started this mess. We have to do something, but what? If we warn the Hagans, someone's going to shoot that old man. If we don't warn them, they're going to shoot him, anyway. Or they'll call Crocker and that yahoo will shoot him." She caught his neck and leaned into him. "This is all my fault. If I'd listened to you in the first—"

"It's not your fault." He hugged her, pressing his face against her hair. "No placing blame. We haven't got time."

He turned to the Jeep. Sliding onto the seat, he reached under the steering column.

"What are you doing? You gave Mr. Waxman the keys."

He jerked the wiring loose. "King of the joyriders, remember?" He fiddled with the wires for a moment.

To Star's utter amazement, the engine sputtered to life. "Teach me how to do that sometime?" she asked with a grin.

"Sure. Hop in."

"So what are we going to do?"

He shoved the transmission into gear. "I haven't the faintest idea. We'll just have to wing it."

"How IN SAM HILL can we miss a doggone bulldozer?" Star stood on the Jeep's seat and scanned the gray horizon for any sign of movement or exhaust. "Don't see hide nor hair of him."

Parked on a dirt road about a mile from Gold Coin, Austin studied the topographical map of the area. "He's lived here all his life. He knows the terrain a lot better than we can learn it from a map." He heard a vehicle at the same time Star spoke a soft warning. It approached from the direction of town.

Austin rubbed the butt of his revolver. Crocker had confiscated their ammunition. Austin had extra rounds, but they were in his car—effectively guarded by five nononsense watchdogs. Fast talk and a cool head, he reminded himself, had gotten him out of hot water before.

A white pickup topped a hill. Recognizing the driver, he said, "It's Isadora."

Star leapt out of the Jeep and ran into the road to flag the rancher down. Austin didn't like it. He didn't trust any of the Hagans. The entire family was twisted as far as he was concerned.

It was too late to stop Star. "Isadora!" she exclaimed. "You won't believe what's going on."

The woman shut off the truck engine and leaned her elbow out the window. "Like hell I wouldn't. I was hoping to catch you two. I overheard Stu and Queenie talking. Is it true? That kiddie-cop ran you out of town?"

"Queenie planted a box of jewelry in the Jeep and said we stole it." High color brightened her indignant face. "She admitted it. Came right out and said it plain as day."

"Now, why would she do a thing like that?"

"To protect your brother!" She caught Isadora's hand in both of hers. "I'm sorry, Miss Ike, so sorry, but I saw it. I remember. Your brother killed Rowena and then he killed my parents. I'm not lying and I'm not imagining it. It's true."

"Stuart..." Her eyes narrowed and her upper lip lifted in a snarl. "Sure wouldn't put it past him. Excuse me for being skeptical, honey, but how can you remember this?"

She turned anguished eyes to Austin. He joined her, wrapping an arm around her narrow waist. Her entire body trembled.

"I just do. At first I thought it was Sloane. He was having an affair with Rowena and she got mad because he was fixing to marry your sister. Only Queenie is involved up to her eyeballs, and why would she do that for Doyle Sloane? It has to be your brother.''

''Do you have any real proof?''

''Not yet,'' Austin answered. Isadora was believing them. He supposed the enmity she felt for her brother made it easy for her to see the truth.

''Queenie said if we come back, she'll throw us in prison. She means it. And she's going to get away with it unless we can find my parents' bodies. I know where they are.''

''You do?''

''Under the spa Doyle Sloane built. Remember? There was a big hole dug around the hot spring. It was the foundation. Stuart knew the concrete pourers were coming. He buried the bodies there. I saw it, Miss Ike. I watched from the window in Queenie's room and I saw it.'' She tucked her chin in; her downcast eyes filled with guilt. ''That's not the worst of it, either. We told Mark Waxman what happened.''

''That crazy old booze-hound?''

''He's on his way to Queen's Cross.'' She snuggled against Austin and sighed. ''With a bulldozer.''

Isadora thought about it a few seconds. ''To knock over the spa?''

''Yes'm. And Stuart will—''

''We'd best cut him off at the pass,'' she said firmly.

''Yes, ma'am,'' Austin said. ''Do you have a CB in your truck?'' He nodded at the long whip antenna. ''You better get the sheriff on the horn before this gets too ugly.''

''Gotcha.''

STAR HUGGED HER FREEZING shoulders, wishing she'd ridden in Isadora's truck instead of the Jeep. Her teeth chattered. The sun had gone down, taking with it all traces of warmth. The Jeep's headlights barely cut through the darkness.

They followed the lights of Isadora's pickup across rocky, rutted terrain. Isadora stopped, killing the engine, but leaving the lights on. Austin pulled the Jeep up behind her. Star looked around, but there was nothing to see except blackness.

"Where are we?" She searched for any signs of house lights or vehicles, but there was nothing to see except for rocks and spindly shrubs illuminated by headlights. "I'm all turned around. Which way is town?"

"Don't know." He slid out of the Jeep. "Is there a problem, Isadora?"

The rancher stepped around the truck. She held a rifle, muzzle up, pointed at them. "Not anymore. Now, be good kids and put your hands up."

Star's heart dropped into her belly. "My God, it was you."

"You always were a pest, Star Bright. Couldn't stay out of trouble to save your life. I guess some things never change. I didn't want it to come to this, but damn it, you're not giving me any choice. You've got Michelle in a state such as I've never seen. She's over at the house demanding to see everybody's handwriting and carrying on about that stupid rug in Stuart's office. Where did it go? Did it really catch fire? She's pestering Queenie and Stuart, asking too many questions."

"Does she suspect you?" Star demanded. "Does she know you're a stone-cold killer?"

"Not yet. But she's going to keep digging and digging in that nasty, mousy little way of hers. It's Stu I'm worried about. He'll make that damned Doyle talk."

Star gasped. "Sloane was in on it?"

"Nah. No guts. But he's smarter than he looks. As soon as he sees that letter you found, it's all over."

"You're Pookie," Austin said softly. "And Doyle is Snuggle Bear."

Isadora grimaced. "I was a fool back then. Trouble was, Doyle wanted the sister he could push around. That wasn't me. I can't believe I ever thought I loved that man. Worthless!"

"If you loved him, why did you kill Rowena? Did you want him marrying Michelle?"

"I get it," Austin said. "It's not Michelle you're worried about, it's Stuart." He chuckled. "If he'd found out you and Doyle were having an affair, not only would he have stopped the wedding, but he'd have retaliated against you. Perhaps driven you off the ranch the way he did Michelle."

"Shut up," she said in an oddly choked voice. "Star, move slow. There's a shovel in the back of the pickup. Fetch it."

"Yep, guess having your way is the only thing that counts, isn't it, Isadora?" Austin said. His face was a mask, his eyes lost in black shadows.

"Shut up, Mr. Private Eye. I'll take care of you, then Waxman, and nobody knows different."

"You're wrong. A lot of people know. Michelle, people we've talked to, Crocker."

"Do you honestly think Stuart will let anyone dig up his precious spa?" She laughed; it had a hollow ring. "He's got lawyers who can fight search warrants until doomsday. And without Star Bright here, who's gonna fight him? No one, that's who. Get the shovel, Star."

"What about Queenie? She knows."

"Don't underestimate her. Only one thing means anything to that old bat. Family. *Her* family. I didn't put her up to stashing those jewels in the Jeep. She did it all herself. 'Course, I knew it wouldn't stop you. That's what I always liked about you, Star Bright. You never let nothing stop you."

"Do you love me, Star?" Austin asked.

"Sweet," Isadora growled. "Now, shut up. I need your muscle, but I can do without."

Star froze halfway between the Jeep and the truck. Isadora meant to kill them both and bury them. She stared at the rifle. Was it the same one she'd used to murder her parents? She stopped feeling the cold, stopped feeling the fear. "I do love you, Austin. I'm sorry—"

"Then trust me. If you love me, do exactly what I say."

"I said, shut up!" Isadora pulled the rifle to her shoulder, aiming it directly at Austin's head. "One more word—"

"Run!" he shouted.

Conflict flashed through her mind, paralyzing her muscles. He was crazy, sacrificing himself for her—trust him, he knew what he was doing. The inner argument seemed to take forever. In slow motion, she watched Isadora swing her body, bringing the rifle around.

Trust him. She bolted.

A bullet zinged past her ear, so close she felt the rushing air and heard it buzzing like an angry wasp. She dived into the darkness, hitting the ground on her shoulder and rolling, scrambling for cover. She hit rocks, feeling the solidity, but not any pain.

The sharp report of the rifle echoed in the night.

She reached a rock big enough for concealment and grasped its icy, rough surface with both hands. She risked a peek at the vehicles. Alone, enraged, Isadora whirled in furious circles, brandishing the rifle.

"I'll hunt you down like vermin!" she screeched. "Star! You can't get away! If I don't get you, the cold will. You'll freeze to death! Star!"

Where was Austin? Star crept a little higher and searched frantically, fearing she'd see his body.

A wet thud. Isadora lurched and cried out in pain. She stumbled, nearly dropping the rifle. Another rock flashed through the light, missing her head by an inch. Quick as a snake, she recovered and spun around, firing wildly into the night.

The rifle clicked empty.

As she fumbled to reload, Austin streaked out of the darkness. Silent, so fast Star could barely comprehend what she saw, he was on top of Isadora, taking her down. They crashed to the dirt and the rifle spun away. Star leapt from behind the rock, intent on helping.

But it was over.

Isadora squirmed on her belly, trapped by Austin's weight. "Punkin, get on the CB emergency channel. Don't bother with Crocker, raise the sheriff."

A great sob wrenched from Isadora as she began to cry.

CROUCHING, STAR TOUCHED her fingertips to the roses she'd laid atop the side-by-side graves. "Looks like this will be my last trip to Colorado, Mama, Daddy. The state gave Queenie a suspended sentence in exchange for testifying. Miss Ike gave up the fight after that. She changed her plea to guilty. No trial. I don't have to testify."

She plucked a few weed shoots trying to grow alongside the fresh sod. The headstones were simple bronze plaques stating her parents' births and deaths. A cottonwood tree grew nearby, and its broad branches cast pretty shadows over the graves.

"Oh, and you know what? Michelle sent me a bunch of stories she wrote about you. Everything she remembered. It's nice. She writes nice. She liked you a lot. She feels just terrible about what happened. I forgave her, though. I mean, I couldn't really expect her to think ill of her family without proof. Right?"

A magpie soared over her head and landed on the grass. It cocked a beady black eye at her, squawked, then flew away. She admired its glossy black-and-white feathers and long tail. Its noise and flash reminded her of the former mayor of Gold Coin.

"You'll like this one. Doyle Sloane lost his election. Not just his gambling issue, but he's not the mayor anymore, either. What with Michelle divorcing him and all, I reckon he'll crawl back under his rock and stay there."

She frowned up at the sky, considering all that had occurred. Mark Waxman's bulldozer had run out of gas before he'd reached Queen's Cross. It hadn't mattered. Between Star's and Austin's testimonies about Isadora, and Michelle raising Cain about the Pookie letter matching Isadora's handwriting, and the rug that had disappeared from Stuart's office the night the Joneses disappeared, and Betty Brownley writing stories, the sheriff had obtained a search warrant to dig up the spa. The investigators had found the bones, and Star had identified her parents through the belt buckle found with the remains.

Star didn't want to think about it anymore.

It was over.

"I can't forget to tell you. Dana is expecting. You'll be grandparents. It'll probably be a big bruiser like its daddy. Don't you worry. I'll make sure her kid knows all about you. No one is ever going to forget you again."

She gave the headstones a final pat, then pushed herself upright and looked around at the rolling acreage of Evergreen Cemetery. She'd thought about taking their remains back to Texas, but her parents had been born and raised in Colorado. Colorado Springs, with the Rockies in the background, seemed fitting, somehow.

She headed for the rental car. Like a silent shadow, Austin fell into step beside her. He looped an arm around her shoulders. She caught his hand and squeezed.

"How are you feeling, punkin?"

She thought about it a while. "Pretty good. Thanks for coming with me. I appreciate the company."

"No problem. So, what's next?"

Finally having a future scared her a little bit, but it was a good kind of scary. For once in her life, anything seemed possible. "Don't know, exactly."

"How about a quick trip to Las Vegas?" His dark eyes sparkled with good humor.

She eyed him askance. "What for? I don't gamble."

"If two people are committed and honest," he said with a grin, "marriage isn't that big a gamble."

She stopped short. Her mouth dropped open.

"Come on, Jones. I don't want your money, but I'll take all the food and sex I can get."

Her insides melted and her knees wobbled. "At the same time?"

"If you say so." He put his arm around her shoulders again and aimed her, unresisting, toward the car. "Might as well say yes. I already changed the airline reservations."

"You're pretty doggoned sure of yourself." Marriage... he had proposed marriage. And when Austin Tack said something, he meant it forever. Her heart threatened to overflow.

"When in doubt, cop an attitude."

"Who are you quoting now?"

"Snooky the cat. So what do you say?"

Her twin came to mind. Sweet, practical Dana, always on top of things and having to do everything just so according to propriety and etiquette. "Dana will have a royal fit if she can't plan a wedding."

"She can throw us a party later." He kissed her. A sweet kiss, full of heat and promise, branding her with his touch and scent. She kissed him back with all the love her heart and soul could muster. When they finally drew apart, he danced her a few steps along the wide concrete pathway.

"Is that a yes?" he asked.

She didn't hesitate. "I love you, Austin Tack, so I reckon it is."

RUGGED. SEXY. HEROIC.

OUTLAWS and HEROES

Stony Carlton—A lone wolf determined never to be tied down.

Gabriel Taylor—Accused and found guilty by small-town gossip.

Clay Barker—At Revenge Unlimited, he *is* the law.

JOAN JOHNSTON, DALLAS SCHULZE and MALLORY RUSH, three of romance fiction's biggest names, have created three unforgettable men—modern heroes who have the courage to fight for what is right....

OUTLAWS AND HEROES—available in September wherever Harlequin books are sold.

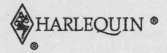

HARLEQUIN ®

HARLEQUIN®

Don't miss these Harlequin favorites by some of our most distin-
guished authors!
And now, you can receive a discount by ordering two or more titles!

HT #25559	JUST ANOTHER PRETTY FACE by Candace Schuler	$2.99	☐
HT #25616	THE BOUNTY HUNTER by Vicki Lewis Thompson	$2.99 U.S./$3.50 CAN.	☐
HP #11667	THE SPANISH CONNECTION by Kay Thorpe	$2.99 U.S./$3.50 CAN.	☐
HP #11701	PRACTISE TO DECEIVE by Sally Wentworth	$2.99 U.S./$3.50 CAN.	☐
HR #03268	THE BAD PENNY by Susan Fox	$2.99	☐
HR #03340	THE NUTCRACKER PRINCE by Rebecca Winters	$2.99 U.S./$3.50 CAN.	☐
HS #70540	FOR THE LOVE OF IVY by Barbara Kaye	$3.39	☐
HS #70596	DANCING IN THE DARK by Lynn Erickson	$3.50	☐
HI #22196	CHILD'S PLAY by Bethany Campbell	$2.89	☐
HI #22304	BEARING GIFTS by Aimée Thurlo	$2.99 U.S./$3.50 CAN.	☐
HAR #16538	KISSED BY THE SEA by Rebecca Flanders	$3.50 U.S./$3.99 CAN.	☐
HAR #16553	THE MARRYING TYPE by Judith Arnold	$3.50 U.S./$3.99 CAN.	☐
HH #28847	DESIRE MY LOVE by Miranda Jarrett	$3.99 U.S./$4.50 CAN	☐
HH #28848	VOWS by Margaret Moore	$3.99 U.S./$4.50 CAN.	☐

(limited quantities available on certain titles)

	AMOUNT	$
DEDUCT:	**10% DISCOUNT FOR 2+ BOOKS**	$
	POSTAGE & HANDLING ($1.00 for one book, 50¢ for each additional)	$
	APPLICABLE TAXES*	$_____
	TOTAL PAYABLE	$_____
	(check or money order—please do not send cash)	

To order, complete this form and send it, along with a check or money order for the
total above, payable to Harlequin Books, to: **In the U.S.:** 3010 Walden Avenue,
P.O. Box 9047, Buffalo, NY 14269-9047; **In Canada:** P.O. Box 613, Fort Erie, Ontario,
L2A 5X3.

Name: _____

Address: _____ City: _____

State/Prov.: _____ Zip/Postal Code: _____

*New York residents remit applicable sales taxes.
 Canadian residents remit applicable GST and provincial taxes.

HBACK-JS2

PRIZE SURPRISE SWEEPSTAKES!

This month's prize:

BEAUTIFUL WEDGWOOD CHINA!

This month, as a special surprise, we're giving away a bone china dinner service for eight by Wedgwood**, one of England's most prestigious manufacturers!

Think how beautiful your table will look, set with lovely Wedgwood china in the casual Countryware pattern! Each five-piece place setting includes dinner plate, salad plate, soup bowl and cup and saucer.

The facing page contains two Entry Coupons (as does every book you received this shipment). Complete and return *all* the entry coupons; **the more times you enter, the better your chances of winning!**

Then keep your fingers crossed, because you'll find out by September 15, 1995 if you're the winner!

Remember: The more times you enter, the better your chances of winning!*

*NO PURCHASE OR OBLIGATION TO CONTINUE BEING A SUBSCRIBER NECESSARY TO ENTER. SEE THE REVERSE SIDE OF ANY ENTRY COUPON FOR ALTERNATE MEANS OF ENTRY.

**THE PROPRIETORS OF THE TRADEMARK ARE NOT ASSOCIATED WITH THIS PROMOTION.

PWW KAL

PRIZE SURPRISE
SWEEPSTAKES

OFFICIAL ENTRY COUPON

This entry must be received by: AUGUST 30, 1995
This month's winner will be notified by: SEPTEMBER 15, 1995

YES, I want to win the Wedgwood china service for eight! Please enter me in the drawing and let me know if I've won!

Name_____

Address _____Apt. _____

City   State/Prov.   Zip/Postal Code

Account #_____

Return entry with invoice in reply envelope.

© 1995 HARLEQUIN ENTERPRISES LTD.   CWW KAL

PRIZE SURPRISE
SWEEPSTAKES

OFFICIAL ENTRY COUPON

This entry must be received by: AUGUST 30, 1995
This month's winner will be notified by: SEPTEMBER 15, 1995

YES, I want to win the Wedgwood china service for eight! Please enter me in the drawing and let me know if I've won!

Name_____

Address _____Apt. _____

City   State/Prov.   Zip/Postal Code

Account #_____

Return entry with invoice in reply envelope.

© 1995 HARLEQUIN ENTERPRISES LTD.   CWW KAL

OFFICIAL RULES
PRIZE SURPRISE SWEEPSTAKES 3448
NO PURCHASE OR OBLIGATION NECESSARY

Three Harlequin Reader Service 1995 shipments will contain respectively, coupons for entry into three different prize drawings, one for a Panasonic 31" wide-screen TV, another for a 5-piece Wedgwood china service for eight and the third for a Sharp ViewCam camcorder. To enter any drawing using an Entry Coupon, simply complete and mail according to directions.

There is no obligation to continue using the Reader Service to enter and be eligible for any prize drawing. You may also enter any drawing by hand printing the words "Prize Surprise," your name and address on a 3"x5" card and the name of the prize you wish that entry to be considered for (i.e., Panasonic wide-screen TV, Wedgwood china or Sharp ViewCam). Send your 3"x5" entries via first-class mail (limit: one per envelope) to: Prize Surprise Sweepstakes 3448, c/o the prize you wish that entry to be considered for, P.O. Box 1315, Buffalo, NY 14269-1315, USA or P.O. Box 610, Fort Erie, Ontario L2A 5X3, Canada.

To be eligible for the Panasonic wide-screen TV, entries must be received by 6/30/95; for the Wedgwood china, 8/30/95; and for the Sharp ViewCam, 10/30/95.

Winners will be determined in random drawings conducted under the supervision of D.L. Blair, Inc., an independent judging organization whose decisions are final, from among all eligible entries received for that drawing. Approximate prize values are as follows: Panasonic wide-screen TV ($1,800); Wedgwood china ($840) and Sharp ViewCam ($2,000). Sweepstakes open to residents of the U.S. (except Puerto Rico) and Canada, 18 years of age or older. Employees and immediate family members of Harlequin Enterprises, Ltd., D.L. Blair, Inc., their affiliates, subsidiaries and all other agencies, entities and persons connected with the use, marketing or conduct of this sweepstakes are not eligible. Odds of winning a prize are dependent upon the number of eligible entries received for that drawing. Prize drawing and winner notification for each drawing will occur no later than 15 days after deadline for entry eligibility for that drawing. Limit: one prize to an individual, family or organization. All applicable laws and regulations apply. Sweepstakes offer void wherever prohibited by law. Any litigation within the province of Quebec respecting the conduct and awarding of the prizes in this sweepstakes must be submitted to the Regies des loteries et Courses du Quebec. In order to win a prize, residents of Canada will be required to correctly answer a time-limited arithmetical skill-testing question. Value of prizes are in U.S. currency.

Winners will be obligated to sign and return an Affidavit of Eligibility within 30 days of notification. In the event of noncompliance within this time period, prize may not be awarded. If any prize or prize notification is returned as undeliverable, that prize will not be awarded. By acceptance of a prize, winner consents to use of his/her name, photograph or other likeness for purposes of advertising, trade and promotion on behalf of Harlequin Enterprises, Ltd., without further compensation, unless prohibited by law.

For the names of prizewinners (available after 12/31/95), send a self-addressed, stamped envelope to: Prize Surprise Sweepstakes 3448 Winners, P.O. Box 4200, Blair, NE 68009.

RPZ KAL